A LANCE KOJO NOVEL

ALL THAT GLITTERS IS NOT GOLD

By FREDERICK L. HARGROVE

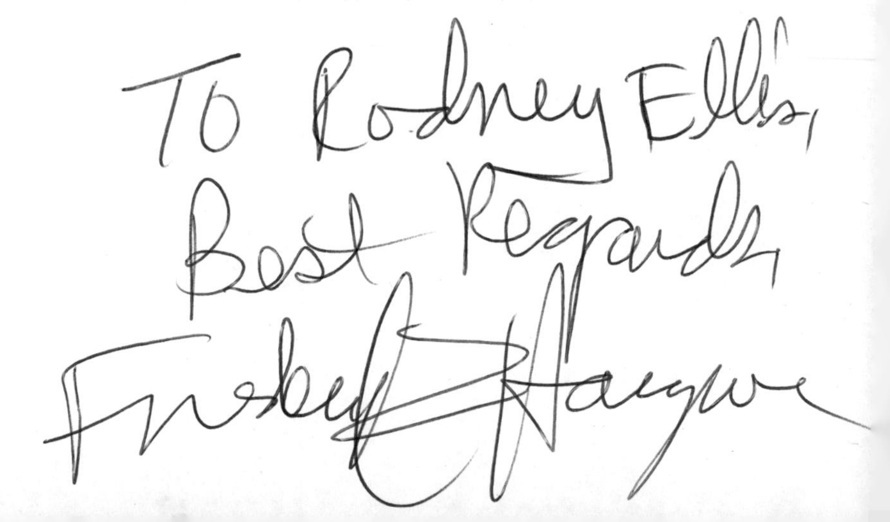

Published by:
Nile River Press, Inc.
P.O. Box 7655
Largo, Md 20792

ISBN: 097629320X

Library of Congress Control Number: 2005902600

This book is a work of fiction.
Names, characters, places and incidents are products of the author's imagination or are used fictitiously.
Any resemblance to actual events or locales or persons, living or dead, is entirely coincidental.

Printed in the United States of America

"There is in this world no such force as
the force of a man determined to rise."

\- W. E. B. Du Bois

Dedication

This book is dedicated to my dearest Mother Lillie.
Thank you for giving me life. I love you.

Acknowledgments

Writing a book is no easy challenge; however, this literary journey has been a labor of love. Writing has allowed me to explore my innermost thoughts, thereby stimulating the creative process of putting ideas to paper. For me, writing is a spiritual act and a forum for social commentary and creative expression. I hope this book will enlighten and entertain my readers. I thank God for giving me the vision and the imagination to write.

I would like to thank those individuals who encouraged me to write. They include Debass Habtemariam, Lonnie Townsend, Robert Brun, Laura Rose, and the countless other people I have encountered over the years.

To Lineo Seotlo, many thanks for reading my manuscript.

Special thanks to Sandi G. Ivey for reading my manuscript and providing technical advice.

I would like to thank Curtis T. Brown Sr. of Teamcujo.com. Curtis designed my book cover and logo. He has enormous skills and patience. I am fortunate to have such great talent in my community.

Special thanks to my talented editor, Carla Dean of U Can Mark My Word (www.ucanmarkmyword.com). Your attention to detail is absolutely incredible. Your professionalism and editing skills are greatly appreciated.

I would like to thank the Black Writer's Guild of Maryland for being a support group for aspiring and published writers. Their workshops and seminars were very informative and useful.

And finally, I would like to thank my immediate family as well as my extended family for giving me the unyielding support for this book project. Their names are acknowledged throughout this book. Special thanks to Donna, Barron, Felicia, Fanta, Cynthia, Barbara, Carrie, Betty, Seba, Jim, Joe, Jerry, Eddie, and the entire McIntyre family.

Peace and Blessings,

Frederick L. Hargrove
Publisher & Author
Nile River Press, Inc.

Chapter One

Traffic was extremely congested on the Baltimore/Washington Parkway, with cars moving at a stop and go pace. The motorists beeped their horns continuously as cars weaved in and out of lanes. As motorists reached the DC area, the speed of traffic increased.

Lance Kojo, an upwardly mobile professional, enjoyed the scenic view of the parkway as he engaged in his morning ritual of commuting to work. The winding lanes of the parkway revealed mostly trees decorated with nature's choice of multicolored leaves. At times, the parkway could seemingly become a wall of ancient forest with glimpses of sumptuous homes along the Potomac River. The temperature was a crisp sixty-two degrees on a clear autumn morning.

As Lance successfully navigated his way through traffic, he drove his blue BMW SUV down Seventh Street into the bustling business district of downtown Washington, DC and entered the parking garage of McIntyre Corporation. After parking, Lance slipped into his dark blue suit jacket, which was neatly folded in the back seat of his truck. As he exited the vehicle, he grabbed his leather briefcase off the floor on the passenger's side, and walked up one flight of stairs to the front of the building.

Lance entered the revolving doors of the newly designed twelve-story building, whose modern architecture represented the transformation and growth of this urban metropolis. This emerging center of commerce was indeed corporate America's playground of success.

Lance arrived at his place of work after a seventy-five minute commute from his home in Mitchellville, Maryland. The elevator door opened on the ninth floor at 8:55 a.m. The lights were muted, and the atmosphere was busy and frantic. The big rectangular shaped office was bright and colorful. The many office cubicles were predominantly light blue, giving the office a uniformed appearance. The office cubicles were primarily occupied by administrative staff and young Account Trainees. The Account Executives' offices were located along the exterior walls.

"Good morning, Kenya. How are you?" Lance asked as he stuck his head in her cubicle before he reached his office.

"I am fine, Lance," Kenya said as she slowly turned around in her chair to locate the voice and place her dancing eyes on Lance's ruggedly handsome face.

"Traffic was terrible on the parkway this morning. I almost didn't make it on time. I'm usually here within forty-five minutes, but it took me forever to get here this morning."

"I think you should consider riding the metro to work. It's a lot less stressful and the commute is faster. Why do you tolerate that crazy traffic everyday?" Kenya asked as she stood up from her chair.

Lance hesitated for a moment as he stood there with his briefcase in his left hand.

"You know, that makes a lot of sense, but I really like having the freedom to go anywhere without depending on the metro."

"Sure, I see you much rather depend on the traffic. Have it your way," Kenya said. She then sat back in her chair and looked up at the mountain of a man who stood six foot two inches tall and smiled with admiration. Lance represented success to Kenya. As she resumed her typing on the computer, she thought about how Lance made her feel. It was usually a feeling of warmth and jubilance.

Lance's arrival to his office solicited stares from other co-workers, especially women, as he walked with rhythmic purpose and athletic grace. His slim, muscular body fit well in his tailored made suit. He was the only African-American Account Executive at this regional office.

When Lance entered his office, he took off his suit coat and hung it up on the coat rack, then immediately opened and read his appointment book to determine his schedule for the day.

Lance had a picturesque view from his office. You could see the U. S. Capitol Building and the astounding architecture of the District of Columbia and its finest landmarks. An MBA diploma from the University of Pennsylvania, Wharton School of Business, hung on his office wall.

A picture of the late Reginald Lewis, who was a successful African-American entrepreneur, hung to the right of his red oak desk. Other pictures of some African art hung at the entrance of his door. Lance had acquired numerous awards at McIntyre Corporation and they were the most prominent along the walls of his office.

Minutes after Lance had sat behind his desk, Kenya entered his office with a notepad to provide him with the status on a pending contract opportunity. Kenya's presence evoked immediate attention from Lance. Her lips were full and painted with subtle red lipstick, and her eyes were dark brown and almond shaped. Her hands appeared to be soft and were adorned with plenty of jewelry, and her nails were freshly polished.

"Nice tie, Lance."

"Thanks."

Lance and Kenya had a comfortable business and professional rapport. Their business relationship exuded a sense of respect and mutual toleration. She frequently complimented Lance on the way he dressed as Lance was a man with an impeccable taste for fashion. Not only did he have a flair for fashion, but Lance also took great pride in his appearance. His hair was cut short with a barely noticeable receding hairline. He had a clean-shaven face and a jaw line that made his full lips more appealing. His smooth chocolate skin and sculptured face, along with his snow-white teeth, made him easy on the eyes.

Kenya, with her pecan brown complexion and short, curly hair, stood in front of Lance's desk and read some specific information about the contract.

"I mailed the bid package to the client. I think we put together a competitive proposal. I hope we win this contract, Lance."

"Good. We did our best, so we'll see."

"Are you ready for the meeting this morning?" Kenya asked carefully, knowing the meeting meant a lot to Lance since he had confided in her on numerous occasions about his desires and goals at McIntyre.

"Yes, indeed. I expect this meeting to be in my favor," Lance replied confidently.

"Well, good luck," Kenya said as she extended her hand in a business-like manner.

"Thank you, Kenya."

Kenya reflected on her career as she walked back to her cubicle, and had long ago decided she wanted to be successful like Lance. She was glad to be working directly with him. Lance frequently shared his knowledge and experience with her, especially as it related to information technology. At twenty-eight years old, Kenya was a quick learner and highly intelligent. She had proved to be successful at the L. Carrie's Advertising Firm, her previous employer. She felt a sense of loyalty to Lance because he was responsible for recruiting her from Howard University's Graduate School of Business.

Lance was a man who was self assured and confident about himself. He was a proud man who was not pretentious about his actions and his approach in the workplace. Lance knew what he wanted in life and his friends often referred to him as extremely ambitious.

Lance's remarkable salesmanship and business savvy enabled him to succeed at McIntyre. He was magnificent at giving marketing and sales presentations. His presentations were electrifying, charismatic, and reminiscent of a motivational speaker. Lance knew how to capture his clients and consistently brought in over twenty million dollars worth of business year after year.

Lance was cautiously optimistic about the meeting. He was expecting Allen Frisco to offer him the position as Vice President of Sales and Marketing. For a fleeting moment, he envisioned a larger office, more challenging opportunities, and a lifestyle of success. Lance had been previously denied the same position last year. However, as he leaned back in his dark brown leather chair, Lance reflected on his accomplishments and felt that he was more than deserving of the promotion.

As Lance put on his suit jacket and caught the elevator to the next floor to meet Allen Frisco, he lost himself in deep thought like a professional boxer before a fight.

Allen Frisco's office was twice the size of Lance's office. Allen, the founder of McIntyre Corporation, had a big portrait of himself in the center of his office. His office had two leather couches and a chair with a table in front. Allen's office exhibited an aura of power and authority. Allen was clearly the man in charge at McIntyre Corporation. On his huge dark brown desk, there was a signed portrait of President George W. Bush.

"Good morning, Allen," Lance said quietly.

"How are you, Lance? What about those Redskins?" Allen said as he stood up, shaking Lance's hand.

Allen was a middle-aged White American who was very cordial and business-like. He was short, standing only five feet five inches tall, and heavyset. Allen was completely bald on the top of his head, but had some hair remaining on the sides.

"Good game. It was very close. The Redskins have a good quarterback this season and their defensive line is awesome," Lance replied like a typical fan. Lance then sat down to the right of Allen's desk with a black notepad in his hand and crossed his legs.

"Oh yeah, great game, and if they keep playing like that, who knows, they might make it to the Super Bowl."

"They certainly have a chance."

"Okay…ah…the job, right?" Allen said as he clapped one time with his hands and gave a hand gesture toward Lance.

"Yes," Lance responded eagerly.

"Well…it was my intention to make a hire this week. However, there has been a change in plans. The position is not going to be filled at this time," Allen said.

"Why?" Lance asked.

"First of all, we have some budgetary issues to resolve. Perhaps we will hire later in the year."

"I see. It was my understanding from our discussion last week that the selection would be made today."

"Yeah, that was our original plan. However, as I said earlier, we have changed our direction. I am just simply not hiring at the moment."

For a moment, Lance was silent as he took a quick glance out of the window. His eyes went south searching for comfort, and then quickly, they refocused to the state of dignity. Lance felt Allen was outright lying to him. Lance knew that McIntyre was a very profitable corporation based on its last quarter earnings. There were no signs of financial problems. Allen's fallacious statements infuriated Lance, especially since Lance had experienced the same rejection last year.

Lance stood up from his chair with his black notepad in his right hand and reluctantly articulated his thoughts to Allen.

"I am disappointed with your decision. I have contributed a lot to this corporation. I have brought in more business than any other Account Executive in this region. I have applied for this position at least twice in my career. This is very frustrating, Allen, but I do understand your constraints," Lance said as he tried to maintain a professional composure without losing it, knowing that his hot temper could erupt like a volcano at any given moment.

"Lance, you have indeed been our top producer for the last three years. You are an outstanding employee. I respect your skills and ability and what you offer McIntyre. However, you just have to understand my position. Believe me, there will be plenty of opportunities for you in this company."

"Okay, but this is not what I expected." Lance nodded his head grudgingly, and then walked out of Allen's office as if the decision hadn't bothered him, but in his soul, he was fed up with the inability to advance within McIntyre. His patience was wearing thin.

Lance went directly to his office and walked around in a circle for about five seconds. "Dammit!" Lance said to himself. "I have to get out of here." Lance could not hold back his anger as his composure collapsed. He quickly snatched his suit coat from the coat rack and hurriedly walked pass Kenya's office cubicle.

"Lance! Lance!" Kenya called out as she got up from her desk and followed him to the elevator. She had been waiting to hear from Lance and was expecting good news.

"Is everything alright? How did the meeting go?" Kenya asked with concern. She could see that Lance was visibly upset.

"Lousy! I didn't get the job. I am tired of his lies, Kenya. I have to get out of here for a few minutes before I explode," Lance replied angrily, momentarily losing control over his emotions. As he took the elevator to the first floor, Kenya was left standing there speechless.

Two co-workers were standing near Lance and Kenya and overheard their conversation.

"What's wrong with that guy?" Buddy asked as he looked to Kenya and gestured with his arms wide open, seeking an answer. Buddy Poretsky was a thirty-seven-year-old co-worker of Lance's and a fierce competitor. He was a redheaded Polish-American Account Executive who had difficulty getting along with Lance.

"I'm not sure," Kenya responded hesitantly as she folded her arms knowing that Buddy was being intrusive. Then she immediately walked back to her office.

Lance went across the street to the local coffee shop and called his girlfriend Valerie on his cell phone to discuss his meeting with Allen Frisco.

"My meeting didn't go well at all. I didn't get the job. I have been with this firm for fourteen years. I came to McIntyre when I was a sophomore in college. This was my first internship. I have been here my entire professional career, and they still will not promote me to senior management. I work hard every year to be the top producer. I work long hours almost everyday. And this is the kind of treatment I get," Lance vented.

"Calm down, Lance. Stay focused and don't allow this to upset you," Valerie declared.

"It's so difficult for me to advance within this corporation. No matter what you do, it's still not good enough. Baby, you just don't understand," Lance said, standing in front of the coffee shop with the cell phone held tightly to his ear.

"What do you mean, I don't understand? Look at me, I'm an attorney. I have been with this law firm for seven years and have not made partner. I know and understand what you're going through, honey. You are still young. You are only thirty-four years old. Most men who become vice presidents of large corporations are usually much older. You really have to analyze this situation in its entirety," Valerie said as she sat at her desk, periodically looking up at the door entrance to make sure no one was listening.

"I don't agree, Valerie. I don't think age has anything to do with me being selected. It's really about your performance, skills, and leadership ability. I know a lot of young corporate executives who are vice presidents, but they are usually white men," Lance responded.

"I understand your frustrations and I feel your pain. Look, honey, I have a meeting in five minutes. Let's have dinner this evening and we can discuss this later. Okay?"

"Alright."

"Bye, Love."

Lance purchased some coffee and then went to sit in the corner of the coffee shop. As soon as he sat down, someone yelled out to him.

"What's up, Lance?" Eddie Patterson said.

"Eddie, what's happening?" Lance replied.

"What are you doing here, man?"

"I'm taking a break. You know how that is. Grab a cup of coffee and sit down." There was only one chair at Lance's table, so Eddie went over to the next table and pulled over a chair, hanging his suit coat on the back of it. He then eased his medium built, five-foot nine-inch body frame into the chair.

"So what have you been up to?"

"I just had a meeting with my boss. I was expecting to hear some good news about a promotion. To say the least, I didn't get it. This is the second time I applied for this position. I am pissed off, man."

"I'm sorry to hear about that, Lance, but I have heard McIntyre Corporation is a very conservative business. They don't hire a lot of minorities," Eddie said as he fixed his horn-rimmed glasses and rubbed his beard.

"You're right, Eddie. I haven't seen many people of color represented in the managerial ranks of this company. I am lucky to have an African-American woman as my trainee. There's not that many of us. I can count them on my fingers," Lance responded. He then poured some cream and sugar into his coffee and slowly sipped the hot beverage.

"Lance, I am thirty-eight years old. I have worked for the Small Business Organization for sixteen years as a Small Business Opportunity Specialist. I have been denied promotions at least four times in my career at SBO. It's tough to break the glass ceiling in these corporations and government organizations," Eddie said as he gestured his fist in the air.

"Yeah...I hear you, Eddie. It's tough for all of us, but you know...we can't let this stop us from achieving our goals in life. "

"Yeah ... I don't know what they want us to do. They want us to act like slaves on a plantation. It's all about control. And believe it or not, these corporations are nothing but plantations. Just give me my forty acres and a mule and let me figure out a way to make it on my own!" Eddie said jokingly. Eddie had quite a sense of humor. He was gregarious and full of fun, but knew how to be serious at the appropriate time.

Lance started laughing and then looked at his watch. "Good point. I hear you, man. Unfortunately, I have to get back to the plantation. You know how that is," Lance said as he chuckled.

"Alright. Don't let them get you down. Hang in there, man."

"Thanks, Eddie. It was good talking to you. Let's talk later. Why don't you meet me at the Upper Nile around eight o'clock tonight? I need to relax and hear a little jazz and poetry."

"Sure, we can hang out a little bit. I don't have anything else planned."

"Okay. After dinner with Valerie, I will come over to the club."

Lance left the coffee shop and walked slowly back to his office. He had his right hand in his pants pocket and his head was high despite the fact that he was deeply hurt by Allen's decision. He didn't want his colleagues to see him looking disappointed, so he wore a mask of confidence to hide his authentic feelings.

"Lance, are you okay?" Kenya asked in a genuine voice as she walked into his office.

"I'm okay, Kenya. Thanks for your concern," Lance replied appreciatively.

"I'm concerned about you. I don't like seeing you upset. I care about you as a friend. Don't let "them" get you upset. You will get your opportunity one day," Kenya said. Kenya was wise beyond her years. Kenya understood the environment that Lance operated within and was determined to stick by his side.

After closing his door, Kenya walked toward Lance's window and started talking. "Don't let them see you stressed, especially Buddy. This is exactly what they want to happen. It just bothers me a lot whenever I see injustice. Okay?"

"I'm not going to let Allen manipulate my emotions. I have to solve this problem on my own. And you are right, Kenya. I have to learn how to control my emotions. I know that this behavior is inappropriate."

Lance rose from his desk, stood next to Kenya, and folded his arms. While listening to Kenya, his eyes had brightened. He was pleasantly surprised at how supportive she was. He smiled to himself because he knew she genuinely understood his struggle.

This was Lance's second outburst in the office. Earlier in the week, he confronted Buddy Poretsky in the hallway about a project. Lance had begun to struggle with his work environment and became increasingly frustrated with his career. His desire to move up the corporate ladder at McIntyre Corporation became problematic. He had witnessed the demons of inequality and injustice, and this made him even more determined to find a solution to his problem.

Lance glanced at the small black book Kenya held in her hand.

"Richard Wright?" Lance asked.

"Yes. I'm reading Black Boy. Maybe this is why I am so fired up today."

"Interesting...I see that we have a serious reader with good taste," Lance said, reflecting again on her earlier comments. In Lance's mind, Kenya's interest in progressive literature explained her social consciousness.

"Thank you. I love to read. I read a lot of books, especially those written by African-American authors," Kenya replied.

"I'm a big fan of Richard Wright and have read most of his books. I love reading, but I am crazy about the spoken word. I could listen to some good poetry all day. As a matter of fact, Eddie and I are going to this Jazz club tonight."

"Where?"

"Upper Nile."

"Yeah, I know where it is. I was there last Tuesday night. It seems like we have a lot in common," Kenya said as her dimpled face smiled.

"I love the Upper Nile. It's a great place to relax after work. Well...maybe I will meet you there some other day."

"Yes, maybe we can do that," Kenya replied as she walked out of his office.

No sooner had Kenya left, Helen Saltenstein, a co-worker, entered.

"Are you doing okay, Lance?"

"I'm fine," Lance said while taking a seat behind his desk.

"Are you sure you're okay? I saw you rushing out of here early this morning," Helen said as she stood in front of Lance's desk with a mug of coffee in her hand.

Helen was a Jewish middle-aged woman, who was very friendly towards Lance but at times, appeared to be somewhat nosey.

"Believe me, I'm okay."

"I'll bring you some of my baked chocolate chip cookies tomorrow. Hopefully, that will cheer you up."

"You really don't have to do that, Helen."

"I want to cheer you up, Lance. Please, I enjoy baking cookies. I will bring some for you tomorrow."

"Okay," Lance replied, giving in.

Just then, the phone rang.

"Hello. Lance Kojo."

"This is Andrew Mason with the Department of Strategic Protection. I would like to discuss a contract opportunity with you." The Department of Strategic Protection was a Federal agency located in Washington DC, and Andrew Mason held the position as a Contracting Officer with DOSP.

"How are you, Andrew?" Lance asked while Helen quietly slipped out of his office.

"I am calling to let you know that McIntyre Corporation has won a three-year contract for fifteen million dollars."

"This is just absolutely fantastic," Lance replied enthusiastically.

"We were pleased with your presentation and McIntyre's pricing and technical approach to this project."

"Well...thank you. This is the best news I have heard today. We are proud to receive this contract."

"This contract is structured in terms of option years. In other words, this is a one-year contract with two option years. Each year will total five million dollars. As you know, this contract requires that you provide us with computer equipment, install software for each of our regional offices, and provide help desk and maintenance for a three-year period."

"Okay, no problem. We will honor the terms and conditions of the contract."

"Great, Lance. We look forward to doing business with you very soon."

Lance was excited and felt good about this opportunity. He knew that he was a true dealmaker. His masterful salesmanship was again instrumental in creating this business for McIntyre Corporation.

* * * * * *

"I'm sorry I'm late, but I had some last minute details to take care of at the office. Luckily, the metro is not very far from my office. Have you been waiting long, Lance?" Valerie asked. She walked immediately towards Lance, giving him an affectionate hug and kiss on his lips. They then proceeded to walk into the restaurant known as Sensations.

"No, only about fifteen minutes. I was lucky to find a parking spot."

"Good."

Valerie was well dressed in a conservative navy blue suit and a beautiful baby blue silk blouse. Her eyes were hazel brown, her nose was narrow with high cheekbones, and she wore a pinkish color lipstick, which blended with her light brown complexion. She stood about five feet nine inches tall and had a model's slim body with few curves.

Lance and Valerie stood in the waiting area to be seated as a young waitress, who could have very well been a college student, greeted them with a friendly smile and escorted them to a candlelit table located in a cozy corner of the restaurant.

"What a roller coaster day. It has been real crazy. I was able to get a contract with DOSP for fifteen million dollars. I was glad to get this call, especially after my morning meeting with Allen. Now you see? I bring in all the business for that company, therefore, I deserve an opportunity," Lance said, leaning forward in his chair and staring beseechingly at Valerie, hoping to gain her support. "Don't you think so, Valerie?"

"Yeah, but Lance...you have to learn how to play the game. I have problems on my job, but I try to understand my boss's psychology," Valerie said as she picked up the food menu from the table.

"What do you mean by playing the game? I am good at what I do. I have skills and have proven this on a consistent basis. I have brought in more business than anyone in my office."

"What I'm saying is that you have to show 'them' that you are on their team. You have to show those guys that you are a team player. You have to go to lunch with them. You have to hangout with your co-workers. They have to feel comfortable with you. Many white people are not comfortable being around black people. They live in predominately white communities. Some of them only interact with people of color during work hours," Valerie insisted, taking a sip of her hot green tea.

"It's not my character to pretend. I call it brown nosing. It's not my job to make white people comfortable. If they can't accept me as I am, then that's too bad. It's not my style, and if it takes that kind of behavior to succeed, I don't want any part of it."

"I'm not saying you should compromise your principles. I just feel you should change your politics if you expect to succeed at McIntyre. You have to play the game. This is how people get ahead, Lance."

"I don't agree with you, Val. I think this is really about institutional racism. You know...this is a very conservative corporation. They don't hire a lot of black people," Lance replied. Lance looked around and saw a white couple sitting two tables away from him. He immediately lowered his voice because he didn't want them listening in on his conversation.

"Perhaps you need to work harder."

"Are you kidding me, Valerie? I just told you that I was the top producer in my office. What are you talking about?" Lance said, taking a sip of his red wine and then wiping his mouth with a napkin. He quickly became silent for a moment, trying to grasp Valerie's interpretation of the issue, his facial expression revealing a cautious disappointment.

"I'm only giving my opinion. Maybe you should improve on your social skills, Lance."

"Alright, enough of my problems," Lance said, wanting to drop the subject. "How was your day at work?"

"It wasn't bad. I got a lot accomplished."

"Is everything okay?" the waitress asked after approaching their table.

"Everything is fine. Can I get the check, please?" Lance said while wiping his mouth with the napkin from his lap after talking to Valerie for about an hour.

"Sure," the waitress replied as she hurried away.

"I love you, Valerie."

"I love you more, Lance."

Lance and Valerie had known each other for more than a year and had been engaged for three months. While looking at Valerie's beautiful face, he smiled proudly. She displayed a conservative demeanor and was a dignified woman. She was often perceived as being "stuck up."

"My girlfriend Julia, whom I met in Law School, is coming to visit me this weekend from Atlanta. She is quite a character and a lot of fun to be around."

"I look forward to meeting her. I remember you told me about her when I first met you."

"Oh Lance, I'm so excited about our wedding. I spoke with my mother last night and she thinks the wedding should be in Philadelphia. What do you think?" Valerie asked.

"I agree. Philadelphia is where you grew up, and your parents live there. So, it seems like the logical place to celebrate with your family and friends. I'm excited about the wedding, too," Lance added.

Valerie had a friendly disposition. She was conservative in her values and espoused the principles of the Christian faith. Being a perfectionist, she was particular about how she approached the wedding. Everything had to be just right.

"I always think about our wedding. I even have dreams about it," Valerie said as she finished her hot tea.

"Val, I know you are a Christian and don't believe in pre-marital sex, but sometimes it gets a little challenging for me. I want to be close to you," Lance expressed with a seriousness Valerie had seen several times before.

"Lance, I understand how you feel, and we have talked about this several times. When you have an urge for me sexually, just say a prayer."

"Well, that's easy for you to say. I'm struggling with this whole pre-marital issue. I respect you enough, and more importantly, I love you. Still, I am human."

"What are you saying, Lance? You can't wait?"

"Yes, I can wait, Valerie. It's just difficult for me, especially when I was sexually active before I met you. It's a tough transition. This relationship means everything to me, and I will wait for you. Now…how about taking a walk with me along the Potomac River?" Lance suggested.

"Sure. Why not," Valerie responded.

As it slowly approached dark, Lance and Valerie left the restaurant and walked down the streets near the river. While they were walking, Lance suddenly stopped, embraced Valerie around her waist, and gently kissed her upon her satin-soft lips. Reciprocating the kiss, Valerie placed both of her hands on Lance's face and moved in closer.

"Mmm, I like holding you, Lance. Hey, why don't you come over to my apartment and watch a movie with me? I'm not ready for the evening to end just yet."

"Sure, I'll come over for a little while. No man in his right mind would pass up an invitation to be with you."

"Oh really?" Valerie said as she smiled shyly.

Lance had a way of making Valerie feel good. He possessed the natural charm many men wished they had. Valerie felt a sense of security with Lance. He knew what he wanted out of life, and with Valerie being the professional woman she was, she needed a man who was purpose driven. There was no doubt in her mind that Lance was the perfect candidate.

Lance drove Valerie to her apartment in Greenbelt, Maryland. "What is that scent? Your apartment smells good," he asked as he entered through her door.

"Those are my scented candles. You know, they really relax me. I'm starting to get into the whole aromatherapy thing. It makes my home a more serene and peaceful place."

"It definitely creates a certain mood."

"Do you want anything to drink? I have water, sodas, and juices."

"Apple juice will be fine."

Valerie attempted to walk towards the kitchen but Lance grabbed her gently, put his arms around her waist, and made a trail of wet kisses from her lips down to her neck.

The sexual tension was becoming increasingly difficult for Lance despite the commitment he had made to Valerie. Valerie was appealing to him and his libido shifted to high gear. He wanted her. He kissed her again as his big hands gently stroked her face and hair.

"Just look at you. Your skin is so soft. You smell good and your lips are sweet. I love kissing them," Lance said as he breathed heavily.

"Oh Lance," Valerie responded in a voice heavy with desire. "It feels good."

They moved slowly backward until they reached the sofa. Valerie collapsed, bringing Lance down on top of her. Lance deepened the kiss as her soft moans mixed with his heavy breathing. They kissed each other in a deeply intimate way as Lance aggressively licked her lips and thrust his tongue inside her mouth. The sexual energy was building as their bodies rubbed up against each other.

"Lance… what are you doing to me, honey?" she cried out while trying to resist Lance's sexual aggression.

"I want you," Lance groaned.

"Ah…Ah…we should stop. Let's calm down. I'm saving myself for you. Let's wait until our honeymoon, baby," Valerie insisted.

Valerie suddenly relinquished control as her arms fell to her sides and Lance continued to run his hand all over her body. Lance caressed her breast as Valerie moaned in heat, her body aching for Lance. As he slid his big hands between her legs, Valerie gasped with pleasure. She simply couldn't resist because it gave her relentless pleasure.

Lance continued to explore her sensual body as his investigative hands located her dripping wet treasure. He kissed her even more passionately as his penetrating tongue found pleasure on her accommodating lips. He gently massaged her and plunged deeper into her erotic zone of wetness.

"Lance, please! We're going too far." Valerie wiggled out from underneath Lance and quickly rolled off the couch, running her fingers through her hair.

As Lance struggled to reclaim his composure, Valerie pleaded, "Let's not do this, okay?" Valerie sat down next to Lance, looked him in the eye, and caressed his face in the palms of her hands. "You must be patient, baby. We have plenty of time for this."

Lance sighed deeply.

"I love you, but I cannot make love to you now. I want it to be special and after we are married, but not just that. What about my religious principles? We have discussed this issue many times."

Lance closed his eyes and leaned his head back over the couch, not giving Valerie any immediate eye contact. He simply sat there in silence for a few moments before speaking. "Okay…I got a little out of control! I am sorry, Valerie. I respect you for your beliefs and conviction, but it's obvious that you want me as much as I want you." Again, there was an uncomfortable silence. "Can I get some juice now?"

"Sure."

Lance took the glass and drank the juice in one gulp. *At least I can satisfy one of my thirsts,* Lance thought to himself.

Lance and Valerie sat in silence as they held each other. After watching half of the movie with her, Lance convinced Valerie he had to leave because of a meeting with Eddie. She reluctantly accepted. As Lance approached the door to leave, Valerie whispered in a soft voice, "Anything good is worth waiting for."

And with those words, the door clicked shut behind him.

Chapter Two

Lance arrived at the Upper Nile Club in Adams Morgan, a trendy community in Washington, DC. The Upper Nile attracted a diverse group of people and was commonly referred to as a "cultural oasis." It was not uncommon to see a local musician or poet engaged in an intense conversation or debating a controversial subject prior to their performance. The young urban professionals were well represented at this popular nightspot. They could be found dressed in their business attire, sitting at the bar and talking on their cell phones while sipping on exotic cocktail drinks. The nightlife was undergoing a dramatic shift in entertainment. The club scene was losing its appeal to many young club goers and they were looking for alternative entertainment, something more substantive. Many were eager to hear the spoken word. Jazz venues that offered poetry were emerging on the scene and becoming very popular in DC. The politically and culturally conscious found refuge here. At the Upper Nile, patrons have a choice to listen to good jazz, poetry slams, performance poetry, and open poetry readings on any particular night.

As Lance entered the club, he could hear the music of Charlie Parker coming from the speakers placed in each corner of the lounge.

"Hello, sir, welcome to the Upper Nile." An Ethiopian waitress with long braids greeted him with a smile.

Lance looked around the club and spotted Eddie sitting alone at a table with a drink in his hand. Eddie's head was turning like a revolving door as he enthusiastically observed the women in the club.

"What's up, Eddie? Stop looking so hard before you break your neck," Lance said jokingly.

"I can't. There are so many gorgeous ladies in here," Eddie grinned.

"Yeah, I'm checking it out." Lance nodded his head, looking at the women Eddie was so hypnotized by.

"I'm glad you made it. I've been here for about twenty minutes. I'm just chillin' – enjoying this magnificent display of pulchritude," Eddie laughed mischievously.

"Nice crowd tonight, huh?"

"Oh yeah."

"I've got some good news."

"What news?"

"McIntyre Corporation won a fifteen million dollar contract today. Without bragging, I must say my efforts played a huge role in securing this contract. And man...I feel good about that."

"Oh really? Congratulations, man," Eddie said. After rubbing his beard and adjusting his glasses, he reached across the table and shook Lance's hand. Eddie was impressed as he smiled.

"Yep, I created this opportunity for McIntyre. It's taken several months to complete, but we beat out the competition. I feel good about this, especially after meeting with Allen Frisco."

"Wow...I think Donald Trump will be calling you soon to work for him," Eddie said jokingly.

"One day soon, Allen will regret holding me back!" Lance declared.

"You should be rewarded for your efforts," Eddie replied.

"It's not easy, man," Lance responded, thinking about Allen, the challenges he confronted at McIntyre, and his meeting with Allen, which still angered him.

"Let me tell you a story I will never forget. His name was Jamie Simpson," Eddie said as he eagerly gestured his hands in the air. "I trained this white guy for ten months for a position as a Small Business

Opportunity Specialist and when a management position became available, I applied for the job and it was given to Jamie after I had adequately trained and groomed him. Jamie Simpson became my boss. I should have been offered the position. How do you explain that to somebody?" Eddie pondered. "This kind of shit happens all the time, especially if you're black. You know what they say: If you're black, you have to work twice as hard," Eddie added.

"Yeah, I've heard that before. Hearing those types of stories makes me angry. If I was qualified for the position and didn't get it, I would have filed a formal complaint," Lance replied shaking his head, easily identifying with Eddie's experience.

"African-Americans experience institutional racism everyday. Many of us just accept this reality and don't do anything about it," Eddie said.

"Did you file an EEO complaint or do anything?" Lance asked.

"I did file a complaint, but it didn't do any good because the guy transferred to another department within the organization after six months and was replaced by another manager. You see, this is how they cover their dirty tracks. It's difficult to break the glass ceiling within a racist corporate structure."

"I have to be more focused on my career goals. Nobody is going to give us anything. I had dinner with Valerie earlier and she told me that I should be more patient. She suggested I learn how to play the corporate game. What do you think?"

"Game? The "game" is not played fairly. They always change the rules. I never knew how to play the game nor am I willing to play the game of compromise or sell out. I don't brown nose too well."

"You're a lot like me. It never worked for me, either. I'm my own man. If we can't get any justice in corporate America, then it seems that the next logical step is to create our own corporations. This is the only way, bro. Either we remain well-educated slaves who are dependent on other people for our economic survival or become self-sufficient." Lance paused, pondering his thoughts and looking around in the club. "You know, Eddie," he placed his right hand on his chin, "I am thinking about starting my own IT business. I've had enough of this corporate B.S."

"Can I get you all another drink?" the waitress asked as she approached their table.

"A Black Russian," Lance replied.

"Apple Martini," Eddie said.

The club was getting crowded as the Jazz band set up to play. Across from Eddie and Lance sat two poets. One poet was wearing dreadlocks with a notebook in his hand, talking while the other listened intently. African art was displayed generously throughout the club. The backdrop of the club revealed a huge picture of the Nile River painted in blue.

"I feel you, man. I think the business idea is fantastic. As a matter of fact, I often think about doing my own thing as a consultant. I always wanted to work with small businesses. Now, let me be straight up with you…the business world is different. Are you prepared for the responsibilities?" Eddie asked as he sipped on his Apple Martini.

"I am prepared for whatever the consequences. Quite frankly, I'm tired of working for other people. I wanna do my own thing. You know what I mean?" Eddie nodded his head. "I want to be in control of my own destiny and that's the honest truth. I'll be the first to admit that I can be very explosive at times. I have a quick temper, and I'm surprised I haven't been fired yet. I just know that it's time for me to make my move, Eddie."

"I want you to see both sides, Lance. I like your kind of energy and passion. I can see you have the experience. However, you also need capital, especially for a start-up business. I see this everyday at SBO since I work directly with small businesses. The process of acquiring financial resources is the biggest obstacle for most businesses. At least that's what I think."

"I agree, Eddie. That is why I am working on a business plan."

A beautiful young lady wearing a red tight skirt that accented her shapely body walked in front of their table.

"Check this out, Lance. Not bad, huh?" Eddie said as he nodded his head toward the young lady.

Eddie was a real flirt and a recent divorcee. Eddie looked at Lance and noticed a somewhat reserved posture when he talked about women. Eddie was responding to women in such an aggressive way because his divorce was very painful to him. He was looking for a new girlfriend to fill the void of his ex-wife.

"That's nice," Lance responded cautiously, knowing that he was engaged to be married. Eddie was Lance's best friend. They were "tight" with each other. Lance knew Eddie was trying to get over his divorce, so he just ignored his constant comments about women.

"I had better stop corrupting you. You're about to get married."

"That's right. My bachelor days will soon be over, but there's no harm in looking," Lance said as he chuckled and rubbed his hand over his head.

"How are the wedding arrangements going?"

"Everything is just fine. Valerie goes up to Philly almost every weekend. She's trying to get things finalized. I really love that woman."

"I never thought you would be getting married so soon. I guess she is that special lady. You're a lucky man," Eddie said cautiously.

Again, Eddie reflected on his ex-wife while looking at the brightly lit stage as the musicians set up to play. Eddie was somewhat cynical towards women because of his divorce, but he respected Lance. He knew Lance extremely well. Lance had a reputation with women and commitment issues before he met Valerie. Lance had only known Valerie for a short while. Eddie knew in his heart that Lance was not ready for marriage, but he kept his private thoughts to himself because he didn't want to be perceived as a "hater".

"Yes, I do consider myself lucky to have Valerie in my life."

"I hear you, man." Eddie directed his attention to the front of the venue. "Is that Bilal coming to the stage?"

"Yeah, that's him."

"I like his poetry. The brother is deep. He knows how to bring it, and the women love him," Eddie added.

Bilal was about average height with a dark ebony complexion, wore an afro hairstyle, and was dressed in all black. Walking over and grabbing the microphone, Bilal introduced himself to the audience while the band began to play

"I would like to read you one of my new poems. As a matter of fact, I wrote this piece last night for a special friend of mine. It's very short. It's called "I See Beauty". Here it goes:

"My eyes wrestle to the sight of your beautiful face;

Missing no angle but simply persistent focus;

You are my kind of beauty;

Open and receptive to my visual desires;

You are the woman with the intoxicating smile;

That I have been looking at for quite a while;

The sight of you inspires my soul;

Indeed, you are a rare creation;

Your beauty makes me smile;

It hypnotically indulges me and forces me into conformity of observation.

I see beauty."

Bilal walked off stage as the audience responded with loud applause.

"I feel you, brother!" a young lady yelled from the audience as she waved at Bilal.

"Thank you for the love, sister," Bilal replied.

"That's my man. He knows how to connect with his audience," Eddie said.

"Yeah, that's a good piece of love poetry," Lance replied.

"Yeah, I dig that," Eddie added.

"We need to talk about this business idea when things aren't so noisy," Lance said, picking up where they had left off in their conversation prior to the poetry reading.

"Okay, I have some ideas for your business plan," Eddie replied.

"I would be interested in hearing them," Lance responded as they sat back, relaxed, and enjoyed the rest of the night's entertainment.

Chapter Three

Lance went to work the next morning a lot more relaxed and confident about his career. He was less concerned about his career advancement at McIntyre Corporation as it seemed he now had a possible plan to escape from his dead-end place of employment. He even contemplated staying at McIntyre until he could finalize his business plans.

Lance entered the elevator on the first floor and stood next to a white woman of mature years who was dressed in a gray business suit. Lance, who was dressed in a light brown suit, stood right next to the woman. As the elevator door closed, the woman grabbed her purse and held it tightly, looking at Lance in fear through her peripheral vision, her eyes racing from left to right. She then walked slowly to the back of the elevator as she continued to hold her purse tightly. He could even hear the woman breathing loudly. Lance looked back at her and shook his head as she immediately looked away from him embarrassingly to avoid any possible eye contact.

He knew intuitively that the woman was uncomfortable being in an elevator alone with a tall black man. As the door opened for her on the fifth floor, she walked off the elevator in a flight. Lance was consumed with anger, shaking his head in disdain for the woman's obvious prejudice. Not wanting the encounter to ruin his day, Lance took it in stride and moved on.

Kenya met with Lance at work, wearing a navy blue business suit and a white silk blouse. She was showing plenty of cleavage and her skirt was above her knees, which displayed her exquisite pair of legs. She often asked Lance for his approval on her appearance. Her inviting presence was an attempt to get Lance's attention. Kenya was attracted to Lance and admired his dignity and strength. However, Lance was so professional and business-focused that he never flirted with her. Although Kenya was a sophisticated young lady, she seemed very insecure on issues concerning intimacy. Her previous relationship was very volatile with an abusive boyfriend.

"Good morning, Mr. Kojo. How are you?"

"I'm doing well."

"You sound so much different from yesterday." Kenya picked up on Lance's suppressed excitement.

"I feel great today. I had time to reflect on my future plans and put things into perspective."

"And what are those plans?" Kenya probed gently, searching and hoping for a revelation from him.

"I'll let you know sooner or later."

"Um, sounds serious."

"Yes, quite ambitious. What kind of perfume are you wearing?" Lance said as he shifted the topic.

"Calvin Klein. It's new."

"Smells good," Lance said, complimenting Kenya. Lance always tried to maintain a friendly relationship with Kenya, clearly respecting her.

"Thank you. Is it too loud?" Kenya asked, seeking his approval.

"No, it's fine."

"So, Lance - when are you going to the Upper Nile again?" Kenya asked. She wanted to get closer to Lance, and felt that socializing outside of work would give her a better opportunity to do so. Kenya sensed that Lance had a personal attraction to her because of the way he looked at her, but she didn't want to be too presumptuous ...simply determined.

Since Lance chose to keep his personal life outside of the workplace, Kenya had no idea of his plans to marry. Therefore, in Kenya's mind, the idea of Lance being attracted to her was not an unrealistic possibility...but one that she secretly entertained.

"I was there last night. With my schedule being so unpredictable, I'm not sure when I'll go again," Lance pondered.

"Oh, well just let me know the next time you plan on going," Kenya replied disappointedly.

* * * * * *

Lance attended an early morning meeting with four Account Executives and the Director of Operations. The discussions focused primarily on how to interact with clients.

As Lance suggested ways to better respond to customers, Buddy Poretsky challenged his comments as if they had no merit. Buddy's comments were blatantly envious and everyone could see his jealousy, especially Helen and Kenya. The other Account Executives made suggestions and their comments were well received. However, they had few business accounts and limited experience. Buddy had little respect for Lance's opinions even though he was the top producer in his department. These confrontations at meetings were very common and Lance felt that his opinions and contributions were being silenced and minimized. Needless to say, this frustrated Lance.

After the meeting, Lance nonchalantly approached Allen Frisco's office, wanting to talk to Allen about his recent contract with the Department of Strategic Protection.

"Good morning, superstar!" Allen said, immediately standing to shake hands with Lance. He was thrilled about the contract. His excitement was similar to a coach supporting a player on a football team who had scored a big touchdown.

"How about a high-five?" Allen grinned, raising his hands.

Lance thought to himself, "*What a phony ass?*"

Lance reluctantly took his right hand out of his pocket and gave Allen a high-five.

"Way to go!" Allen shouted.

A smile quickly appeared on Lance's serious visage.

"I guess you heard about the deal with DOSP," Lance chuckled, relaxing a bit.

"Yes, Helen told me this morning. I'm proud of you. You can expect a big bonus for your efforts. Good job!"

"Thank you."

While Lance appreciated the accolades, he was still angry about Allen's obvious intentions to deny him a much deserved promotion. These comments from Allen did nothing to satisfy his soul and ego. Instead, they reassured him that his plans to start his own business were timely.

As Lance left the office, he ran into Buddy Poretsky.

"Congratulations on your contract, Lance," Buddy said disingenuously.

"Thank you," Lance replied.

"What is your hustle? You must be threatening these clients, because you are getting a lot of business," Buddy asked sarcastically as he looked at Lance, hoping to provoke a negative response.

"What do you mean by hustle, Buddy? This is not a hustle. I'm just damn good at what I do, unlike other people." Lance knew that Buddy was trying to make him angry.

"Don't get upset, cowboy. I am just giving you a compliment."

"Sure. Right! I don't need it. And by the way, I didn't appreciate your comments in the meeting this morning. It's too bad people like you have to stoop to such a low level in order to make a point."

"You think you know it all, Lance. I have an opinion too, cowboy."

Ignoring his comment, Lance brushed past him and continued on to his office. Once he entered, he noticed a small bag of chocolate chip cookies on his desk. There was a note attached with Helen's signature. It read: "I hope these cookies make you feel better."

Wanting to thank her, he proceeded to her office, but she had already left for a meeting. After making a mental note to express his thanks to her later, he returned to his office to await the end of his workday, anxiously looking forward to seeing Valerie at her apartment that evening.

* * * * * *

Eddie was hanging out over a friend's house in Northwest DC, sitting in her living room, watching TV, and drinking grapefruit and vodka. Eddie did not handle the divorce very well. He internalized the pain and tried to drown it by drinking. Before his marriage ended, Eddie caught his wife in bed with another man. After leaving work early one day, he walked into his bedroom and saw them having sex. It devastated him. The scene was constantly replaying in his mind. He even had nightmares that frequently woke him in the middle of the night.

"I'm so glad to have you in my life. Thank you for the dinner," Eddie said.

"No problem. I enjoy cooking for you, Eddie," Regina replied. She was a dark brown complexioned, medium-built woman, who was a few years older than Eddie. He had met Regina on the rebound, and although he was not serious about her, she had given him a lot of support after his divorce.

"Hey Regina, I'm looking for something new, a positive change in my life. Maybe I should go into business with my buddy, Lance. He's a decent man. I have known him for many years."

"That's a good idea. Try something new. Maybe this will help you get over your divorce," Regina said as she held Eddie's hand.

"Yeah, you're right," Eddie replied as he took another sip of vodka.

"Eddie…you have to stop drinking so much. You can't drink your problems away. I don't like seeing you this way."

Eddie had already finished one bottle of vodka, his eyes were bloodshot red, and he smelled like a liquor factory.

"Hun, I'm going to take this drink away from you. No more, Eddie!" Regina demanded.

"You wanna make love?" Eddie asked unconvincingly as his voice slowly faded out.

"Eddie…you're not in the condition to do anything. Just look at you."

Eddie looked at her, nodded his head, closed his eyes, and passed out in a drunken slumber.

******

When Lance arrived, Valerie was entertaining her friend Julia, who was an attorney like Valerie.

"I'm glad you came over. I wasn't expecting you so soon," Valerie said as she shut the door behind him.

"I wanted to surprise you. I remember you telling me that your friend was coming up from Atlanta," Lance replied, looking around the apartment in hopes of seeing her girlfriend.

"That's right. As a matter of fact, Julia is in the kitchen right now."

As if on cue, Julia emerged from the kitchen displaying a beautiful smile. She had long hair and dazzling light brown eyes.

"Julia, I would like to introduce you to my fiancé," Valerie said proudly.

Lance and Julia greeted each other and shook hands.

"Have you all decided on the location of the wedding?" Julia asked.

"We're planning to get married in Philadelphia at Friendship Baptist Church," Valerie responded.

"Oh yeah, interesting."

"How do you like the DC area?" Lance asked curiously.

"It's fine. I have been here before and love visiting. There are certain parts that remind me of Atlanta, especially the Maryland Area," Julia replied.

"Oh really? I've heard so much about Atlanta. I hear it is a great business climate for African-Americans down there," Lance said.

"Oh yeah, a lot of the major corporations are based in Atlanta," Julia responded.

"Interesting… I have family in Atlanta and would someday like to move there. What do you think about that idea, Valerie?" Lance asked, smiling with a look of persuasion.

"I could see it happening, but I don't know if I'm ready for that hot weather," Valerie said as she smiled and looked at Julia.

"Oh yeah, it gets hot in Atlanta, but I *love* the warm weather," Julia replied.

Realizing he had left his cell phone in his car, Lance excused himself to retrieve it. When he returned, they were deeply engaged in a discussion about men.

"You know, Valerie, you were lucky to find a good man. I think good men are a dying species," Julia laughed.

"It can't be that bad, girl. Come on. You have a great career. You have a lot to offer. I know there are a lot of nice southern gentlemen in Atlanta," Valerie replied.

Lance stood in silence as he continued to listen to their discussion.

"I know what the problem is, Valerie. These so-called good black men are choosing to marry outside of their race more often than not. Most men are either married, gay, or in jail. All the good ones are accounted for, especially the professional type," Julia expressed in a tone that would make any man angry.

Lance, who felt a little disturbed by her comment, decided to intervene. "I don't agree with that, Julia. There are a lot of decent men out here. They may not be doctors and lawyers, but they do exist. Not all black men exclusively pursue women of other races. It's a matter of choice," Lance reluctantly responded as he looked at Valerie, hoping to get her support. Lance didn't like indulging in "male bashing" conversations, but he was willing to defend his position.

"I don't know about that, Lance. Just look at some of those professional athletes. It seems like as soon as the brothers become rich and successful in their careers, they dump the sisters," Julia responded sarcastically. Julia looked at Lance as if he was on trial in court, placing her hands on her hips and waiting for Lance's defense.

"I think you're being a bit too hard on black men. There are a few brothers who marry outside of their race, and I feel a man should marry whoever makes him happy. I do understand your frustration, though, and I can relate to your concerns, but I think in the final analysis, believe it or not… love has no color," Lance argued.

Broaching a subject that clearly was deviating from the discussion at hand, but was still pertinent, Valerie said, "The church is a good place to meet men. I go to church every Sunday and I see plenty of black men in the congregation." Being the daughter of a minister, Valerie thought about all the men who belonged to her father's church.

"The church is a good place, but I have not met any men there," Julia replied.

"Why don't you go to church with us on Sunday?" Valerie asked.

"Sure. Why not? Maybe God will bless me with a good man. But he has to meet a certain criteria for me. For one, he has to have money."

"Interesting...why does he have to have money?" Lance replied cautiously.

"I want to live comfortably. I don't want to struggle. I don't want to end up marrying a broke man who is trying to get his career together. I want someone who is established," Julia responded.

"I don't understand. You have just eliminated half of the men out there," Lance replied.

"In other words, I want a man to bring something to the table. There is nothing wrong with having standards."

Lance shook his head. "Different strokes for different folks. I didn't fall in love with Valerie because of her material possessions. I fell in love with her because she is a wonderful person," Lance declared, and then he became silent, turned off by Julia's opinion of men. He hoped Valerie didn't harbor such thoughts.

Trying to dissolve the tension in the air, Valerie interjected while releasing a nervous chuckle. "You guys are really getting into this crazy discussion. You both have made your point." She could see Lance was getting upset and didn't want any problems between the two of them.

"I hope I didn't offend you, Lance. I appreciate a male's point of view and respect your honesty," Julia said apologetically.

"I appreciate your candor, as well. I hope you enjoy your stay in Maryland. Valerie, honey, I have to go. I have some things to take care of."

"Why don't you stay and have dinner?" Valerie asked.

"I have a lot of things to do this evening. I didn't plan on staying long. I'll let you ladies catch up on ole times and I'll talk to you later," Lance said as he exited Valerie's apartment after placing a feather-soft kiss on her lips.

Chapter Four

Fleming Brown's Barbershop was where Lance visited bi-monthly for his hair grooming needs. This popular barbershop was a hot spot where mostly black men came to get a haircut and talk about sports, women, politics, and every other thing you could imagine. It was located in Southeast, DC on Burbank Street. Lance was comfortable in his surroundings, at ease navigating in both worlds from his old neighborhood of Southeast to the upscale community of Mitchellville.

Along this street, you could see a lot of trees with moderately maintained homes. At the end of the street were four small businesses: the Korean-owned nail salon, a Laundromat, grocery store, and the barbershop. The barbershop had been in existence since 1967 and was a historic institution in the community. Many black leaders during the sixties frequented Fleming Brown's Barbershop for haircuts and to share news with the community, and even today, you may see the mayor of DC in one of the shop's chairs getting a trim.

It was Saturday morning and the barbershop was full with customers, both young and old, anxiously waiting to get a haircut. Lance walked in the busy barbershop and looked around for a seat, locating one in the corner near the entrance. Fleming, meticulously cutting the hair of a young man, finally spotted Lance and took the hair clippers away from the young man's head to acknowledge his presence.

"Hey, Lance. How you doing, young blood? You're right on time for your appointment," Big Flem said.

"Yep, I can't afford to miss my spot. I need a haircut badly."

Fleming Brown, affectionately known as Big Flem, was the owner of the barbershop. Fleming's tall body of about 6'5" reached over and grabbed a black apron, placing it around Lance's neck and body as he took a seat in the barber's chair. While settling into the chair, Lance witnessed a classic barbershop debate between a young skinny guy, who appeared to be in his late twenties, and an older gentleman he stood over. The older gentleman was sitting in a chair and holding a soft drink. They were quite colorful as they argued about who was the best basketball player of all times.

"There was never a player as good as Wilt Chamberlain. There were times when he was simply unstoppable. He scored 100 points in one game," the older gentleman argued as he stood up from his chair and pointed his finger toward the younger guy in order to make his point. "Wilt Chamberlain could do it all, man. I use to love watching him play against Bill Russell. He was a great offensive and defensive player," the old guy continued.

"Oh yeah! That sounds good, but Michael Jordan could score points just like Chamberlain! I think as an all-around player, Michael was the greatest. Look how many championships Mike won," the young guy responded.

Fleming intervened, taking the hair clippers away from Lance's head for a moment. "Hey, ole fella," Big Flem said as he turned toward the older gentleman. "I have to agree with, young blood. I think Michael Jordan is the greatest basketball player ever. Just look at his statistics. He was a great defensive player and phenomenal scorer. He made the Chicago Bulls a successful franchise," Fleming stated. "What do you think, Lance?" Fleming asked as he solicited Lance's opinion.

"Jordan, no question. You have to respect the fact that he took his team to six championships," Lance responded.

"That's right. You have to take that into consideration. Chamberlain did score one hundred points in one game, but so what? How many championships did he win?" the young guy retorted.

"I don't care. I just know that there was no player who could dominate a basketball game like Wilt Chamberlain. They use to call him 'Wilt the Stilt'. That's my man!" the old man shouted. "You young cats just weren't even around to see Wilt play in the sixties and seventies. And of course, you are gonna say that Michael is the best," the older gentleman said, looking at Big Flem and hoping to convince him.

"Michael Jordan can dominate a game, too. How many players can play like that, even at the age of forty?" Fleming said as he shook his head and surrendered. He then resumed cutting Lance's hair. "I haven't seen you in a while, Lance. I thought you gave up on me."

"No, I can't do that. There's no barber that can cut hair like you," Lance replied.

"Those are kind words, brother. I try my best. So, where you been hiding?"

"Just working hard and trying to stay focused. And you know…I've been thinking about going into business for myself."

"Wait a minute now. Aren't you the man that works for McIntyre Corporation? Good job and everything. You got it good, man."

"Not really. The money is nice, but you have to put up with a lot of B.S."

"What do you mean?"

"I applied for a position twice within the organization and got rejected. My boss keeps coming up with excuses."

"Yeah, I understand. It's all by design. They don't want a black man in any position of authority, especially if he thinks for himself. They want "yes" men only."

"What are you saying, Big Flem? Is this some kind of conspiracy theory or something?"

"Hell no, this is fact!" He then placed his hair clippers on the table to make his point. Fleming's tall body stood in front of Lance with his protruding belly. Big Flem looked like a man in his fifties and had a completely baldhead that shined in the light. He had a dark chocolate complexion with a boomerang-shaped scar on the right side of his neck. His face was very mature with prominently well-defined facial lines.

"You have to do what is best for you. I bet if you were a white man, you probably would have been promoted several times by now. They ain't gonna give a black man a damn thing in this country! You have to fight for it!" Fleming said angrily as he turned the clippers on to evenly fade Lance's hair in the back.

"That makes a lot of sense. And this is why economic independence is the key," Lance stated in a serious tone.

There were about fifteen chairs in the barbershop. Pictures of men with different hairstyles were plastered on the walls. Some of the patrons were engaged in their own personal discussions and debates, while some listened attentively to the dialog between Lance and Fleming and others waited eagerly for the next haircut.

"I went over to Vietnam to fight a war for America, which we had no business being over there in the first place. When I came back to the States, I couldn't get a job for almost three years, and because of that experience, I decided to start my own business. This barbershop may not be a whole lot, but I call the shots here. I don't have a boss telling me how to run my barbershop. For me, Lance, it's peace of mind."

"I can relate to that, Big Flem. I definitely want to be in control of my own destiny."

Just then, the door opened and a young lady entered with her son who looked to be about four or five years old. The young lady appeared to be in her mid-twenties and was wearing a dress that exposed her curvaceous legs and a tattoo on her left ankle. Her entrance drew the attention of all the male patrons.

"Who is that?" a young guy whispered to his friend.

"Well, hello, Tasha. You're looking good, baby doll. Are you coming to see Big Daddy? And when are you going to let me take you out to dinner?" Big Flem asked flirtatiously.

Big Flem had a reputation for flirting with young girls. He preferred them young and had a particular attraction to Tasha. He had even been known to give her money.

"I'm going to take you up on your offer one day, but right now, I have to go to a wedding in two hours. Can you cut my son's hair?" Tasha asked, looking at Big Flem like a little girl pleading for some candy in a store as she slowly leaned her head to the left and batted the long lashes of her dark brown eyes at him. "I am really in a hurry," Tasha continued.

"Now you know there are other people ahead of you. You really have to make an appointment. But for you, I will cut your son's hair after I finish with Lance," Big Flem replied. Big Flem was a sucker for Tasha and had been pursuing her for many months.

"Thanks, hun," Tasha said, pouring on the charm heavily. "And did I tell you that I'm trying to find me an apartment?"

"You don't need to find an apartment. I have a big house in Southeast. You can come stay with me, baby. As a matter of fact, I will let you rent one of my rooms for little or nothing," Big Flem insisted as he rubbed his bald head. Big Flem was serious about his offer. "And how're you doing, little guy? Ready for a haircut?" Big Flem asked as Demetrius nodded his head. Just then, Tasha began taking Demetrius' coat off.

"I don't know about that, Big Flem. I need my own place with my son," Tasha replied.

"Lance...have you met Tasha?" Big Flem asked.

"No, I haven't. How're you doing, Tasha?"

"I'm fine."

"Nice to meet you. Hey Big Flem, thanks for the haircut," Lance said as he rose from the chair. "I have to go to the gym and sweat a little. I'll holler at you."

"Alright, man. Take care."

******

The gym in Largo, Maryland was one of Lance's favorite hangouts. Lance was an active member of the Spinning Bike Club, where he worked out several days a week.

"Hello, Reina. What's up?"

"Not much, just trying to get ready for my spinning class. I got some new music for the class that I hope you guys like," Reina said.

"It doesn't matter as long as the music sounds good and I get a good workout."

"I will definitely give you a good workout. You can believe that. You're here early. The class doesn't start for another hour," Reina said as she looked Lance up and down.

"I know. I just wanted to get an early workout before class."

"Okay. I see you are taking good care of your body," Reina commented as she continued her inspection of Lance, her eyes finding pleasure in looking at his toned physique.

Reina Perez, a charming Latin beauty with long brown hair, bushy eyebrows, and enticing lips, was a spinning and aerobic instructor at the gym. Reina had well-defined muscles in her arms, stomach, and legs. Her body was evident of intense and relentless physical activity.

"Gracias, Senorita! I try to work out on a consistent basis. I'm still trying to get those six pack abs," Lance said as he attempted to speak a bit of Spanish.

"Keep up the good work and you'll get there, Papi?" Reina replied affectionately in her native Spanish tongue as she looked at Lance bashfully and smiled. Reina had always been friendly with Lance and smiled frequently whenever he was around.

"Maybe you can give me some tips on my abs. My abs is not bad, but I want six packs." Lance waited for her response, knowing this would be a way to get closer to Reina. He sensed a strong sexual vibe based on her body language. And even though Lance was sexually frustrated, he needed to confirm her interest.

"Sure. Now, diet and nutrition play a major role in getting nice-looking abs. Maybe I will give you a counseling session next week," Reina responded anxiously.

"So you will advise me on fitness? I wouldn't pass up that offer, especially coming from a beautiful woman."

"Well, thank you. Aren't you kind." She blushed as she smiled at Lance's complimentary words.

As if rehearsed, Reina dropped her towel on the floor. Lance's roving eyes took a quick peek as her nylon shorts slowly diminished to a smaller size when she bent over, her butt cheeks in clear view of Lance's lustful eyes.

"I look forward to training with you," Lance said.

"It will be fun. I have to go upstairs now, but I'll see you later," Reina responded.

"Alright."

******

Lance met Eddie at Cynthia's Tastebuds, an upscale establishment in Arlington, Virginia that attracted a certain type of clientele. Upon their arrival, the waitress escorted them to a non-smoking area of the restaurant.

"I have an idea," Lance said after they were seated.

"What is it?" Eddie replied.

"Do you remember last week I told you about my business idea?"

"Yeah, what about it?"

"Well, I'm ready to execute that plan, and I want you to be a major part of my business... like the Chief Executive Officer."

"Really?"

"Yes. I have known you for over ten years, and there is no one else I would trust more. I have the technical expertise in the IT arena and can definitely sell a product, while you have the expertise in business development. You would be a great asset to my team," Lance said as his eyes sparkled with excitement.

"Well, I really have to think about this. It sounds like a great idea, though. I have been thinking about a career change and I even expressed this thought to my friend Regina. You and I have discussed this idea numerous times, but maybe now the timing is right. My only concern is financing," Eddie replied, rubbing his chin like he always did whenever he was in deep thought.

Eddie then looked around for the waitress, hoping that a drink would help him think more clearly. However, he did not see one in sight. Eddie thought about his drinking problem, which wasn't actually a problem in his eyes since he felt he could stop if given a mission or purpose.

"I understand your concern, Eddie. I will get a business loan and once that happens, we can move forward. How does that sound?"

"It sounds good...but give me a little time to consider your offer. You kind of caught me off guard. I was wondering why you wanted to meet at this expensive restaurant," Eddie said, chuckling.

Eddie was surprised Lance had asked him. However, he felt honored that Lance had confidence in him. Eddie rubbed his beard and looked away from Lance for a moment.

"That's fine. You don't have to make a decision right at this moment. I know you need time to reflect on everything I said."

Forty-five minutes passed as Lance and Eddie continued to talk business.

"We've been waiting here for over forty-five minutes and I haven't seen a waitress yet," Eddie declared.

"Yeah, I thought it was just me thinking that. I was so caught up with our discussion, I completely forgot about the time. Frankly, I'm getting a little pissed off," Lance replied. "Look at this couple sitting across from our table," Lance said as he pointed in their direction. "They came in twenty minutes after us and have already been served their food. This is crazy, man. Are we invisible?"

"Maybe we should wait a few more minutes and then ask to speak to the manager," Eddie suggested.

Not wanting to wait another second, let alone a few more minutes, Lance called over the waiter who was serving the table next to theirs.

"Yes, sir, can I help you?"

"I have been waiting here almost an hour and haven't seen my server. Do you know where he or she is?" Lance asked.

"Sir, I am sorry. I don't know, but I could find out," the waiter replied right before scurrying off to the kitchen.

After waiting another five minutes and still not seeing a server, Lance became even more furious. As soon as he attempted to get up from his table to find the manager, a waitress approached his table, but before she could apologize, Lance erupted like a volcano.

"Why in hell do you have us waiting here? What kind of service is this?" Lance shouted in a loud voice as his quick temper unleashed.

"Hey, Lance, don't let these people upset you," Eddie said, motioning his hand and shaking his head as if to say don't do it. Eddie could detect Lance's anger and was well aware of his quick temper.

"Sir, I am sorry. I was so busy. I just totally forgot," the waitress apologized, standing in front of Lance.

"What do you mean by you forgot? This is unacceptable. Where's your manager?" Lance asked.

Within seconds, a short chubby man came over.

"What can I do for you, sir?" the manager asked.

"We've been waiting here for almost an hour and haven't gotten served. Not so much as a menu has been handed to us. Is this how you do business?"

"Of course not, sir, and I would like to extend my sincere apologies. Tonight is very busy. We'll take care of you right away. I am really sorry, sir. Would you like a free dessert after your meal?"

"I don't think so. Let's go, Eddie. There's another restaurant across the street. I don't need to be patronized," Lance said.

"You're right, Lance. We don't need to be disrespected. She didn't forget. She just didn't care to serve two black men, or maybe it wasn't her priority," Eddie spat.

The couple sitting next to their table turned and looked at them in a strange way as Lance and Eddie left the restaurant.

* * * * * *

That Monday, Lance was informed by his boss that there was an opportunity for some business in Ohio. Lance was told to visit the Department of Information Security (DOIS), which was located in Dayton. The Planning and Logistics Office of DOIS had an opportunity for McIntyre to bid on a solicitation, and Lance was requested to develop a cost and technical proposal. The business opportunity was worth twenty-five million dollars over a five-year period. If Lance could win this government contract, it would be Lance's largest business account.

"How're you doing?" Kenya asked, walking into Lance's office.

"Busy. I'm working on this business opportunity. I'll definitely be consumed with this project for a couple of weeks," Lance responded. "How are things with you, Kenya?"

"Okay. You seem to spend most of your time in the office. If you need help, I'm here."

"Sure thing. I'll certainly need some help with collecting the cost data for this proposal."

"Okay, no problem. I can also help you with the technical proposal, especially with the Quality Assurance Plan."

"Sounds good. You are really a big help around the office, Kenya, especially on my team."

"Well...thank you, Lance. I like being on your team. Do you like my new earrings?" Kenya asked, seeking validation and wanting the focus of conversation to be more on her than work.

"They're lovely and they look good on you," Lance replied as he wondered privately to himself why such a question was asked.

"Thanks," Kenya responded as Lance's approval gave her a sense of temporary security.

"By the way, Kenya, I won't be able to make it to Upper Nile this week because of the time I have to commit to this proposal. Sorry."

"Okay, I understand." Truth is, Kenya understood but was still a little disappointed as indicated in her facial expression. Her smiling face quickly transformed into a stoic face.

"It will probably be in another two weeks. I will definitely let you know, Kenya."

As Kenya walked out of his office, wearing a tight fitting skirt that highlighted the curves of her lower body, Lance stared at her body discreetly. Once she was out of view, he shook off the impure thoughts and reached for the phone to call Valerie.

"Hello, Valerie. How you doing?"

"Fine, just sitting here talking with Julia and reminiscing about old times."

"There's nothing wrong with that. Hey, I called to let you know I will not be able to come by tonight. I'm working on a big project and it's taking up a lot of my time. But I'll come by to see you soon, okay?"

"Alright. Julia and I have a lot to do anyway."

"I love you," Lance said.

"I love you, too, honey. By the way, I spoke with my mother earlier today and she is really excited about our wedding. She's practically told everyone in her neighborhood. Can you believe that?"

"Oh really?"

"Yes. And, oh yeah, I have to drive up to Philly on Sunday to take a look at some wedding dresses and to finish with the wedding invitations. There's so much to do."

"I know…you have your plate full. Just keep me posted on what I need to do."

"All you need to do is show up at the church," Valerie said jokingly. But in Lance's mind, he knew there was a serious undertone to the statement she had made.

"Well, baby, I have to get back to work. I'll talk to you a little later."

As Lance was leaving work, he ran into Trey, an old high school buddy he hadn't seen in two years. Last time he had seen Trey was when he had gotten in some trouble with the law for assaulting his girlfriend and had to serve thirty days in jail. Trey was a burly dude with a well-defined muscular body and smooth dark skin, almost jet-black, who worked as a security guard at night and indulged in excessive bodybuilding during the day.

"What's up, Trey?"

"Yo, Lance, what's up, man?" Trey spoke in his street vernacular. "I almost didn't recognize you. Long time no see, dawg."

"It has been a while. What have you been up to?"

"Still working in security and trying to qualify for this bodybuilding contest."

"I hear you, man. I guess you're determined to be Mr. Universe, huh?"

"Definitely, I'm working on it. I'm serious about my body. Are you still making the big bucks? Living like a king, huh?" Trey said as he laughed.

"I'm trying, brother. I'm still employed with McIntyre Corporation, but I am starting my own company."

"Oh really?"

"Oh yeah, I have to do my own thing."

"Hey, you the man. If anyone can do it, it's you, my man."

Trey was a blue collar kind of guy who always admired Lance. Lance and Trey use to be running buddies when they were in high school, and they even attended some wild parties together back in the day. Lance had learned a lot of things about women from Trey, who had a reputation of being a womanizer. Despite his reputation, though, women couldn't resist his muscular body.

"How are the women treating you?" Trey asked.

"I don't pursue women like before when we used to hangout at the Ritz Night Club," Lance replied, although he knew that he still lusted for women like Reina and Kenya.

"That's hard for me to believe because I know how much you love women, especially the pretty ones. Come on, Lance… you know that you will always be a player. It's in your blood."

"Now, I am trying to do right. When I was younger, I didn't know what I wanted. As a matter of fact, I am planning to get married in few months."

"Get out of here! Serious?" Trey responded.

"Yeah, that's right. I think I've found the right one. I have put my past behind me."

"Congratulations and good luck. I have to respect that."

"We have to exchange numbers and keep in touch because it's so hard to keep up with you, man. I'll send you an invitation to the wedding."

"Okay, man. Cool."

* * * * * *

Lance and Eddie met for lunch at Lillie's Café. Eddie was anxiously waiting to talk to Lance, who arrived five minutes after Eddie.

"I thought about your business proposal long and hard. I even considered my fifteen-year career at SBO. I am fully aware of what I'm giving up, but I'm willing to make the sacrifice at this point in my life. Therefore, count me in."

"Cool, man! I needed to hear that. I am glad you are coming aboard, and I will do my best to make sure we succeed."

Lance and Eddie shook hands and drank to their future business relationship.

"I'm here to help. So, let's talk about the business plan. Your marketing strategy is great, but I think we should begin focusing on how to obtain a business loan. If we don't have the sufficient amount of start-up capital, our ship will quickly sink into the ocean of lost dreams. I want to be on the winning team," Eddie voiced with optimism.

"I completely agree, Eddie."

"Have you figured out the estimated start-up cost?"

"It's approximately two hundred thousand dollars based on my market research. This includes office space, equipment, marketing, advertising, etc.," Lance responded as he reached into his briefcase and pulled out his business plan.

"What financial institutions do you have in mind? I have a list of banks at my office that may be helpful. My research has found Andrew Financial Bank to be quite liberal in its lending practices," Eddie suggested.

"I haven't thought about any bank at this point, but Andrew Financial Bank sounds interesting. I will leave this business plan with you for review. Maybe some of your colleagues at SBO could also take a look at it," Lance suggested, putting ketchup on his French fries.

"Okay. I'll run it by them and see what their opinion is. I will treat your business like you were another small business seeking assistance through SBO. I will be leaving SBO soon, so I don't see this as a conflict of interest or anything. I'm just preparing my nest egg before leaving."

"I understand, bro. I think we're getting started on the right track, and I have a good feeling about this venture. Once we receive the financing for this business, we can then officially quit our jobs."

"That's right, Lance... we can leave the plantation," Eddie said, taking a bite of his turkey sandwich.

"That's right, partner. No more whips," Lance laughed.

* * * * * *

After lunch, Lance decided to go to the gym and work out for a while.

"Ola. Como esta bien?" Reina greeted as Lance entered her office.

"Bien," Lance replied.

"Well. . .you're trying," she said in response to Lance's attempt at speaking Spanish.

"I'm still depending on you to teach me more."

"I see, or should I say 'I hear'," she giggled.

"I came by to see when you would be available to give me one session of fitness counseling. Also, I would like you to show me some abdomen training techniques."

"Well, this week I'm booked, and next week I am traveling to Puerto Rico to see my grandmother for two weeks. How about I let you know when I can fit you in when I return?"

"Okay. Puerto Rico, huh? Sounds like fun."

"I am looking forward to seeing my grandmother because I haven't seen her in five years. I understand that she is sick. Can you close the door a little?" Reina requested before continuing. "That noise is loud outside. WKYS is here today having some promotional campaign for fitness."

Reina's office was small, compact, windowless, and with lots of papers strewn about on her desk. There was nothing spectacular about the office. In fact, it really appeared to be a place simply for immediate privacy.

"That's better," she said after he had pushed the door shut. "So, tell me, what have you been up to?"

"Not too much besides working. My partner and I are in the process of starting a business."

"Wow, that's great. You seem like the business type, Lance."

"Oh really? And you say that because…?"

"Sometimes you can be so serious. I like a serious man who knows what he wants and takes charge."

"Thanks. I've always been this way. I just know what I want."

"How 'bout this? I'll give you two sessions. I will give you the counseling aspect and then the demonstration."

As she rose from her office chair, the sight of Reina's tight shorts immediately turned Lance on. Standing as well, Lance said, "You look good."

"Thank you. I have been doing a lot of training lately and teaching two spinning classes a day."

"I can see the results."

"I guess all the hard work is paying off then."

Lance walked over near Reina and extended his immense hand to her. Knowing that being affectionate was a custom of her Latin culture, and that Reina was the type of woman who hugged a lot, he took advantage of the situation. "Didn't you forget to give me my hug? Can I get a hug?" Lance asked.

"Sure, Papi."

Lance placed his arms around Reina's waist and kissed her on both cheeks, holding her close for longer than he should have.

"Aren't we frisky? Don't get carried away. Don't you have a girlfriend?" Reina said reluctantly, appearing to be somewhat embarrassed. She was attracted to Lance but didn't know how to express it. She was painfully shy.

"I have friends," Lance replied, refusing to disclose his engagement. He still had some of the "player instinct" in him. "I'm sorry. I just needed a little love," Lance said as he smiled and rubbed his chin, knowing full well he wanted to be with Reina sexually since he had not had sex in a while.

"Do you like to dance?" Reina asked, changing the subject.

"Oh yeah, I can shake my booty," Lance said as he laughed and did a little funny dance move.

"Well when I get back from Puerto Rico, I will take you to a Latin club with me."

"I look forward to it." And with that said, he made his exit out the door while he was still on his best behavior.

Feeling a sense of guilt after flirting with Reina, Lance drove to visit Valerie at her apartment later that evening after work. Lance's interest in Reina was primarily sexual, although she was a nice and friendly woman.

"How's my future wife doing?"

"Lovely. And how is my future husband doing?"

"Great. I brought you some flowers."

"Oh, how sweet of you. Thank you, honey," Valerie said, placing her soft lips against his. "I have to go back to Philly on Saturday and I want you to come with me. My parents asked about you."

"Okay. I haven't been to Philly in a while. How are your mom and Reverend Melbourne doing?" Lance asked.

"They're fine," Valerie replied. "And how is your family?"

"They are doing well. They're also excited. They keep asking me questions about the wedding. You know how that is."

"Oh yeah, I know very well. We'll have to make it a point to go to DC to visit your parents soon," Valerie declared.

"Absolutely."

Valerie's apartment was impeccably clean, unusually organized, and had a serene effect with the contemporary gospel music playing in the background. It was a simple abode, with few pictures hanging on the walls. There was a black bible on her living room table and a picture of her mother and father in a gold frame nearby.

"Come sit next to me and hold me."

Lance joined Valerie on the sofa and slowly put his muscular arms around her waist. She leaned into him, resting her head on his shoulder. This was comforting to both of them; two people in love.

Lance wanted to share his business plans with Valerie. However, he decided to wait, not wanting to ruin the moment. In addition, Lance was somewhat apprehensive about telling Valerie because she didn't seemingly display a strong interest based on previous conversations.

******

The next day, Lance met with Allen Frisco in his office to discuss his DOIS project.

"How's the project coming along?" Allen asked.

"Not bad. I'm just trying to get the best pricing and make sure our technical approach to this project is sound," Lance replied with confidence.

"Great! We have two more weeks left before we submit the proposal to DOIS. I'm confident you will do a great job."

"No worries, I will provide a good proposal. This is a big opportunity for McIntyre."

"If you need any help with the pricing or any aspect of the proposal, I have hired an outside consultant to provide guidance on technical and marketing matters. His name is Nathaniel Watson, and he has over twenty years of IT and marketing experience."

"Oh really! Are we experiencing problems with sales and production?" Lance asked in a surprised manner as he straightened his bright yellow necktie.

"Not necessarily, but we could always improve our production. We want to be number one in our region. I also want to make you fully aware that this new consultant is not a replacement for the Vice-President's position we discussed weeks ago. It is still my intentions to fill the position at some point."

"Well, that's good to know," Lance responded indifferently.

"Nathaniel is not in the office at the moment. However, I will introduce him to you when he comes in. He's only in the office about three days out of the week."

"Okay. I look forward to meeting him."

"Oh yeah, I forgot to give you your five-thousand-dollar bonus check. Here it is," he said while retrieving it from the center drawer of his desk. "Again, congratulations on the fifteen-million-dollar contract with DOSP. Keep up the good work."

"Thank you very much, Allen." Lance shook his hand, ending their conversation, and proceeded to carry on with his day.

Lance was happy to have received the bonus. However, he was suspicious about the hiring of a consultant in the sales department. The Marketing Department had consistently done well over the last four years and the sales continued to climb each year. Lance thought that perhaps this consultant could be positioning himself for the Vice-President's position. Lance thought it was strange that Allen hadn't informed his employees of his decision prior to hiring the consultant.

"Hi, Helen, those cookies were delicious," Lance said, stopping by her office.

"Thank you, Lance. They were fresh out of the oven."

"I could tell. They practically melted in my mouth."

"Have you met our new consultant?" Helen asked in an investigative manner, seeking an explanation.

"No. I just met with Allen. Hopefully, I will meet him today."

"Just between you and me, Lance, I don't have the slightest idea of why we need a consultant. It doesn't make sense."

"I agree, Helen."

"Well, I have to run to a meeting. I'll talk to you later."

Helen confirmed Lance's suspicion.

"What's up, Lance? Have you met the new consultant?" Buddy asked as he ran into Lance coming out of Helen's office.

"No," Lance said nonchalantly.

"Is everything okay?" Buddy asked as his lanky body stood in front of Lance.

"I'm fine, Buddy," Lance responded flatly. He didn't like talking to Buddy outside of what had to do with business and professional matters.

"I got a joke for you, Lance."

"Um...I really don't have the time to--"

"It's only going to take a few seconds. Laughter is good for you. It's just a joke."

"Go head," Lance grudgingly replied.

"What did the black soldiers do when the General told them to 'get down' during combat with the enemy?"

"I don't know. What?"

"They started dancing," Buddy said as he burst out in loud laughter while holding his stomach.

"You think that's funny? I will not dignify your statement with a response. Excuse me, please." Lance walked away, clearly pissed off. He knew Buddy was trying to provoke him.

* * * * * *

During his lunch break, Lance made a visit to the loan officer at Andrew Financial Bank, an African-American owned bank located in Silver Spring, Maryland. Upon Eddie and Lance's agreement to name the business Freedom Technologies, since it represented freedom for both of them in terms of their jobs, Lance submitted the business plan to the bank for approval.

"Good afternoon, Mr. Kojo," the female loan officer said, greeting Lance with a friendly smile and a soft voice. She was an African-American woman with streaks of gray in her hair.

"How are you?"

"I am fine for a Tuesday. Is it still raining outside?"

"Yes, it's drizzling a little."

"You know, our office has really been busy processing loans this week."

"I can imagine," Lance said as he smiled with immense curiosity.

"It is my understanding that you are requesting a two hundred thousand dollar loan for your business," the loan officer said.

"That's correct," Lance replied.

"What I need is for you to fill out this application. It will take at least twenty-four to forty-eight hours to review your application and business plan. After a complete review, I will provide you with a decision regarding your loan. You certainly have provided us with a lot of information to review. If we have any further questions concerning your application, I will contact you immediately."

"Okay."

"Here's a pen for you to complete the form. Feel free to fill it out at my desk, but please excuse me while I go speak with my colleague," the loan officer said while exiting the office.

Lance felt he had a good chance of getting the loan, appearing quite relaxed and confident as he walked out of the bank.

* * * * * *

Later that day, Lance went to visit his parents, who lived in a spacious townhouse in Southwest, DC near the waterfront. As Lance pulled up behind his father's Lincoln Town car in the small driveway of his parents' townhouse, he took notice of the changes the community had undergone as a result of recent gentrification.

Lance walked in the house and proceeded to the kitchen where his mother was cooking. Mrs. Kojo, a retired schoolteacher, was a petite woman of about five feet four inches tall. She was in her late fifties, had gray hair, wore glasses, and always displayed a dazzling smile.

"How are things, son?"

"I've been busy doing many things lately. Where's Dad?" Lance asked as he planted a kiss on Mrs. Kojo's cheek. Mrs. Kojo was sitting at the kitchen table reading the local newspaper, having just finished cooking.

"He's in bed sleeping," Mrs. Kojo replied as she looked up over her reading glasses at Lance.

Lance's mother, who was active in the community, had just returned from doing some volunteer work for DC's Public School System.

"I've been preparing myself for this wedding, and Valerie has been busy with the wedding plans. It seems like she goes to Philly every weekend." Lance pulled the kitchen chair back and sat down in front of his mother at the table.

"How is Valerie?"

"She's doing well. I'm supposed to bring her to see you next week," Lance said as he glanced at the sports section of the newspaper.

"You better tell her to come see her future mother-in-law! Valerie is such a sweet young lady. I'm proud of you and Valerie. Do you need any help with the wedding?"

"Not really. I think Valerie's family is taking care most of it."

"Do you want anything to eat? I have some jerk chicken, peas, and rice," Mrs. Kojo asked. Mrs. Kojo was an excellent cook and enjoyed cooking food from back home where she grew up in Black River, Jamaica.

"No…no… I just ate, Mom. Maybe I will take some food with me when I leave, though. What I came over for was to let you know about my business plans. I will be starting a business in the next couple of weeks. I have already applied for a business loan and am waiting to see if I get approved. As a matter of fact, I just came from the bank. What do you think about this idea?"

"Son, I think it is great! You're following in your father's footsteps. You know, he had a very successful real estate business. Remember, son, I want you to do what makes you happy. I support you."

"Thanks, Mom," Lance replied as the comforting words of his mother made him feel at ease. He then rubbed his right hand over his face.

"What does Valerie think?"

"I haven't really told her yet."

"I'm sure she would understand. You guys will be able to work things out no matter what."

"Yeah," Lance said reluctantly. He had not told Valerie about everything, especially the loan.

"Is that my son in there talking?" Lance's father said as he walked in the kitchen with his bathrobe on. He went to the refrigerator and poured himself a glass of grape juice. "Honey, that food smells good," Mr. Kojo continued.

"Hi, Dad. How you doing?"

"I'm fine for an old sixty-five-year-old man with arthritis in his left wrist," Lance's father said as he laughed in an uncanny manner. Lance's father had quite a sense of humor, his laugh being unique and contagious, and was very protective of his son. Lance looked a lot like his father, only a little taller and thinner.

Lance's father, who grew up in DC, was a retired real estate broker and had been very active in the civil rights movement during the sixties. He even changed his last name from Williams to Kojo as a form of protest.

"I don't see you that much, son. What have you been up to?" Lance's father asked as he finished his glass of grape juice.

"I've been working on a business plan for the business I will be starting soon."

"Congratulations! Like father like son, huh? How does Valerie feel about this?"

"Mom asked the same question. I haven't told her yet," Lance replied.

"Well, your mother and I think a lot alike. Now, I want you to know I'm with you, son. Just make sure that your future wife is on board, because if she does not support you, you may have some serious problems in your marriage. I was fortunate enough to have your mother's support in my real estate business. And you know how we struggled in the beginning."

"I appreciate your advice, Dad, and I have thought about this idea for quite some time now."

"I hear you loud and clear, son. Just think about what I said. That's all I'm saying."

"How was the trip to Jamaica?" Lance asked, changing the subject.

"It was very nice. But those mosquitoes in Black River nearly ate me alive! I was glad to see my family and the beaches were so beautiful. Your father was ready to come back to DC after the first week, though. The mosquitoes gave him a tough time. Otherwise, it was fun," Mrs. Kojo replied.

"Your mother is right. I couldn't take those mosquitoes, but I brought back a whole lot of fruit. You like mangos?" Lance's father asked.

"Yeah, I will definitely get some, Dad, but I gotta run right now," Lance responded as he started walking toward the door.

"Please say hi to Valerie and her family for us," Mr. Kojo said.

"Okay, Dad."

Lance had a strong family that supported him. And while Lance seemed to have garnered up a lot of support for his business, he still had not gotten the approval from the most significant person is his life: Valerie. Later that evening, Lance went to his house in Mitchellville and received an unexpected visit from Valerie.

"Hey, baby, I'm surprised to see you here this time of day."

"Yeah, I know. I got off from work early and had to drop off a package to a client, so I thought I would pay my honey a visit," Valerie said.

"Well, I'm glad you did. You seem to be in a good mood today."

"Yes, I am, especially when I see you. How was your day, honey?" Valerie asked as she hugged and kissed Lance on the lips, and then put her arms around his waist.

"It was okay. Busy as usual."

"I love you, Lance."

"Not as much as I love you, Valerie."

"I love you more."

"I love you so much until I have decided to marry you," Lance said as he smiled and his eyes twinkled.

"Okay, enough of this mushy stuff. Remember, we are going to Philly on Saturday, so I will be by to pick you up at nine o'clock that morning. I want you to drive, though."

"If you insist, baby."

"Is everything okay, Lance?"

"Yeah. Why?"

"You look a little preoccupied."

"Not really. Well... I am working on something."

"You mean with your job?"

"No. You remember when I told you that I had some business ideas?"

"Yeah."

"Well... I have been thinking seriously about this for quite a while and have begun to execute my business plan."

"What business plans are you talking about, Lance?"

"I'm starting a business, Valerie. I'm working out the details with Eddie. As a matter of fact, I am waiting to hear from this bank about my loan."

"Why haven't you discussed this with me before now? I didn't think you were serious about your business plans. Are you sure you're doing the right thing? What about McIntyre Corporation? You have a great career there."

"Truth is, you seemed somewhat disinterested."

"Listen, Lance...I am not going to get into this any further with you. Maybe you need more time to reflect on this business stuff. Hopefully, you will come back to your senses."

"I know what I want, Valerie. Let me explain my plan to you."

"You know, Lance… let's not spoil our time together right now. Why don't we talk about this later, okay?"

"If that's how you feel, but I want you to know this is very important to me," Lance said as he looked Valerie directly in the eyes and placed his hands on both of her shoulders in order to emphasize his point.

"Apparently, it is very important to you because you didn't include me in your decision," Valerie said as she turned her head in another direction to avoid eye contact.

It was evident that they did not see eye to eye on this matter. Valerie's idea of success was a job that was visible and accompanied with the trappings, whereas, Lance was willing to take a step out on faith.

"Lance, I have to go now. I'll talk with you later," Valerie said abruptly. Lance felt a little disappointed in Valerie's reaction to his news. However, he thought perhaps he could convince her later that he was making the right decision. Despite Valerie's lack of support and "bourgie" ways, he loved her deeply and was optimistic about their future.

Chapter Five

Thursday evening, after returning home from work, Lance opened a letter he received from Andrew Financial Bank. To his disappointment, the bank had not approved his loan. At that moment, it seemed like his whole world was crashing down around him. Lance sat in his brown reclining chair, trying to make sense of the loan rejection. He looked distraught and felt uneasy. He had received a wake-up call about life: Things don't always come easy. Lance knew the pursuit of financing would be incredibly daunting, but he thought it would be an easy loan based on Eddie's recommendation. He dragged himself into the kitchen like a wounded soldier on a battlefield and opened a bottle of red wine. He wanted to be relaxed. Lance pondered for a while as he sipped on his wine and leaned against the kitchen counter. Finally, he decided he needed to talk to someone about it, so he called Eddie.

"Hey Eddie, I need to talk man," Lance blurted out, hardly giving Eddie a chance to say hello.

"Sure. Is everything okay, Lance?"

"Not really. I just received a letter from Andrew Financial Bank. I didn't get the loan. I thought it would be quick and easy to obtain the loan from the institution you suggested, but...I don't know."

"You're kidding me, right?"

"No, I wish that I were. I'm serious."

"Gosh! I'm really surprised. Did they give you a reason for not approving the loan?"

"No. The letter was very general and didn't identify any specific reasons. In my opinion, we put together a very good business plan, and I was expecting a positive response. You know...approval? Mind you, this bank is African-American owned. On top of that, I have good credit, Eddie."

"Yes, this bank is black owned, but not all banks' lending policies are the same. We can't allow this to hold us back, you know. We just have to keep applying to other banks."

"Do you think I should go back to Andrew Financial to ask for a more detailed explanation?"

"No, let's keep moving on. I didn't say this would be easy. Let's try Seba Security Bank. It's a large commercial bank. Maybe those small banks are tight on their cash."

"Okay. I agree. We can't allow this small setback to stop us. No matter what, I am not going to let them stop me!" Lance declared.

"That's the spirit, Lance. You know how hard it is for black folks to get financing for a business. It's a bitch. But we must keep fighting!" Eddie added.

* * * * * *

Although Lance was a little depressed, he wanted to bring sunshine into Valerie's life after their little spat about his business plans. So, he sent a dozen of red roses and a box of Godiva chocolates to her law firm. The flowers arrived that morning and the secretary buzzed Valerie's office by way of intercom, happily informing her of the pleasant surprise. As she emerged from her office, a big smile appeared on her face upon seeing the flowers on the secretary's desk.

While returning to her office, one of the lawyers of the firm saw her with the floral arrangement and chocolates. "I see someone likes you, Valerie. Nice flowers," the young lawyer said.

"Oh thanks. I have no idea who they are from," Valerie replied bashfully, quickly disappearing into her office. She wanted a private moment to enjoy her flowers and read the card attached. *"Valerie...I am sorry about our disagreement yesterday. You are as sweet as these chocolates. I love you. Lance."*

* * * * * *

While at his office, Lance worked primarily on the DOIS proposal. As he was reviewing the proposal, Allen Frisco came into his office to introduce Nathaniel Watson, the new consultant. Nathaniel was a man of average height with blond hair and blue eyes, who appeared to be in his early forties.

"Hi, Lance. I hope I didn't disturb you. I would like to introduce you to Nathaniel Watson. You remember I told you about him. Nathaniel will be providing some technical assistance to our team."

"Oh yeah, I remember in our last meeting. Hello, Nathaniel. It's nice to finally meet you," Lance said.

"It's nice to meet you, also. I have heard so many good things about you, Lance. Let me know if you need any help with your proposals. I am excited about being here at McIntyre," Nathaniel said as he gave Lance a firm handshake and no-nonsense look.

"Okay. Thank you. I look forward to working with you," Lance replied. Nathaniel then excused himself and left the office.

"How is the proposal coming along?" Allen asked.

"Great. As a matter of fact, I am mailing the proposal certified within the next hour."

"Okay, but in the future, Lance, I would like Nathaniel to review all of your work, especially the proposals."

"I wasn't aware of this, Allen. I don't understand. Is this a new procedure?" Lance was baffled by this news.

"Yes, we use to do this when Barbara Taylor was Vice President of Sales and Marketing. I have decided to re-institute this old policy since it seemed to work well in the past. I believe in the concept of quality assurance. A system of checks and balances is always good."

"Oh? Okay. No problem."

Lance felt terribly suspicious about Nathaniel. This further confirmed the fact that Nathaniel was being secretly trained for the position as Vice President. Lance did not feel good about this. He could read between the lines of Allen's hidden agenda.

After talking with Allen, Lance went to Seba Security Bank on his lunch break and made a second attempt at applying for a business loan for his proposed business. When he returned to his office, he checked his voice mail and listened to the message from Valerie.

"Thanks for the flowers, sweetie. You are full of surprises, you rascal!"

"At least someone's day is much brighter," he thought out loud to himself.

******

Lance drove to Philly with Valerie on Saturday morning from his house, arriving late that afternoon. Valerie rang the doorbell of the well-maintained row house and her mother answered wearing a white baseball cap, a pair of worn blue jeans, and a pair of yellow plastic gloves with a tiny shovel in her right hand.

"Hello, Valerie. Hi, Lance. How are the two of you doing? I was out back working in the garden. I've been waiting for you all the last three hours," Mrs. Melbourne said as she walked them into the living room.

"Hello, Mom," Valerie said, planting a kiss on her cheek. "We were stuck in traffic on I-95 North and then there was a car accident at Broad and Market streets. It took us forever to get here."

"How you doing, Mrs. Melbourne," Lance said while noticing the strong resemblance between her and Valerie. She was an older version of Valerie.

"I'm so glad to see you, Lance. It's been a while. I was just picking some tomatoes from my garden. I am such a mess right now," Mrs. Melbourne said as she pointed to the dirt on her gloves and knees of her jeans.

"You look fine. A little dirt can't hurt your appearance," Lance responded humorously.

Reverend Melbourne slowly descended the stairs, stopping midway and placing his right hand on his lower back before continuing to the bottom. He was a light-skinned heavyset man with a bushy mustache mixed with gray that stood out prominently on his face. He wore a pair of black slacks and a dark blue shirt.

"How're you doing, young man?" Reverend Melbourne said, extending his right hand to Lance.

"I am fine and how are you doing, Reverend Melbourne?" Lance replied in a gentleman-like way.

"How's my baby girl doing?" he asked while hugging Valerie.

"I am good, Dad. How's your back?" Valerie asked.

"It's getting better. The doctor gave me this new medication, so I'm feeling a little better...Praise God! I was upstairs reading my bible."

"I'm glad you are getting better. Preparing for church tomorrow, huh?" Valerie said.

"Oh yeah, and I would like to invite you and Lance out to Sunday service. It's a tradition in the Melbourne family to attend church every Sunday. I don't accept any excuses unless you are sick," Reverend Melbourne demanded as he looked back and forth between Lance and Valerie.

"We'll try, but we may have to leave tomorrow morning. We have so much work to do before the wedding," Valerie responded apologetically.

As with Valerie's apartment, the house was impeccably clean. The sun shined brightly into the living room, which reflected on the shiny antique table. There was an antique magazine rack placed right next to a seemingly old piano. The hardwood floors in the living room looked virtually spotless, and there was a fresh fragrance that permeated throughout the house.

"Do you attend church frequently, Lance?" Reverend Melbourne asked while standing at the base of the stairway with his arms crossed.

"I don't attend church as much as I should. I travel quite a bit with my job and don't always have the time," Lance replied cautiously.

"As I said earlier, it is part of our tradition. You know, Lance...you can never get too busy to worship the Lord. Remember, young man, my daughter is a woman of God," Reverend Melbourne declared.

Lance hesitated for a moment and then looked at Valerie nervously. He didn't feel that Reverend Melbourne had a right to make demands on him. This was only Lance's second meeting with Valerie's father, and he felt his views were imposing and a bit intrusive. Lance felt momentarily uncomfortable and folded his hands in a defensive posture. Moreover, Lance was a product of a religious upbringing and didn't feel he had to prove his commitment to God to anyone. Besides, he was tired from traveling and did not want to hear the Reverend's pontification.

"Are you making demands on me?" Lance replied in an agitated way, the look of discomfort engulfing his face. Visiting with the intentions of making a good impression on Valerie's family, engaging in a debate with Reverend Melbourne was the last thing on his mind.

Feeling some tension between Lance and her father, Valerie intervened. "Dad, stop your preaching. We get your point."

"I am just trying to tell you what is right," Reverend Melbourne said, noticing the irritated expression on Lance's face.

"I understand your concern, Dad, and I know you mean well, but we are adults and you don't have to tell us how to conduct our lives. The church will be a very vital part of our marriage. Lance is a good Christian man. Isn't that right, baby?" Valerie said as she looked at Lance, hoping he would echo her sentiments.

"Yes, I believe in worshipping the Lord," Lance said confidently as he smiled at Valerie.

"Are you guys hungry? Valerie told me that your favorite cake was red velvet so I baked one for dessert," Mrs. Melbourne asked, attempting to help ease the tension in the room.

"I could eat a little food. Thank you, Mrs. Melbourne," Lance uttered.

"Good. Dinner will be ready in about fifteen minutes."

"Amen to that," said the Reverend.

******

The next morning, Lance and Valerie drove back to Maryland after attending Reverend Melbourne's service, which was spiritually enlightening.

"Did you have a nice time?" Valerie asked.

"It was okay. I think your mother is very friendly, but your father is a little pushy. I'm sure he means well, though."

"He's just very protective. When I was growing up in Philly, I was not allowed to date until I was seventeen years old. I couldn't go out dancing like my other friends. I couldn't watch certain television shows or listen to secular music. These are some of the rules I had to adhere to as a child. I was known as the minister's daughter."

"I hope this doesn't create any problems with our marriage, because I am not going to have him running our lives. I don't mean any disrespect to your father, but this is the way it has to be."

"I understand, Lance. And trust me, it won't be a problem."

"Okay."

"Are you still leaving McIntyre? I know you're not really serious, are you?" Valerie asked, hoping to convince Lance to change his mind.

"Yes, I'm moving in that direction," Lance said diplomatically, not wanting to create another disagreement.

"Oh really? Why would you want to do that when we both have two good incomes? In the initial stages of our marriage, I want stability. Being a lawyer, I know start-up businesses can be very risky. Is it possible for you to wait a few years?"

"No. I'm not happy at McIntyre Corporation. I believe it is time to make my move at this point in my life while I'm still young."

"Do you know that over fifty percent of small businesses fail in their first year?" Valerie asked rhetorically, looking at Lance with concern as they drove down I-95 South. Her intent was to discourage Lance from pursuing his business interest.

"Yes, but what does that have to do with my business? I don't think in a negative way. I am determined to put a lot into this business, including my time. I can't wait another five or six years. I've always wanted to have my own business. It was one of my dreams," Lance argued as he paid the toll in Baltimore.

"When will you have time for me? I need you in my life. I don't want a part-time husband. I want things for us to be right. I believe this business will take you away from me," Valerie cried out.

"I will always make time for you. And I may even need your advice on some legal issues. This way, I can get you involved in the business. I need your support, Val."

"I want you, Lance, not your business. I have a career of my own. You're being unreasonable and selfish. Think about the other people in your life. Suppose we want to have children?"

"I am not selfish. I just have to do this. Sure, there is a price to pay, but I am willing to make sacrifices for my freedom and our financial independence in the future. I have always been supportive of your career. So why can't you show me the same support?"

"I don't understand you. It's simply just not practical to start a business at this point," Valerie insisted.

Without speaking another word during the remainder of the drive, they arrived at Valerie's apartment, Lance helped her with the luggage, and they kissed goodbye.

Chapter Six

The next day, Lance traveled to DOIS in Dayton, Ohio to do an oral presentation on behalf of McIntyre Corporation. Lance met with a contracting officer and his technical team. Conducting himself like a consummate executive, he sold the quality assurance approach to DOIS, with his presentation being quite convincing. After his presentation in Ohio, Lance flew back to DC.

Two days later, he received a call from Jerry Patton, an African-American contracting officer with DOIS.

"I would like to congratulate you on your contract award?" Jerry said.

"Thank you," Lance replied while smiling and holding the phone close to his ear as he sat down in his big leather chair, his eyes showing excitement.

"We were pleased with your presentation, but more importantly, your technical approach to our requirement and your proven Quality Assurance Program contributed to our final decision. In addition, your price was competitive and favorable to our cost estimate for this project. This contract is valued at twenty-five million dollars over a five year period. That translates into approximately five million per year. I look forward to doing business with McIntyre Corporation."

"Thank you, and we are excited about this opportunity," Lance responded.

"We will be scheduling a meeting to notify all parties associated with this contract, including my technical team."

"Okay. I look forward to meeting with you again. By the way, do you know of any good golf courses in Ohio?" Lance asked.

"Yes, I know of several golf courses. I see we have another golf enthusiast, huh?" Jerry replied.

"Yes, indeed. I love the game."

"There's a golf course about twenty minutes from Dayton. The Bobby James Williams' Golf Resort is really nice. I play there all the time. Let me know when you will be in Ohio again. Perhaps we will play the next time you are here."

"Absolutely, sounds like a plan. Again, thank you for the opportunity."

Lance was extremely excited about the contract deal with DOIS and immediately called Allen Frisco on his office phone, being too excited to walk upstairs and tell him.

"We just won the contract with DOIS," Lance said as he struggled to hold his phone to his ear.

"Great! Lance, you are unbelievable. Congratulations! You really know how to bring it home," Allen said as he cheered Lance on.

"Thank you. I am so happy, Allen! This was a big opportunity. I'm glad we could land this contract. This is what it's all about: winning," Lance said as he immersed himself in a feeling of accomplishment.

"Why don't you come up to my office and tell me more about the contract arrangements."

"Okay, I'll be right up."

******

Thursday evening, Lance met with Kenya at the Upper Nile for a private celebration between just the two of them. He wanted to thank Kenya for her help with the DOIS Project.

"Ladies first," Lance said as he entered the club, giving Kenya the lead.

"Thank you, Lance. I can't believe you finally decided to come to the Upper Nile."

"Yes, it took a while, but we are here for a good reason. It's to celebrate our contract deal. We made the big twenty-five million dollar score, and I couldn't have done it without your help. We make a good team."

"Well, I'm proud to be on your team. I am learning a lot from you."

"Good. I'm also proud to have you on my team. You are very intelligent and a fast learner. Hey, let's sit near the stage. That way, we can hear the poets and the band without straining our ears," Lance suggested.

"Excuse me, sir. Is anyone sitting at this table?" Lance asked, quickly grabbing a table toward the front of the crowded club.

"No, just let me move my coat from off the chair," the man replied.

"Thanks."

"Excuse me for one minute, Lance, while I go to the ladies room," Kenya said.

"Sure," Lance responded.

A few minutes passed and Kenya returned to the table.

"How is my make up? Is it too much?" Kenya asked.

"It's fine, Kenya. It looks perfect."

"Thanks. Do you like my new dress? I actually made it," Kenya asked as she raised her hands up in a way to say, 'how do I look'. Kenya looked regal in the beautiful dark blue dress with lace around the collar and arms. She yearned for Lance's approval, which meant a lot to her.

"I see you have other talents too, huh? Your dress looks wonderful. I must say you look marvelous. I say, just marvelous, dear!" Lance said jokingly in a fake British accent.

Kenya started to laugh as she smiled bashfully. Her glowing eyes sparkled to the symphony of Lance's complimentary words.

"You're so funny, Lance. You know, I have a poem, but I am too shy to read it. I have to develop a little more courage before I attempt to go on stage."

"Come on, Kenya," he coaxed. "I would love to hear your poem."

"Well…it's actually a love poem. Maybe next time I will read it. Do you have a poem? Didn't you tell me you wrote poetry?"

"Yes, I do write poetry. I would read my poem on stage tonight since I'm in a good mood, but I don't have my material with me."

"I'm in a good mood too, Lance."

"I am curious as to what you are reading these days."

"I'm reading Invisible Man by Ralph Ellison."

"Good book! I've read it."

"I'm just finishing up the first chapter, so I can't give you my opinion on it yet."

"I love a woman who reads. I like to be engaged intellectually and introduced to new ideas. Reading allows me to explore the world. I particularly enjoy reading about the black experience and other cultures," Lance said as he emphasized his point with hand gestures.

"This is really intriguing. I didn't know this side of you. In the office, you are so professional. My father is a Black History Professor at Morgan State University. As a matter of fact, he named me after the African country of Kenya. My father introduced me to reading when I was a child, especially books on black history."

"What's your father's name?"

"Professor Kwame Harden."

"Is he still teaching?"

"Yes, but he took time off at Morgan State. He is on a sabbatical leave doing research in West Africa on the Atlantic slave trade.

"Wow! This is fascinating to me. I love that kind of stuff. I would love to meet your father one day. I am so curious about history. It seems your father had a big influence in your life."

"Absolutely, my father taught me a lot. When he gets back to the states, I will let you meet him. You know…you remind me of my father, just a little."

Kenya was enthralled by Lance. She really liked him a lot. She smiled throughout the conversation, and at one point, she just starred at him while they listened to the band and poets who came to the stage. To Kenya, their encounter was like a date where two individuals, strangely enough, enjoyed each other.

"So, Lance...are you dating anyone? You never talk about your personal life."

"I try not to talk about my personal life. I like to keep it on a business level. But since you asked, I'm not only dating, but I will be getting married in a couple of months."

"You kidding me?"

"No, I am not kidding."

"Oh...that's great. What a surprise," Kenya said, struggling to appear happy for Lance, even though her feelings were of disappointment and her eyes showed gloom.

"Thank you. What about you?" Lance asked as he wondered what life would be like with Kenya because she was so interesting to him.

"I'm not dating at the moment. I was dating this guy a few months ago, but it didn't work out. It's not that easy to find a good man."

"That's hard to believe. I'm sure a fine woman like you will not have a problem finding Mr. Right."

"So tell me about your fiancée."

"She is a beautiful woman and a very successful attorney. I'll just leave it at that."

"Okay. I guess you think I'm being too nosey, huh?"

"No. Not really. I just don't like to talk about myself too much, you know?" This was Lance's way of being evasive, not wanting to shine the spotlight on himself. He also knew that talking about his fiancée would make Kenya jealous.

"Are you going to tell the folks at McIntyre?" Kenya asked, seeking to get a better sense of Lance's intentions as she sipped on her wine, leaving lipstick on the glass.

"I don't know yet. I'm a very private guy," Lance said.

"My lips are sealed."

"Okay."

"Since you are about to get married, I want to say..." Kenya paused and hesitated.

"Say what?"

"I just want to tell you that I respect and admire you, and quite frankly, I am attracted to you. I have been since day one."

"Oh really? Why are you telling me this, Kenya?"

"I don't know. It's just the way I feel, okay?" Kenya said as she looked away from Lance to avoid eye contact. This was her last effort to let him know that she liked him in a serious way, and just maybe, he would change his mind about Valerie.

"I understand. I think you are an interesting woman. As a matter of fact, there seems to be a little chemistry. You and I seem to like the same things. But as you know, I have already made a commitment."

"I'm sorry. I didn't mean to be so straightforward."

"No problem, Kenya. Are there any more revelations?"

"No. "

"I am really happy about this contract but I am not happy at McIntyre," Lance said, changing the subject. "Believe it or not, I'm working on a business plan."

"What do you mean? Are you leaving, Lance?"

"Not yet. I am working on getting finance for this new business venture. Who knows…maybe one day you could come work with me."

"I tell you, Lance…you are full of surprises tonight. Sure, I would love to work with you, but the idea is a little premature at this point. You have proven yourself to be a winner and I definitely want to be on a winning team, but are you really serious about this business?"

"Oh yeah, it's time to make my move. You have been a witness to the last two years of my struggles with McIntyre. Let's just say I am having difficulty climbing the corporate ladder. I'm really frustrated. I am not going to keep waiting for the generosity of Allen to pour down on me."

"With your intelligence and leadership skills, Lance, I think you would be successful in business. I support you one hundred percent.

Just let me know how things develop with your business," Kenya said as she stared Lance in the eye, knowing this association would bring her closer to him.

"I wish my fiancée understood," he mumbled.

"Interesting," Kenya thought to herself silently. The opportunity for her to lend Lance her infinite support had presented itself. Kenya thought it would give her bonus points in Lance's popularity contest. Somehow, she sensed Lance was somewhat hesitant about his marriage plans.

"What an inspirational poem. I like that!" Lance said as the young lady with dreadlocks walked off the stage.

"I like the band. They're hot! I'm feeling this!" Kenya said while gyrating in her seat and thinking about when would be the next time she would be able to have Lance all to herself.

Later in the week, Lance dropped by Fleming Brown's Barbershop, which was practically empty with the exception of two other barbers sitting in their chairs.

"What's happening, Big Flem?" Lance said.

"I'm okay?" Big Flem replied. "Life must be treating you well, Lance."

"I'm hanging in there."

"Hey Lance, you remember that young lady I introduced you to the last time?"

"I believe so, the young lady with the kid."

"Yeah, yeah...Tasha. That cute little honey is living with me now. She couldn't find an apartment and asked me if she could stay with me. I gladly agreed. What can I say, man?"

"You move fast, Big Flem, but she is definitely cute. Now, aren't you robbing the cradle?" Lance asked as he laughed and shook his head and quickly eased into the barber's chair.

"Not really. I like my women young and tender. An older woman can't do a damn thing for me. I had my share in my lifetime. They are too bitter, especially if they are older, and they usually carry a lot of baggage."

"I don't agree. You can't say that for all older women. I hear that some older women have more patience. Tasha is young. You know what young girls want most of the time. They usually want your money, especially if you are an older man. It's all about money for sex with them."

"Yeah, they want a damn Sugar Daddy. That's what you are to her, Big Flem," Ardell said as he intervened in the conversation between Lance and Big Flem. Ardell was a slim and light complexion guy who appeared to be in his early forties. He was an opinionated barber whose chair was located next to Big Flem's.

"Okay, Ardell, you made your point. I don't mind giving Tasha a little money. So what? I'll be her Sugar Daddy. I don't care. You have to spend money on women anyway, especially when you're dating them. So what's the difference?"

"I understand, bro. I see you'd rather pay for sex, huh? I remember my uncle got involved with a young girl. I think he was like forty-seven or forty-eight years old, something like that. That young girl gave him hell. In fact, he was locked up twice for assault charges," Ardell said.

"Ardell, why are you in my business? I'm talking to Lance. I already know what your opinion is," Big Flem said, pointing his finger in the direction of Ardell. "Besides, she definitely knows how to satisfy a man. We get along well, and I'm happy," Big Flem added.

"That's cool. Just watch your pockets. These young girls come and go. Then again, maybe you have a good one," Lance said as he admonished Big Flem in a serious way.

"Everything is under control. Tasha understands Big Daddy," Big Flem grinned with confidence.

"You the man!" Lance shouted.

"I try to take care of business, brother. Speaking of business, are you still moving forward with your business endeavor? How's that going?" Big Flem asked.

"It's okay. I'm making some progress, but the loan process has not been favorable. I hope it works out. I'm still determined, though. I just wish I had the support from my fiancée. She is not with me on this business thing."

"You will get there. No one said it would be easy. But if your woman ain't behind you, then you gonna have some problems, brother. You're going in one direction and she's going in the opposite. This same kind of shit happened to me in my first marriage. She has to be with you, man."

"You're right. I'm sure she will eventually come around and show support. Still, no matter what, I'm going to pursue my dream."

"I am happy for you, Lance. Stay focused on your goals."

As Lance left out the barbershop, his cell phone rang.

"Hello, Lance. How you doing?"

"Hello, Reina. It's good to hear your voice. How was Puerto Rico?"

"Great, the weather was fantastic. My grandmother is doing a lot better. She was so glad to see me. I even got a chance to see some of my old friends. It was nice being home."

"I'm glad you had a nice time. I missed you at the gym."

"I missed you too, Lance. I want to see you. How about we go dancing tonight?"

"Are you serious? This is definitely short notice." Lance hesitated as he thought about Valerie for a fleeting moment, but he was anxious to see Reina.

"Yes, I am serious. I want to have some fun. I love dancing."

"I have a better idea. Let me take you out to this nice restaurant in Columbia, Maryland and maybe next time we could go dancing." Lance knew he had no intentions of going dancing with Reina. He was sexually curious and didn't want to miss this opportunity, but he couldn't risk being seen in public with Reina.

"You don't want to dance with me? Okay. We can go next time. A restaurant would be fine. Let's say eight o'clock tonight."

"Sounds good to me. I'll pick you up at your place."

After jotting down the address, Lance hung up the phone in shock. He couldn't believe Reina actually made the first move. He had never gone out with her and only talked to her at the gym.

Lance picked up Reina and they had dinner at a Thai restaurant in a safe and isolated location where he was certain he wouldn't see Valerie or any of her friends. Later that night, Lance drove Reina back to her apartment in Laurel, Maryland.

"Would you like to come up for a minute?" Reina asked while batting her sexy eyes at Lance and smoothing down her long, fluffy hair. Wearing a nice red dress that stopped two inches above her knee, she appeared vulnerable and somewhat suggestive in her behavior and appearance.

"Sure," Lance anxiously replied.

As Reina walked upstairs to her apartment on the second floor, Lance walked right behind her, staring at her stockingless, muscular, and well-defined legs as her round butt gave definition through the dress.

"Would you like anything to drink?"

Reina's apartment was small and unimpressive with few pictures on the walls, one being a framed photo of her with the beach in the background. Gym bags cluttered a corner of her living room and lots of CDs were strewn about on her living room table.

"What do you have?"

"I have Coke, Sprite, fruit juice, and Puerto Rican rum I brought back from my trip."

"Let me try some of that rum mixed with Coke."

"Okay. I think I'll have some, as well."

After pouring them both a glass, Reina returned to the living room with the bottle in hand and sat in a chair facing the couch where Lance was sitting.

"I had a great time at dinner tonight," Reina said while making room on the coffee table to place the bottle of rum and taking a sip of her drink.

"I had a great time, also, Reina," Lance replied. "This rum has an interesting taste."

"Yeah, it's not bad. It has sort of a fruity taste. It's a genuine import from Puerto Rico."

As Lance complimented her apartment, he noticed her black thong peeking from underneath her dress and slightly opened legs. Initially, Lance felt a little surprised, but he soon became turned on by her tease. As she reached over to pour some more rum into her glass, she opened her legs wider, giving him a full view of her most valued possession. Immediately, his penis inflated in his pants.

"Why don't you come and sit next to me," Lance said, signaling with his hand and patting the empty space on the couch beside him.

"Oh, I'm sorry. I'm just so use to sitting here in my favorite chair," Reina replied as she stood and then took a seat next to Lance.

"I can't believe we are finally hanging out after having known each other for almost a year now. You're really cool. You know that?"

"Yeah, it has been almost a year. I like you too, Lance. I like your confidence."

"Thank you, my friend. Can I get a hug?"

Lance turned toward Reina and hugged her. Next thing he knew, and without warning, she kissed him fully on the lips. Lance sat there stunned as Reina explored his lips with her tongue, but after a period of momentary shock, he returned the kiss with intensity. His thick tongue wet her sweet red lips and delved deep into her welcoming mouth. As they continued kissing, Reina hiked her dress up higher near her beautiful toned thighs, which Lance started rubbing as he planted kisses on her ear and down the length of her neck. Clearly, they were in the heat of the moment.

"Don't stop. I want you, Papi," Reina moaned.

"I want you too, baby," Lance replied as his hand inched toward her black thong. She reciprocated by rubbing and grabbing his crotch.

"Make love to me, Lance," Reina demanded.

Pushing the thin piece of material covering her love canal to the side, he inserted his right middle finger into her erotic zone of wetness, stroking her flesh inside and out. His left hand squeezed her breasts through the dress and her nipples hardened as she moaned, groaned, and squirmed at his touch. He could feel the effects of the Puerto Rican rum and apparently Reina was "feeling good" too.

"Lance, you're making me so wet. I want you inside of me." As she unlocked from their kiss and pulled off her thong, Lance quickly kicked off his shoes, one landing on the chair and the other under the table. He then pulled down his pants below his knees while continuing to sit on the sofa.

"Where are the condoms?"

"They're right here in my purse. Here, put it on," Reina insisted. Not bothering to remove her dress or pumps, she stood up from the sofa and pulled her breasts from underneath the dress and then turned her beautiful sculptured butt toward Lance's face as she raised the red material. Lance could not believe his eyes. Her body was absolutely spectacular. He had fantasized about this moment for a long time. Suddenly, she spread her legs wide so that she could position her body overtop Lance. Reina then lowered and anchored her flesh doggy style on Lance while rotating her hips and sucking up his throbbing penis into her wet and pulsating walls. Her athletic body bounced up and down as she delivered and received pleasure with Lance grabbing her hair and breasts from behind. Before long, they both screamed out in ecstasy.

Chapter Seven

As Lance drove home from Reina's house late that night, he was overcome by guilt over their sexual encounter. The drive seemed to take an eternity. During the ride, he was preoccupied with periodic flashes of Reina, the smell of sex and her perfume permeated his senses. At that moment, Lance began to ponder the viability of marriage to Valerie. He thought about how their life would be if they were married. He even questioned whether he *should* get married. "*Could I be faithful to Valerie*?" he thought.

* * * * * *

After his weekend break, Lance returned to work and was busy at his computer when Kenya entered his office and stood in front of his desk dressed in a conservative blue suit. She wanted to alert Lance to the fact that everyone was talking about his twenty-five million dollar contract. Lance was intrigued by her information, however, he appeared be somewhat absorbed.

Kenya thanked Lance for taking her to the Upper Nile and then walked out of his office, thinking to herself that Lance seemed preoccupied. After returning to her office cubicle, she began daydreaming about Lance as she did everyday.

As Lance turned his attention back to his computer, Nathaniel Watson entered his office, congratulating him on his recent contract and praising him for his success as the top producer. Somehow, though, Lance did not feel Nathaniel's praise was sincere, but instead driven by professional courtesy. Lance picked up on his attitude immediately. From Nathaniel's poor eye contact and the stiffness he displayed, Lance could detect he had a hidden agenda, although he could not yet ascertain his motives. Nathaniel strongly reminded him of Buddy.

Minutes after Nathaniel left, Allen entered Lance's office.

"Hello, Superstar!" Allen greeted Lance in a roaring cheer. "I have a little surprise for you. Here's your bonus check for your efforts, and we also have a chocolate cake for you in the conference room."

"Oh, really? Thank you, Allen," Lance said as he shook hands with Allen.

Several people stood about the conference room as they entered. Most of the account executives were present, with the exception of Buddy.

"I hope you enjoy the cake, Lance. I baked it last night," Helen greeted Lance excitedly with a genuine smile.

"Thank you so much, Helen. You never cease to amaze me," Lance replied with a smile of embarrassment as he stood in the center of the room. The attention made him a little uneasy because he didn't particularly like the accolades of his colleagues. It simply wasn't his style.

After Allen gave a five-minute speech about Lance's contributions, Lance thanked everyone for their support and then cut a slice of the chocolate cake. Kenya walked up to Lance, shook his hand, and congratulated him. Nathaniel stood quietly and observed everyone in the room surreptitiously. Another account executive, a young Irish woman, approached Lance and congratulated him as she held a piece of cake in her left hand with a small plate. Lance made his rounds, accepting the praise and comments of his colleagues. Finally, everyone began to filter out and return to their offices, with Lance being the last to leave.

As Lance left the conference room, he noticed Nathaniel's name on the door of the former Vice-President's office. As they had many times before, Lance's suspicions about Allen's motives resurfaced.

"Excuse me, Lance. Can I talk to you for a brief moment?" Allen said as he approached Lance with ease.

"Sure."

"Nathaniel has been doing a fantastic job working with the employees here, and I was just wondering if you could talk to Nathaniel about your specific job functions. Perhaps you could give him an overview of what you do, and even share some of your experiences in the sales and contract arena. He's trying to get a good understanding of how McIntyre operates. He has been working with Buddy Poretsky for the last week. "Hey...," Allen paused and continued instigating, "I tell you...it seems like those guys are working fine together."

"Okay, I'll talk to Nathaniel," Lance said reluctantly, ignoring Allen's insinuations.

Lance was no fool. He knew Allen was "grooming" Nathaniel for the Vice-President's position. He didn't understand why Nathaniel was so involved with the management aspect of the account executives when he was merely a technical advisor. There was definitely something foul taking place.

When Allen finished talking to Lance, Kenya rushed into Lance's office as she carefully monitored Allen's departure.

"Lance, I have to tell you something, and I hope that I am not overreacting," Kenya said as her eyes darted across the room and back to Lance's face.

"What is it, Kenya?" Lance asked with a look of concern on his face.

"I am suspicious of Buddy. I've seen him in your office at least twice today. Does he normally come in your office when your door is closed?"

"No. That's strange. Um...what the hell is he doing in my office? No one should be in my office, especially not Buddy. I don't trust him!" Lance replied in disgust.

"I don't blame you. You should probably keep your door locked when you are gone for a while," Kenya suggested.

"Good idea, and thanks for watching my back," Lance said, patting her shoulder as she departed. Lance knew Buddy was up to no good. He wanted to walk over to his office and express his anger to Buddy, but he decided otherwise.

Lance hesitated for a moment, breathing slowly in and out, and thought about Buddy's actions for a moment. He knew Buddy was trying to manipulate his emotions, so he remained calm and tried to figure out a way to outsmart him. Lance also reflected on Kenya. He appreciated her loyalty to him and thought about how she would be a great woman in his life as well as a supporter of his business. He wished

Valerie possessed those same qualities. His phone rang jarring Lance from his deep thought.

"Hello."

"Hi, Lance. How are you, honey?" Valerie greeted, sweetly.

Valerie had spent the past two days in Philly and Lance hadn't spoken to her since she left. Upon hearing Valerie's voice, his guilt re-emerged.

"Hi, baby. I hope you had a nice weekend in Philly." Lance responded enthusiastically.

"It could have been better. I'm still working on the wedding and all the details associated with this event, and you know how stressful that can be. I miss you and want to see you, honey."

"I miss you, too, and would love to see you, but I have a lot of work to do. If I don't see you tonight, I will come by tomorrow. Okay?" Lance evaded. He didn't feel good about seeing Valerie right away. He wanted to prepare himself psychologically after his misadventure.

"Okay." Valerie responded in disappointment. "Is everything okay, Lance?" she asked, hearing a little hesitancy in Lance's voice.

"Oh sure, everything is fine," he responded, nonchalantly. "I just have a lot on my mind and a lot of work on my desk."

"I understand. I know you are a busy man!"

"Alright, baby. I'll talk to you later."

Later that evening while on his way home, he called Reina from his cell phone.

"I just called to let you know that I really enjoyed spending time with you. You are a special woman."

"I enjoyed being with you, too, Lance. I'm just a little embarrassed, though." Reina laughed nervously.

"Why?"

"I don't want you to think that I am an easy lay. I have respect for myself, but you just turn me on. Let's start over. We should be friends and really get to know each other first. Is that okay with you?"

"That's fine. Just give me a little time. There are some things that I need to resolve."

"What do you mean, Lance? Is there another woman in your life?"

"Well…yes. I do have a friend. You know, just a friend," Lance replied in a dishonest manner, knowing he had a serious relationship with Valerie.

"You didn't tell me that you had a girlfriend. Do you want to talk about it? I don't want to get my feelings hurt."

"No, not right now. It's very complicated. We can discuss this at a later time."

"Lance...I want to talk about it now," Reina demanded.

"Do we have to talk now, Reina, because I have something to do?" Lance wanted to avoid this discussion, but Reina persisted.

"Are you serious with this woman, Lance? How could you do this knowing that you have a girlfriend?" Reina asked, ignoring his protest.

"I will explain all of this to you, Reina. I wouldn't hurt you. I'm not that type of guy, just give me some time. I'll call you later, okay? Maybe, I will see you at the gym next week. I'll talk to you later," Lance replied with finality.

"Okay, but I'm not letting you off the hook. Bye, Lance."

When Lance arrived home, he sorted through the mail and came across an envelope from Seba Security Bank. He opened the letter expecting good news, but instead was greeted by another loan rejection. Lance stood in his kitchen and shook his head. He was not as disappointed as with the previous rejection letter. He took it in stride, chuckling as if it didn't affect him.

Seba Security Bank did mention that they would consider Lance's application in the future if he could provide two hundred thousand dollars worth of collateral. Lance thought their proposition was unreasonable, so he simply accepted the letter as a rejection. This time, he did not call Eddie right away, but began to re-evaluate his options. He questioned whether Valerie was correct and if perhaps, he should wait or simply abandon the idea of entrepreneurship.

After work the following day, Lance met Eddie a local bar on 18th street in DC. "Eddie, I've got more bad news."

"And what is that, man?"

"I just received another loan rejection from Seba Security Bank. I don't know what to do now," Lance said casually, straightening his bright red tie.

"I told you this would be an uphill battle, but we *will* win. We'll just have to apply to another bank. We should come up with a different approach," Eddie said.

"What do you mean?" Lance asked.

"Perhaps we should consider using investors. Who knows, Lance…we could find some individuals who are willing to invest. There are a lot of investments clubs out there. They just might be interested in investing in an IT business."

"The idea sounds great, but I don't think it would work. It's very difficult to get people to give their money to a start-up business unless you can overwhelmingly prove that you can generate immediate profit. It's not easy."

"That may be true, however, we shouldn't rule out the possibility," Eddie insisted.

"I agree. It is worthy of consideration, but I don't know of any investor at this time. Hey, I have a better idea. Maybe we should look outside of Maryland for financing."

"Interesting. I think that's a viable option. It gives us a wider selection."

"Yes, I have a friend who lives in Boston. His name is Jim Earp, and he's a Branch Manager at State Street Bank in Roxbury. He may have some connections. We went to grad school together. He's doing pretty well up there in Bean town. I'll give him a call," Lance said as he smiled thinking about the endless possibilities.

"Why not? I think it's time for you to take a trip to Boston. As I told you, Lance, it's difficult for black folks to get access to capital. We have to keep applying over and over again until we get it, though."

"You know, last night I thought about this business venture and how I'm not getting any support from Valerie. She doesn't like the idea of me starting my own business."

"Really? But you know, Lance…you gotta do what is right for you."

"Yeah, I hear you. You know, Eddie, things have been a little strange lately. I've been messing around with this Puerto Rican honey."

"You mean that babe over at the gym?"

"Yeah, that's the one."

"You hit it? What's up with that? What about the wedding?" Eddie prodded.

"The wedding is still on. I love Valerie. I haven't had sex in a while, like several months. Valerie is against us having sex until we get married. I must admit that I feel guilty about it. I messed up, okay?" Lance defended.

"Hey man, it happens to the best of us. A man's gotta do what a man's gotta do." Suddenly, Eddie wasted his beer on the counter. "Damn it!" Eddie yelled out as he wiped the beer off the counter with a napkin. A little of the beer spilled on his suit jacket.

"Are you okay, Eddie?" Lance asked, noticing that Eddie appeared to be almost drunk.

"I'm okay, man." Eddie said while standing up.

"Are you sure you're okay, Eddie? You have been seriously drinking those beers. You've gulped down at least six since I've been here." Eddie's eyes looked red and his hand and face gestures had become increasingly slow and sluggish.

"I know how to hold my alcohol. Let me go to the bathroom," Eddie replied.

As he walked to the bathroom, he staggered twice and almost fell against one of the tables.

"Are you okay, sir?" the bartender yelled out.

In a few seconds, Eddie straightened himself. "I'm okay," he replied.

When Eddie returned, Lance offered to drive Eddie home.

"I'm going to have to drive you home because I think you've just had too much to drink." He had never seen Eddie get drunk like this before at a bar.

"Do I look like I'm drunk, Lance?" Eddie asked as his red eyes stared back at Lance. He then grinned and started to sing.

"Come on, man. Let's go. Did you drive?"

"No," Eddie replied

"Good. I'll drive you home. Now let's get the hell out of this bar before you do something crazy."

Chapter Eight

The rain poured heavily that cold and raw morning in New England. Lance's flight landed in Boston at Logan International Airport at 7:10 a.m. and from there Lance took a taxi to the Sheraton Hotel in the Back Bay section of Boston. He was anxious about his morning interview with his longtime college friend, Jim Earp. Lance felt optimistic about the interview despite the fact that he had been unsuccessful in obtaining a loan. He had a gut feeling this trip would produce favorable results for his business.

He walked to the registration desk to check in at the hotel and as he was standing there, he recognized a well-known record company owner, Ernest Ross, who sold and promoted R&B and Hip Hop music. Ernest was standing in the lobby with his entourage waiting for his limousine. At that instant moment, Lance's eyes glistened as he looked at Ernest with admiration and respect. He wanted to say hello to him but decided not to because there were too many people around him trying to get an autograph. Lance saw Ernest as a man in charge, and the sight of him evoked a sense of motivation about his business goals. He had read about Ernest in Ebony Magazine on how he got started in the music business, selling records out of the trunk of his car. Lance was fascinated by Ernest's drive, determination to succeed, and the wealth he had accumulated. It was reported that Ernest Ross's music empire was worth three hundred and fifty million dollars.

Lance's hotel was three blocks from the John Hancock Building where State Street Bank was located. Once he checked into the hotel and placed his bag inside his room, he walked from his hotel to Copley Square. He entered the John Hancock Building and took the elevator to the 42nd floor. After getting off the elevator, he shook the water from his umbrella onto the dark blue carpet of the bank and then placed it in the corner near a tall green artificial plant. He walked up to a desk and the beautiful smile of the African-American woman receptionist caught his attention. Her teeth were conspicuously white and well aligned like a movie star. Lance appreciated a beautiful smile.

"Good Morning. Can I help you, sir?" the receptionist greeted, speaking in a soft and professional voice.

"Yes, I am here to see Jim Earp," Lance answered cheerfully.

"And you are?" the receptionist replied.

"Lance Kojo."

"Sure. He is expecting you. Why don't you have a seat? Jim should be here shortly."

"Thanks."

As Lance sat in the lobby dressed in a dark blue suit with his legs crossed and hands folded, he thought about Valerie for a brief moment. His guilt kicked in for the one hundredth time. He thought about how to make his relationship better with Valerie. He yearned for her support. He looked around the lobby area and said a quick prayer to himself. Then at once, Jim approached Lance.

"You finally made it to Boston, huh? Why don't you come in my office?" Jim said as he extended his hand to Lance.

Jim's office was considerably large and overlooked the west part of the Back Bay. The view from his office was magnificent. You could see the Charles River despite the poor weather conditions.

"I almost didn't recognize you with that beard. I guess this is the distinguished look, huh?" Lance said.

"Not really…I just decided to change the look. I like trying different looks. I may even shave my head bald one day. You remember back in college when I use to wear those army pants and the dreadlocks," Jim replied as he reminisced about the old days.

"Yes, indeed, I remember. You were quite the rebel back in those days. We both were a little on the wild side. I had my wild outfits, too. I finally stopped wearing the crazy hats."

"Yeah, those were the fun days. You are still looking sharp. It looks like you've been working out," Jim commented.

"I try to stay in some kind of shape. I have to take care of the body. You know once you get in your thirties, your metabolism slows down and you can easily gain weight," Lance said as he laughed and rubbed his hand backwards over his head.

"I know what you mean. You got to watch that diet," Jim said as he patted his stomach. He then leaned back in his black leather chair and smiled as the reflection from the unusually bright office light shined on his wavy hair and light complexion face.

"Yeah, no question about that," Lance replied.

"So, are you ready for the business world?" Jim asked as his big bulging eyes looked at Lance.

"Absolutely, this is why I came to see you," Lance responded.

Lance thought to himself how critical this loan was to his future. Although he was still cautious, he felt comfortable and confident talking to Jim. He knew that Jim had significant influence at State Street Bank.

"It's my intent to process this loan as quickly as possible. It usually takes about two to three weeks for approval. As you know, we discussed this loan weeks ago. Now, I just have to submit the request through the normal channels. I have already reviewed your business plan and application. I am impressed with your package. You have a realistic business plan and would probably get a loan approval without my assistance, but I am here as a friend to facilitate the process. I wish you all the luck with your business."

"Thank you. I appreciate your support. I owe you, man. This has not been an easy journey," Lance said as he stood up, shook his head, and then glanced out of the window.

"I can imagine, but you will do fine. Hey look, let's do something tonight. Why don't we hook up later for happy hour?" Jim asked.

"Definitely, I'm staying at the Sheraton in Room 4561."

"Okay, Lance. I will come by around six o'clock. We have a lot to talk about man!"

"Alright, man. Again, thanks." Lance left State Street Bank and proceeded to walk in the direction of his hotel. His cell phone rang, and it was Valerie.

"I called your office this morning and they said you would be out for two days. Is there something wrong?" Valerie asked as if Lance might be sick.

"No. I am in Boston right now."

"Boston! For what?"

"Relax, Valerie. I am here in Boston on business. I went to visit my friend Jim about a loan."

"Lance, you didn't tell me that you were going to Boston."

"I didn't tell you because I knew you wouldn't like the idea. If I get this loan, I will be resigning from McIntyre soon."

"Listen, Lance, we seem to have a communication problem all of a sudden. Obviously, you don't care what I think. You're just doing what you want to do as usual, while I'm feeling stressed and running around preparing for this wedding. You've been acting really strange lately. Look, you're going to have to either choose me or the business!"

"That's ridiculous. What kind of ultimatum is that? I want both. It's obvious that you don't have any faith in me, and I'm tired of you underestimating me. I will not allow anyone to limit my ambition, including you, Valerie."

"Well…I don't get it, Lance. We're supposed to be getting married and we argue all the time. I support your business endeavors, but I don't think the timing is good."

"I have heard that too many times, Valerie. I don't want to argue about this anymore. I am tired of it."

There was complete silence on the phone.

"Valerie, are you there?" Lance asked. He wasn't sure if he had lost her call, if she couldn't hear him, or if she had hung up.

"I'm here. Maybe we should put this wedding on hold until we can both decide what is best," Valerie replied in a voice of frustration.

"Why should we do that? Valerie, this is such a small issue. We will work this problem out. I think you are being too reactionary right now!"

"Maybe I am being reactionary, but I want stability in my life, Lance. I had a cousin who was married to a wonderful woman. He had a great job working at an insurance company. He quit his job to go into some multilevel marketing business. I think it was Amway. They lost their house and everything. I have big plans for us. I want a good life that will include a nice big house and kids. I want you to be a part of that," Valerie said as tears rolled down her face. Lance could hear the sniffle of her cry.

"I am sorry, Valerie, but I have to make this point," Lance interrupted, hearing the sniffle of her cry. "Your cousin failed in the Amway business. It doesn't mean that I will not be successful. You can't equate your cousin's situation with mine. It's totally different. You can't make a person do something they don't want to do. You want nice things out of life, and that's great. But you have to learn to support your man, especially a black man. This society doesn't always treat black men in a favorable light. Our abilities are always questioned. I need you in my corner. I need you to believe in me," Lance insisted.

Lance stood outside the Sheraton Hotel talking on his cell phone in the rain with his umbrella.

"I do support you, Lance. I have always been there for you, especially when you had problems at McIntyre. I don't want to hear that poor excuse about being a black man. I've heard enough of that. You need to deal with reality," Valerie countered.

"Come on, Val. I'm surprised you would say such an insensitive thing. You simply don't seem to understand the black struggle. You are definitely out of touch with reality. I need a strong woman on my side. I need a woman that shares my vision and knows herself."

"That really sounds selfish. You only seem to care about your career. What about me? What about us and our future, Lance?" Valerie pleaded.

"That's not true, Val, and you know it. What do you want me to do? Just forget about this business?"

"No, I'm not saying that. You're confusing me, Lance. I need to think about all of this. When are you coming back to Maryland?" Valerie asked as she wiped the tears from her eyes.

"I will be home tomorrow. My cell phone battery is getting low, so I'll call you later. Bye."

Later that evening, Jim came by to pick up Lance at the hotel.

"Where are we going?" Lance asked as he slid his tall body into Jim's Lexus, carrying his folded coat in his right arm.

"I know this really nice place in Government Center. A lot of nice professional ladies hangout there. You know the spot...Lola's Lounge. That's right. I have to remember you're about to get married. You know how it is being a single brother. We are always on the chase, man," Jim said as he grinned and then reached over and fastened his seat belt. Jim seemed to be a lot more relaxed outside of work. He could talk like he wanted to without putting on his professional face.

"Lola's Lounge, huh? Nice spot. We went there last time. I don't know about this wedding, though. I might have to postpone it. Valerie and I just can't see eye to eye on this business. I don't know, man. Valerie is a sweetheart and I love her to death, but I have to admit she can be a bit too demanding sometimes."

"I see you have issues with your girl already. Why are you getting married? Hey, man, if your relationship is not right up front, don't get yourself involved in a marriage you will regret down the road. You know, Lance, I have a friend who got married not too long ago. He married this woman from New Bedford, Mass. And I tell you, her family basically destroyed his marriage. They separated after four months of marriage. Can you believe that? His in-laws were very controlling. I'm not telling you what to do, just be careful. If you are focused on having your own business, you should have a woman that is going to support you," Jim said as he took his eyes off the road to glance at Lance, looking for a reaction.

"You're right, Jim." Lance nodded his head.

As they drove down Massachusetts Avenue, they heard a police siren. Jim looked out of his rearview mirror and saw a police car tailgating him. For Lance, the sound of a police siren resonated concern and fear ever since he had been racially profiled by cops in Maryland. Jim pulled to the right shoulder of the street.

"What the hell is he pulling you over for?" Lance said angrily.

"I don't have the slightest idea. Let's just relax. Fucking cop!" Jim responded nervously as he looked carefully in his rearview mirror. The redheaded Irish cop walked slowly up to the car, his eyes examining Jim's car as he stopped and began writing down the number of the license plate.

"Sir, can I see your license and registration?" the officer asked.

"Sure, officer. What did I do?" Jim replied as he reached over to get his registration from the glove compartment.

The cop didn't say anything, just kept examining Jim's car. The cop walked back to his car for about five minutes and then returned. "Both of you get out of the car right now," the cop demanded. Jim immediately looked at Lance in disbelief.

"What is the problem, officer?" Jim asked again.

"There was a robbery on Hemingway Street. Two black men robbed an elderly woman about forty-five minutes ago as she was entering her apartment. A neighbor witnessed a car that looked like a Lexus, so we are stopping all cars that fit the description."

"Officer, we did not rob anybody. I'm just coming from work. You can call my office to verify my whereabouts at that time. This must be a mistake. Besides, I'm not the only person in Boston who is driving a Lexus," Jim said as he slowly got out of the car, being particularly cautious and watching the cop closely. He did not want to be a victim of a trigger-happy cop.

"I don't believe this. We didn't rob anybody. We are decent human beings," Lance declared as he stood next to Jim, looking at the cop with the same intensity as Jim.

"Shut up! I need to search your car. Now...both of you put your hands behind your head, legs spread eagle style," the cop said authoritatively as he relished in giving the two black men instructions. His tone was cocky and arrogant.

Jim stood up against the car with his black trench coat on in the rainy, cold New England weather. His legs spread wide as directed. Lance stood in a similar position like Jim with his long wool coat and big hat on his head. Jim looked flabbergasted as he kept looking back and forth between Lance and the cop.

Lance was incensed, his face showing fear at the imminent threat. His mind raced with thoughts of the Rodney King incident. He then thought about the Amadou Diallo incident in New York, where an African immigrant was shot and killed while reaching for his wallet. Lance's hand shook nervously while the cop searched him. He felt violated and humiliated by the act. The traffic slowed down as people in cars witnessed two African-American men being searched. After minutes of searching Lance and Jim, a second police car drove up.

"We have the wrong people. Let these gentlemen go about their business," the Italian-looking cop said after exiting his vehicle.

As Lance looked across the street, there was a small crowd of people gathering as they watched in amusement. Jim felt ashamed and embarrassed, hoping no one recognized him. Jim wanted this harassment to be over as soon as possible, and was glad to see this cop rescue them.

"We are very sorry about the misunderstanding, gentlemen, and apologize for the inconvenience. These things happen all the time. I am just doing my job," the Irish cop said sarcastically.

Lance looked at the Irish cop and for a quick second, he conjured up a thought about what would be the best way to kill this racist cop. Then suddenly, he snapped back into reality, knowing the idea was not rational.

"This is so humiliating and dehumanizing. The Boston Police Department will definitely hear from my attorney," Jim said adamantly.

"Sir…have a nice day!" the cop said arrogantly.

"Let's go, Jim, before they find a reason to arrest us. It's not worth it," Lance said as he grabbed Jim by the arm and directed him into the car.

Jim and Lance left feeling disgusted as they drove to Lola's Lounge. Even after the incident with the police, Lance was convinced his meeting with Jim Earp had been productive and that he had a great chance of getting a loan through State Street Bank.

Upon returning home, he called Eddie to let him know about his trip to Boston.

"Eddie, I met with my friend in Boston. Jim said I should get an approval in about two to three weeks. I'm very optimistic," Lance said.

"Good. Hopefully, this trip will reap some benefits," Eddie replied.

"I was just thinking, we need to get another person involved with this business," Lance said, knowing he was already considering Kenya. Lance wanted to get Eddie's reaction and didn't want to appear arbitrary.

"Do you know anyone?" Eddie asked.

"Well, as a matter of fact, I do...my co-worker, Kenya. I have talked to her about the idea of coming aboard once I start my business and she expressed a strong interest. She is a very intelligent woman with a strong background in marketing. We could definitely use her skills."

"Does she know the IT field?"

"Absolutely, I have worked with her for two years. She is really good."

"Great. If she is talented and reliable, we should try to recruit her."

"Okay, Eddie, I will definitely talk to her."

"Lance...we may have a business opportunity over at the Prince George's County Public School System. PG has been allocated five million dollars through the state budget to update their software and is looking for small 8A firms to upgrade their system. However, this opportunity will not be available for another three months, which gives us time to secure the 8A Minority Business Certification. At that point, the only thing we need to do is submit a bid."

"That sounds like a deal," Lance said.

"You know, Lance, I believe in this mission. Brothers got to do for self, and we must stick together no matter what," Eddie expressed his heartfelt opinion. In Eddie's mind, he wanted to convey to Lance that he was with him one hundred percent.

"This business idea is bigger than us. It's about black people taking ownership of their destiny. Corporate America will never play fair, so we must create our own opportunities. I want us to become partners in this venture so that you will have a vested interest. We are in this together, man," Lance said.

"It's good to know you feel that way. It's also reassuring to me," Eddie replied.

* * * * * *

Later that day, Lance showed up at the gym.

"Where have you been the last two weeks? I haven't seen you at my spinning classes lately," Reina inquired petulantly.

"I've been busy. You know...taking care of business."

"Oh, okay. Now, how do I say this? Let's just say that I think about you a lot, Lance, but I can't be the other woman. I know you have a girlfriend." Reina looked at Lance with disappointment as she stood in front of him with her arms crossed. Her social life was miserable and Lance had helped fill a void in her life. Although she questioned Lance's sincerity, she was hoping things would work out.

"Yeah, I have a girlfriend, but I enjoy being around you. I am going through a lot in my relationship. Who knows what may happen." Lance replied evasively.

"You should have told me this earlier. I have feelings for you, Lance. I just don't want to get hurt."

"You are incredible, Reina. What happened the other night was special and maybe we should just leave it at that."

"Maybe, we'll see. Anyway, my grandmother passed away yesterday. I have to go to Puerto Rico in two days."

"I'm sorry to hear that, Reina. My condolences go to you and your family. You know...you were just in Puerto Rico last month."

"That's right, and she appeared to be fine. However, she had a massive heart attack. I probably will be over there for at least six months. I have to take care of her finances and house. She included me in her will."

"It looks like you will be gone for a while," Lance said. Lance felt bad about how he handled the affair with Reina, knowing he had made a mistake when he led her on.

"Yes, and it may even take longer than six months. But I will keep in touch. I have your e-mail address." Reina paused. "I will miss you, Papi," she said, then hugged Lance.

"I will miss you, too, Reina." Lance replied, quickly changing the subject. "Hey, let's go upstairs and spin because I haven't worked out in two weeks, and I need a good workout."

******

After his hour-long workout, Lance drove up to Fleming Brown Barbershop to get a haircut. Big Flem was sitting in a chair with his right hand supporting his chin as he stared intently at the television. He appeared to be in a melancholy mood. His facial expression revealed he was deep in thought or depressed about something.

"Is everything okay, Big Flem?" Lance asked concerned, noticing immediately that Big Flem was not his usual self. Lance could feel his energy and he knew Big Flem very well. Lance thought of Big Flem as sort of a father figure. He could talk to Big Flem about virtually anything.

"I'm fine, Lance. Business is a little slow, but it will get better. Things have been a little crazy lately, though," Big Flem said as he adjusted the barber's chair to fit Lance.

"Crazy like how? What do you mean?"

"Tasha and I are having some problems."

"I thought everything was fine the last time I talked to you. As a matter of fact, you were happy about her staying with you."

"I was happy at first. But it seems like she's always asking me for money. I am not a goddamn bank. Ardell told me that Tasha was a stripper… exotic dancer or whatever they call them. Can you believe that shit? Tasha told me that she was a waitress at a restaurant. Ardell said one of his friends saw her dancing on stage at the Playboy Club. I haven't been down there to confirm it, though. It's not so much that the dancing bothers me. It's the fact that she lied to me. I asked her about it and she denied it," Big Flem said as he shook his head and tightened his lips.

"It may be true. You need to check it out for yourself. Not to say I told you so, but I did warn you about those young girls," Lance replied.

"I thought I had the situation under control. Check this out, Lance. She even used my credit card to purchase a pair of shoes over the internet without my permission. This young girl is out of control, man," Big Flem said as he ceased cutting Lance's hair to see his reaction.

"Hey, man, it seems like you got trouble on your hands. You may have to let her go," Lance responded nodding his head with certainty.

"I know, but I do like her. I like her company and it's nice to have a young "thang" like her around. When I confronted her about this, she denied it and then started crying. I'm just trying to help her get on her feet. You know, she has a little son that is just crazy about me. Demetrius is like a son to me," Big Flem smiled for a moment, reflecting on the good aspects of his relationship.

"I understand all of that, Big Flem, but you have to watch your money. If Tasha is stripping, I would ask her to leave. Who knows what else she's doing." Lance hoped Big Flem would read between the lines. Lance also feared Tasha's dancing might have gone one step further and that she might be engaged in prostitution.

"I don't know, Lance. I haven't seen her stripping. This is just hearsay," Big Flem defended.

"Why don't you go down to the Playboy Club one night and find out?"

"I'll think about it, Lance."

"I have learned a lot from you, Big Flem, but I don't understand why you can't see through her games. Maybe you are in love with her," Lance said.

"I will work this out. Nobody can run the game on Big Flem, especially a woman. I have been in the game too long," Big Flem assured him.

* * * * * *

Lance left the barbershop and went to visit his family in DC.

"There must be a problem," Mamie Kojo said as Lance entered the house.

"Why do you say that, Mom, and what are you cooking?" Lance asked as he walked into the kitchen.

"Rice and peas. I can tell when something is not right with my son. What's bothering you, Lance?" Mrs. Kojo gently demanded.

"Sometimes I wonder if you are a psychic, Mom. You're right once again. Valerie and I are having problems, and I'm not so sure about going through with this wedding. We keep fighting about my plans to start my own business and we can't get beyond that. Valerie is a nice woman, but I am not sure if it will work."

"What are you all talking about in there? Is it about Valerie?" Mr. Kojo interrupted as he came out of the living room and into the kitchen to talk to Lance.

"Yeah, Dad," Lance replied.

"I knew it. We can't decide whether you should marry Valerie. But I can tell you one thing, son. Go with your heart. If it is not right, then move on with your life." Mr. Kojo spoke as if he knew he had the right solution to Lance's problem.

"Son, just leave it in God's hand. I am sure you and Valerie will work things out. I am looking forward to this wedding in August," Mrs. Kojo soothed, silently admonishing her husband with a stern look.

"Mamie, you can't make the man marry the woman! He has to do what is best for him. I wouldn't want him to marry her and six months later, they file for divorce. Marriage is serious business," Mr. Kojo voiced as he walked to the living room, buttoning his shirt and then plopping down in his reclining chair.

"I know, but Valerie seems like a nice young lady. All couples have disagreements. You don't run at the first sign of trouble," Mrs. Kojo replied.

"I think its best that we give this marriage idea some time. Maybe things will work itself out down the road. She doesn't support my business and that is extremely important to me. Therefore, I need time to myself to think things through," Lance said.

Chapter Nine

After work, Eddie entered his car and sat with his hands on the steering wheel as he stared out the window at the pigeons searching for food in the freshly fallen snow. Eddie was in deep thought about the opportunity Lance had presented to him. He was flattered, but still, he felt a sense of uneasiness. *Would Lance demand too much from me? Can I overcome my drinking and effectively function as a CEO?"*

Eddie was a smart guy, but he justified his drinking as a temporary problem he could conquer. He knew his excessive drinking had become a zone of comfort in which to ease the pain of his divorce, but this was a personal problem of his that he was not willing to share with anyone, including Lance. The familiar scene of his ex-wife in bed with another man tortured his mind with horror and grief. Without consciously being aware of it, Eddie had lost trust in women as a result of this experience.

Before driving down Vermont Avenue towards Southwest to a local bar on the waterfront, he put his seat belt on, adjusted his rearview mirror, and turned the car's radio dial to his favorite station, WHUR. Upon reaching his destination, he parked his car and loosened his blue necktie, giving him a sense of ease. His eight hours at SBO were officially over, and he wanted nothing more than to have a drink and unwind from the stress of the day.

"What can I get you, sir?" The young, attractive bartender, who wore her hair in a ponytail and had a middle-eastern look to her, greeted him with a smile.

"Remy on the rocks," Eddie replied, rubbing his beard while giving her a full-body scan.

Removing his black suit jacket, he placed it on the back of his chair. After thirty minutes of drinking four strong drinks, Eddie relaxed a bit and started swaying in his seat to the beat of the music videos playing on the small television screens located throughout the bar and restaurant. A young couple, from out of nowhere, seated themselves in the empty stools to the right of Eddie at the bar.

"Who is that? I have seen this video before," the woman asked her boyfriend who didn't have a clue.

"Amerie," Eddie responded after overhearing the question to her boyfriend. At this point, Eddie was feeling good about now. He was indeed intoxicated.

"Oh, okay. Amerie, huh? She's hot," the woman responded while turning toward Eddie, the cleavage from her low-cut blouse calling out to him.

"Hello, my name is Eddie, and yours?" he said, extending his hand to the young lady.

"My name is Pam, and this is my boyfriend, Robert." Her boyfriend acknowledged Eddie with a simple nod.

"I see you guys don't watch music videos, huh? Not that I watch them a lot myself."

"Not really. I listen to songs on the radio and I don't always know the artist. I just like the song. These videos all appear to be the same, with most of them having young girls shake their booties. Ain't that right, Robert?" Pam started laughing as she looked at her boyfriend and then back at Eddie for his reaction.

Robert smiled, not knowing what to say. "If you say so, Pam. Excuse me for a minute while I go to the men's room. Hun, can you order me a Budweiser?"

"I tell you, you do see a lot of booty shaking on these videos. It sells, though." With Robert now out of sight, Eddie became loose with his words and less discreet as his eyes targeted her breast with precision and delight. "I bet you can shake your booty. You know something, your man is lucky to have a woman like you. You're sexy." Eddie stole another glance at her chest.

"Why…thank you, but…" Before she could finish her statement, Eddie continued with his words of admiration.

"You know, I'm looking for a nice, cute thing like you."

"Hold up, you don't really know me like that, and you are disrespecting my boyfriend. You better check yourself." Pam rolled her eyes at Eddie. From the smell of the alcohol on his breath, she could tell he was intoxicated.

"I'm sorry. I didn't mean any harm, baby. I'm just giving you compliments." Eddie patted her hand, leaned back, and stared at her with a smile, laughing to himself as the alcohol made him more talkative.

"Yeah, right," Pam replied angrily.

"Let me tell you about what my ex-wife did to me," Eddie insisted with his slurred speech.

"I 'm sorry, but I don't feel like hearing it." Looking up, Pam was glad to see her boyfriend coming back to the bar so Eddie could get out of her face. After he had eased onto the stool, Pam whispered into Robert's ear and told him about Eddie's behavior. Pam had been deeply offended by Eddie's flirting and constant stares at her breast.

After being fully updated about Eddie's actions, Robert asked, "I see you have acquainted yourself with my girl. What's your name again?"

"Eddie, my man."

"Okay, Eddie, this is the deal. I would appreciate if you would not talk to my girl again, and I think it is disrespectful how you keep staring at her chest. So just chill the fuck out."

Like most drunks, Eddie immediately jumped on the defensive. "I didn't say anything to offend your girlfriend. I was being friendly. We were just talking about the music video. Besides, you don't tell me what to do, man," Eddie slurred, his eyes displaying a look of confusion. By now, their loud tone had grabbed the attention of the bartender who was watching them closely.

"He's drunk, Robert Just forget about it," Pam said.

Robert was an extremely jealous man and quick to defend his woman.
"I'm not telling you what to do, but if you say anything else to my girl, I will kick your ass."

Eddie hesitated for moment as he took a drink from his glass. His eyes were red and his movement was slow.

"You're not going to kick my ass, and I don't need to hear this shit, man," Eddie said as hc stood up from the bar.

"What did you say?" Robert was a slim guy in his late twenties. He wore an oversized long sleeve white shirt, baggy FUBU sweatpants, a backwards baseball cap, and corn rolls in his head. Displaying his street mentality, he stared Eddie up and down and shook his head as if he was ready to fight him at the bar.

Not to be intimidated, Eddie replied, "You heard me," while putting on his coat.

"Listen, if you open your mouth again, I'm gonna fuck you up. Do you understand that, punk?"

The bartender intervened as the other patrons looked on in shock. "Is everything okay, gentlemen?"

"Hell no! This guy is disrespecting my girl."

"Are you okay, sir?" the bartender asked Eddie.

"I'm okay. I was just leaving." Eddie placed fifty dollars on the counter and walked away, looking back at the guy with a funny stare before exiting the establishment. Robert became increasingly angry by Eddie's actions and refused to drop the dispute.

"Excuse me, Pam. I have to go to the men's room again."

Already aware of Robert's intentions, Pam called out, "Leave him alone, Robert!" She knew Robert was capable of doing crazy shit.

While ignoring her pleads for him to return to his seat, Robert followed Eddie to his car. As he walked up on Eddie from behind, Robert yelled out, "What are you going to do now? You were talking all that shit in the bar with your bitch ass."

"Man, let's just drop it, okay? I am sorry if I offended your girlfriend," Eddie said as he stood up straight from unlocking his door and looked Robert in the eye.

Robert turned as if he was walking away and then suddenly spun around, punching Eddie in the face with a solid blow. "Take that, motherfucker!" The punch connected to the left side of Eddie's face, sending him into the side of his car and to the ground.

Eddie immediately grabbed where Robert's fist had impacted and started breathing loudly. "Oh shit!" Eddie yelled in pain as Robert fled the scene where no witnesses were present.

Drunk and incapable of defending himself, he laid on the ground with one leg folded behind him while rubbing the blood from his left eye. He attempted to get up from the ground, but slid back down the side of the car in a state of dizziness. On his second attempt to get up from the ground, he was successful and finally managed to get inside the car while holding onto the door for balance. He sat there for about twenty minutes wiping away the blood with a napkin from the glove compartment before driving away.

For the next two days, Eddie decided to stay home from work so he could recuperate from his badly bruised left eye. He didn't want to have to explain to anyone about his embarrassing encounter with the thug. After his time off, he returned to work with shades to hide his stitched left eye. While standing in line to order lunch at Lillie's Café, he ran into Lance, who he definitely didn't want to see at this point.

"What's up, Eddie?"

"Oh hey, man. What's up? I'm just trying to order me a sandwich."

"It's a wonder you can even see the menu. I almost didn't recognize you with those dark shades on. What's up with the shades? I usually see you with the horn-rimmed glasses."

Eddie became silent as he racked his brain for an excuse.

Noticing Eddie's slow reaction to his question, Lance asked, "Is everything okay, Eddie?"

Knowing he would not be able to hide his injury from Lance for much longer, Eddie snatched the shades from his face. "This is my problem, Lance." The young black lady standing behind them in line turned her head and grimaced.

"Damn! Put those shades back on, man. What the hell happened to your eye?" Lance asked, temporarily taken aback.

"I got punched in the eye when I was outside a bar two nights ago. I guess I had too many beers that night."

"Shit, I'm sorry to hear that. Why did he, she, or they punch you?"

"This guy socked me in the eye when I was walking to my car for talking to his girlfriend. He thought I was flirting with her."

"Were you?"

"No, the guy was just a jealous man."

"Listen, Eddie, you're my boy and all, but I have noticed you've been getting drunk a lot lately. Is this about the divorce? Are you okay, Eddie? Let's talk, man. I need you on my team, and I want you to be in the condition to take care of business. I have total respect for you, but I am a little concerned."

Both men moved up with the line.

"What are you saying, Lance? I don't have a drinking problem. I am in control of things. I've just been a little heavy on the booze as of lately, but I'm fine. And for the record, my divorce has nothing to do with it," Eddie replied, refusing to accept reality and be honest with Lance. On the inside, the divorce was eating him up.

"I'm just trying to help you, man. I didn't say you had a drinking problem. Don't get upset with me because you have a black eye."

"I'm fine, Lance. Now let's just drop the subject, okay?" Eddie's face said differently, showing an uncomfortable look as if something was deeply bothering him. Eddie handed the cashier a ten-dollar bill, grabbed up his change along with his juice, chips, and sandwich, and walked away without another word.

"I'll call you later, man," Lance called out to Eddie who just threw his hand up in the air in response.

"*What's wrong with, Eddie*?" He had known him long enough to know that Eddie had incredible will and tenacity. Therefore, there wasn't any doubt in his mind that Eddie would overcome his problem.

* * * * * *

It was late Tuesday night around 10:20 p.m., and Kenya was dressed in her red silk pajamas eating popcorn on her sofa while watching the old film *Carmen Jones* on her 52-inch television screen. She smiled as Dorothy Dandridge engaged in a romantic encounter with Harry Belafonte during a scene in the movie. Immediately, she began fantasizing about Lance and wondering what he would be like as a lover. In a strange way, she wanted to be married and have a family. She was tired of being alone and wanted things to be right in her personal life. As she sat on the sofa chewing on her lightly buttered popcorn, her doorbell rang.

"*Who is this at this time of night?*" Kenya thought. Usually, her friends would call before coming over to her apartment located in Northwest, DC on Sixteen Street. Kenya put her popcorn bowl on the wooden coffee table, slipped into her bathrobe and slippers, and walked slowly across the light brown plush carpet toward the door.

She had a small apartment with little furniture; however, she lived in an expensive neighborhood. Large pillows were neatly place throughout her apartment.

"Who is it?" Kenya said cautiously as she stood in suspense.

"Kenya…it's me, Jason."

"Jason? What do you want and what are you doing here?" Kenya began to get nervous. Jason was the ex-boyfriend she had broken up with five months ago. Their relationship had been one filled with violence and abuse.

"Kenya, I need to talk to you. I really do. I am having some problems in my life, and I need to talk to you, baby," Jason pleaded. He knew Kenya was vulnerable and had a generous heart when it came to helping people.

"Jason, do you realize what time it is? I don't feel like talking. It's my bedtime," Kenya replied, hesitating for a moment. She quickly moved away from the door. She didn't want to be bothered with Jason. Jason was nothing but trouble.

"Please, Kenya, I need to talk to you. Please, just a few minutes, baby."

Kenya hesitated again. However, the sound of Jason's voice resonated with her and evoked a familiar emotional response. She sensed Jason's desperation. For some strange reason, she couldn't resist his demands. Quickly, she unlocked the chain on the door and opened it.

"Thanks, baby. I'm not going to hurt you. I just wanted to talk for a few minutes."

"Okay, Jason, but you better make this quick," Kenya demanded as she stood with her arms folded across her chest, allowing him to pass by her extensive library of books and vintage video tapes filed neatly on a bookcase near the doorway.

Jason had an imposing figure, about six feet tall with good looks and a round face. He wore his head bald with an earring in the left ear. He had a gap between his front teeth and a dark skin complexion. Jason was an aspiring singer but had fell bad on his luck as a result of his touring band breaking up.

"Kenya...I was evicted from my apartment. I'm having some major financial problems. I have been on the road touring, but the gigs are not happening right now. I know you and I have been through tough times in our relationship and that I have not been the best person I could be to you, but I always think about you. Kenya, I messed up. I just can't stop thinking about you, baby," Jason whined as he stood in Kenya's living room dressed in a black mid-length leather jacket and blue jeans.

As Kenya approached him, she kicked the couch's pillows that were on the floor from out of her way. "Jason, you just don't get it. Our relationship was over five months ago after you broke my wrist. I have moved on with my life. I am sorry you are having financial problems, but I can't help you."

"Kenya, I just need a few dollars. I know you understand me better than anyone else. You and I had a relationship for three years. I need your help, baby. I need fifty dollars to get some food."

Under normal circumstances, Kenya would give in to Jason. But clearly, she was over Jason.

"I don't have fifty dollars to give you. Now it's time for you to go, Jason. It's getting late."

"Why are you being so difficult, Kenya? I know you have the money."

His eyes pleaded with her, and she knew she had to get him out of her apartment before she gave in.

"Listen, Jason, I was kind enough to listen to your problem. Our relationship is over. My obligations to you have come to an end. Do you understand that? Now, I am asking you to leave my apartment."

"So it's like that, huh?" Jason slowly approached the door with his shoulders hung low in defeat.

"Yes, Jason, it's like that. I don't owe you anything. You were abusive to me, and I just want to move on with my life. Now please leave." Kenya reached for the door's handle, swung it open, and waited with her hand on her hip for him to make his exit.

"Alright, I'm leaving, but let me tell you one thing, Kenya. You're still the same bitch you were five months ago."

"Leave my house, Jason!" Kenya yelled as he walked out of her apartment. Kenya then slammed the door closed, cursing herself for having opened it in the first place.

Sensing that evil had dispersed itself, her Siamese cat, Persia, came from out of Kenya's bedroom and rubbed up against her leg. After scooping her up in her arms, Kenya began rubbing Persia on the head as she reflected on her encounter with Jason five months ago. She played out the scene in her mind when Jason pushed her against the kitchen table in her apartment and broke her left wrist. This incident occurred as a result of an argument over money. Kenya had loaned eight hundred dollars to Jason for some band equipment, and he refused to pay her back. She had indeed learned a lesson from the violent experience, and was determined not to make the same mistake twice.

The next day, she received a telephone call from Jason.

"Kenya, I gotta talk to you. Please don't hang up on me," Jason said as he begged for Kenya to talk to him.

"Jason, please don't call my house again."

CLICK!

The following day after she left work, Jason was standing next to her car. Kenya stopped about ten feet away, stunned at first, and then proceeded walking to her car.

"Jason, what are you doing here?" Her voice took on a tone more of irritation than fear. "I thought I told you to leave me alone."

"Kenya, I am sorry for what I said to you the other night, but I love you. I need some money, baby. Please understand my situation." Jason looked unkempt, his fingernails were dirty and he badly needed a shave and bath, the white shirt under his leather jacket was dirty and stained.

"Get away from me, Jason." Kenya attempted to go around him.

"Stop being so damn dramatic. I'm not going to hurt you." He blocked her from opening the car door by pressing his hand against it. He then grabbed her left arm in a tight grip with his big hands. Kenya struggled to break free from his grasp.

"Take your damn hands off of me, Jason! Why are you stalking me? Leave me alone. I don't want to talk to you, and if you bother me again, I swear I will put a restraining order on your ass. I'm not playing with you. If I hear from you again, I will report this to the police." She began to back away slowly from her car while looking directly at Jason, fearing he may try to attack her.

Jason stood there with his arms folded looking at Kenya. "What are you gonna do? You know you love me."

As if her prayers had been answered, two of McIntyre's employees walking to the parking lot overheard Kenya and Jason arguing and rushed to her side.

"Is everything okay?" one gentleman asked while the other looked in the direction of Jason who was running down the street.

"I'm okay, guys. Thank you for your concern. We were just having a little disagreement."

For the next three nights, Kenya's girlfriend, Diane, stayed at her apartment with her. To her relief, weeks passed and she never heard from Jason again.

Chapter Ten

Lance turned on his computer to read his e-mails. Kenya approached his office and knocked gently on the door, which was halfway open. She stood with a white folder in her right hand.

"You can come in," Lance announced turning around in his chair and looking towards the door. "Oh, Kenya, come in. You don't have to always knock," Lance insisted as he looked attentively at Kenya. He quickly placed his right hand on his desk and crossed his legs, assuming the "man-in-charge" position. Kenya slowly approached his desk but stopped a little distance from it. Lance was pleasantly surprised as he observed Kenya in a particularly fashionable outfit. She wore a beige business suit with a large belt around her waist. A pearl necklace adorned her smooth brown neck, and her hair was shiny with a frizzled look. Lance smiled as he appreciated her beauty.

"Have you heard the news?" Kenya asked.

"What news?" Lance responded.

"Can I close your office door?" Kenya asked as she proceeded to close the door, not waiting for his response.

"Sure," Lance replied.

"Allen Frisco mysteriously decided to go on vacation for two weeks. I don't believe he informed anybody in this office. We were told by e-mail that Nathaniel would be the new Vice President of Sales and Marketing. You should read the e-mail. Strange things are happening around here, Lance," Kenya said as she rolled her eyes and shook her head. Kenya feared her news would solicit an unpleasant response from Lance. She'd witnessed several of Lance's temper tantrums.

"I agree. This is real strange, but it doesn't surprise me. I knew he was grooming Nathaniel for the position. You know, Kenya...I don't care anymore. I have bigger goals. I'm not even worried about that," Lance said calmly as he sat straight in his leather chair and clenched his hands. Lance smiled, showing no overt emotions, reaffirming his prediction and accepting the reality.

"Good for you, Lance. I don't like the sneaky way in which this was handled by Allen, but you know...he is the boss."

"I am tired of the corporate games. We don't get easy breaks in corporate America because we are not part of the old white boy network. You and I know this. Why sweat it? I will put this behind me and focus on what is really important -- Freedom Technologies. I spoke with Eddie Patterson yesterday, and as you know, we are looking for another person to help us get this business off the ground. I would like for you to officially join us," Lance offered.

Kenya's eyes shone with gratitude. "As I told you before, Lance, I will gladly join you," Kenya replied with absolute acceptance.

Kenya thought for a moment of how big a risk she would be taking, but she was willing to do anything to be with Lance. She knew their business relationship would bring her closer to Lance. Kenya was also becoming increasingly dissatisfied with McIntyre based on recent events, which made her decision to join Lance in his business endeavor an easy one. She felt confident about her talents and was willing to help him. Leaning her head slightly to the side, she smiled appreciatively at Lance Kenya felt Lance's passion, and he could feel her energy. He knew she was the right person. He stood up, shook her hand, and then gave her a fierce hug.

"I am flattered. You have made my day," Lance said, knowing Kenya would provide tremendous support for his business.

"I am honored you would ask me," Kenya smiled, showing her deep, pretty dimples.

* * * * * *

That afternoon, Lance left work and showed up at Valerie's apartment unexpectedly. Lance was concerned because he had not heard from her since their conversation in Boston. This was unusual, especially since they normally talked everyday. As Lance exited his car, he noticed a car with a Georgia license plate parked next to Valerie's but didn't think much of it. Lance rang Valerie's doorbell. The door opened slowly, revealing only a partial view of Julia's face.

"Hi, Julia. Is Valerie home?"

Julia hesitated for a moment before shaking her head and clenching her lips.

"Yeah, she's in the kitchen," Julia said in an unfriendly tone, turning her head quickly away, as if she was Valerie's guardian. This greeting immediately angered Lance. He was pissed. Lance walked into the kitchen to find Valerie eating an apple.

"Why did Julia answer the door like that?" Lance said, questioning Valerie who was dressed in a blue sweat suit and sitting on a white kitchen stool.

"What do you mean? I wasn't at the door," Valerie greeted Lance in a lukewarm tone, taking another bite of her apple. She shrugged and looked at Lance as if she hadn't the slightest clue about Julia's behavior.

"Well, she has an attitude problem."

"I don't have an attitude, Mr. Lance," Julia said, walking up to Lance with her arms folded.

Lance looked at Julia as his tall body towered over her shorter one. Wanting to avoid any type of confrontation with her, he immediately directed his attention to Valerie.

"I'm not talking to you, Julia. I'm talking to Valerie, and you should mind your own damn business! You understand that?"

"Hey! Watch your mouth, buddy!" Julia shouted.

"Julia, I'm okay. I will handle this. Just go in the other room," Valerie instructed as she intervened and stood up from the stool, throwing her finished apple in the wastebasket. With her arms around Julia's shoulders, she slowly walked her back into the living room.

"What's going on Valerie?" Lance asked when she returned to the kitchen. "Are you telling your girlfriend about our personal matters? I don't like when you do that. I feel like you have told your friend something bad about me."

"I feel like you're cross-examining me, Lance. The only thing I know is that you hurt me and that bothers me greatly. I've made some significant investments in this relationship. We are supposed to be partners, but we are not acting like it. You seem to have your own agenda. I have thought about this for a few days and I have decided to put this wedding on hold like I told you until we can figure things out. And yes…I have told the people who care about me of my decision," Valerie said.

"I didn't tell you to call off the wedding! We can resolve this issue, Valerie! Are you crazy?" Lance folded his fingers into a fist and swung at the air, expressing his disappointment.

"No, I am perfectly sane, and don't raise your voice at me like that. I can read between the lines, Lance. As I have said numerous times, you have put your business ahead of our relationship," Valerie asserted passionately.

"You know something…I have figured this out. You are the selfish person. Not me. You are a professional woman, and for God sake, you should be more understanding than anyone! There is no need for this type of drama. It's really unnecessary. You are making too much out of this. I am just a black man trying to pursue his dreams. Do you understand that?" Lance shouted in anger as he leaned against the kitchen counter with his arms wide open seeking an immediate response from Valerie. After a few moments, he walked up to Valerie and gently placed both of his hands on her shoulders and looked into her eyes, searching for an answer within her soul. Valerie looked back at Lance and then warily turned away.

"I disagree with you, Lance. I believe couples should be in the same accord, and if not, they shouldn't be together," Valerie stated.

"Okay. If that's how you feel, why didn't you tell me that Julia was in town?" Lance whispered to Valerie, not wanting Julia to hear him over the gospel music playing in the background.

"You didn't tell me when you decided to go to Boston. You have some nerve, Lance. Julia is my friend. I need her support. My family is very disappointed with this situation. I put so much energy into planning for this wedding." Tears welled in her eyes; she wiped them away and gave Lance a look of surrender, turning her head away from him.

"I can't make you change your mind, Val. I have tried my best."

"It is abundantly clear that this discussion is going nowhere. Therefore, I rest my case," Valerie replied, as if she was arguing a case in court.

"Val, if you want time, I will give you the time," Lance said as he put on his gray suit jacket while looking at Valerie. His somber eyes were pleading for her understanding.

He slowly walked towards the door and then took a second look at Valerie. He walked pass the living room as Julia sat watching TV. He shot Julia a look of anger and displeasure, knowing she was a negative force and influence on Valerie. After anchoring himself into his car, he sat there for about five minutes, thinking about Valerie and conducting a mental inventory of their relationship. At this point, he knew his future with Valerie was uncertain.

Within minutes of his departure, Valerie and Julia began to assess Lance's visit. Valerie walked into the living room where Julia was sitting on the couch, wearing a pair of gray sweat pants and a baggy pink tee shirt. Julia had taken off her bedroom slippers and had one leg folded underneath her.

Valerie released a long sigh as she sat next to Julia with a cup of tea in her hand. "Lance…I tell you," she started as she shook her head. "He is so stubborn. I have put all this work into the planning our wedding and look at what I have to go through. He doesn't seem to care about what I think. I will pray for Lance, though. He needs God in his life. Maybe this wasn't meant to be," Valerie said, smoothing back the stray hairs from her ponytail, and then leaned back on the couch with her eyes closed for a brief moment.

"Listen, Valerie…please…you don't have to be so hard on yourself. Lance may be the man for you, but…I really think he has some issues. He thinks the world revolves around him, and it shouldn't be that way. Maybe you should just move on with your life. I'm tired of these selfish ass men. And like I have told you several times, most of these men that I have met lately are full of themselves. If you don't jump on their bandwagon, they will accuse you of not being supportive. I don't buy it. Would Lance support you if the tables were turned?" Julia asked rhetorically, stabbing her finger in the air emphasizing her point.

Valerie looked at Julia and nodded in agreement. However, she knew Julia didn't always bring a balanced view of men. Valerie lamented over her conflict with Lance as she sat there listening to Julia's man bashing. She loved Lance, and deep inside her heart, she wanted the relationship to work. The question was, could it?

Chapter Eleven

Big Flem was the last to leave the barbershop on Friday evening. He put on his blue jacket, his old baseball cap and locked up the barbershop. After he eased into his Lincoln Continental, he decided to take Lance's advice and drive down to the Playboy Club on Georgia Avenue. As he approached the club, he saw several cars parked in front. For a few minutes, he drove up and down the avenue looking for a parking space. Finally, he found a parking spot north on Georgia Avenue after a patron of the Playboy Club decided to leave.

Once he parked his car in the space, which was almost too small, he walked into the dark and smoke-filled club. He cautiously strolled through the club, and saw three young nude girls dancing on different stages and a woman sitting at the bar wearing a skimpy bikini exposing her big butt cheeks. Big Flem did not want to appear conspicuous, so he sat in the back of the club.

After the three girls finished their exotic routines and collected dollar bills from the sexually hungry men, three new girls came onto the stage. To his dismay, Tasha appeared, dressed in high heels and a see-through miniskirt. Big Flem looked keenly at Tasha, and then stood to make sure it was her. Tasha, not seeing Big Flem, immersed herself into a sexually suggestive dance as the rap music blasted in the background. His facial expression conveyed utter shock. He felt a sense of betrayal because she had lied to him.

Big Flem rushed to the exit of the club. He walked so quickly until he accidentally bumped into a younger gentleman standing near the exit. "Excuse me, man. I'm sorry," Big Flem nervously said as he walked out of the club.

Tasha was living a life he didn't know about. All along, he thought she was a waitress at a restaurant. He was tired of people telling him about Tasha's nightlife. The notion of Tasha being a stripper bothered him greatly because he knew her body was for sale and the thought of Tasha engaged in prostitution irked him.

During his short visit at the club, one of Tasha's girlfriends recognized Big Flem. When Tasha came off stage, the girlfriend whispered in her ear about Big Flem's visit. Tasha simply shook her head as if she didn't care, walked into the dressing room, picked up her cell phone, and called Big Flem, who didn't answer.

******

Eddie drove over to Lance's house in his silver Mercedes Benz. Expecting Eddie's arrival, Lance greeted him at the door. It was around 6:00 p.m., and Lance and Eddie were dressed in their business attire. Both men were neat in appearance, with the only difference being Lance had his necktie loosened.

"Hey, man, come on in. You came at the right time. I just got here." Eddie walked in and sat in the living room. "Kenya gave me her commitment today. She wants to work with us at Freedom Technologies," Lance announced from within his kitchen while pouring himself a glass of apple juice.

"Great!" Eddie replied.

"I think Kenya would make a good VP of Marketing and Sales. She is very assertive. Not to mention, she has a good background in software development and IT security. She understands the product and how to market it," Lance said confidently, entering the living room.

"Can I get you something to drink, Eddie?" Lance asked, spilling the apple juice on the sleeve of his shirt. "Damn, I am wasting this all over the place."

"Yeah, man. I'll have a beer if you have one," Eddie replied.

"Okay."

"We should all meet very soon to talk about our business opportunities," Eddie suggested after Lance had returned from retrieving his beer. "Believe it or not, we may have our first contract with the PG's County Public School System. They want us to submit a bid."

"I spoke with a representative over at PG's budget office," Eddie informed him while cracking open the can. "They would like for us to install security software in their high schools' computers. We can get started on this project within the next thirty days. It's a small job, and pays about $250,000.00. We only need about three analysts to do this job. This opportunity will be a sole source contract, which means we don't have to compete on this requirement. I have contacts at SBO, so I am trying to expedite the 8A certification process."

"That sounds great. I remember you discussing this with me last week. Your SBO contacts will also be helpful. To tell you the truth, Eddie, I didn't think this would happen so soon."

"I will definitely utilize my SBO experience in order to get the business. There are a lot of opportunities under the 8A and Small Business Program, especially in the area of subcontracting. There are many large firms who are looking for small IT companies to do subcontracting work," Eddie explained.

"Oh really? This means we have to start making contact with the large IT firms," Lance replied.

"Definitely. We also have to meet with a SBO representative in Largo, Maryland next week in order to finalize this deal with PG," Eddie added as he took a sip of his beer.

"When do we submit an offer to SBO?"

"They will let us know next week."

"Good."

"We could definitely use the start-up capital. Have you heard from State Street Bank?" Eddie asked.

"No, Eddie, and it's been almost three weeks. Jim told me he should have the loan approved within two weeks. I don't know what's going on. I will wait another week, and then I'm going to contact them."

"I hope everything is okay, Lance."

"Yeah, but I can't jump to any conclusions at this point," Lance said, leaning back on his sofa as he rubbed his chin while reflecting on Eddie's comment. Lance thought to himself, "*I hope I get this money soon.*"

"Let me know what time you would like to meet this week."

"Okay. I need to look at my schedule first, and then I'll let you know, as well as Kenya."

Eddie and Lance stood up from the sofa almost simultaneously. Eddie finished his beer with one gulp and they shook hands before Eddie exited out the front door.

After Eddie left, Lance thought about the role of Valerie in his life and decided to give her a break for a while until things cooled off. He wanted to focus his energy towards the development of his business. Lance called Kenya at home.

"I told Eddie about our business deal. He was very excited about this arrangement."

"Great! So how will I fit into the business scheme of things?" Kenya asked excitedly as she sat in a chair of her apartment looking at TV with the volume muted.

"Just wait. Don't quit your job yet until the loan is approved. We really need your experience at Freedom Technologies, though. We are going to schedule a meeting to discuss the business structure," Lance said while opening the refrigerator with the phone to his ear.

"Alright, just let me know what time and where," Kenya responded.

"What are you doing tonight?" Lance asked, hoping to spend time with her.

"I have a lot of work to do at home. You know, like cleaning, errands, etc. Why?"

"Would you like to go out for dinner?" Lance asked, grabbing a bowl of baby carrots to munch on. He was ready to have a nice meal.

"I wish I could, but thank you anyway." Kenya was flattered by the offer from Lance. However, she decided to change her approach towards Lance. Kenya thought it would be clever to play "hard to get" for a while. She thought to herself that if Lance really wanted her, he would have to prove it.

"I can understand," Lance said.

"Maybe next time," Kenya replied.

"Okay. I'll call and let you know as soon as we decide on a day for the meeting."

Lance hung up the phone and reflected on Kenya's response. He knew Kenya liked him, which is why he was terribly surprised at her unresponsiveness to his dinner request. He thought back to her confession during their last dinner at the Upper Nile. He felt a real chemistry. He pondered for a moment and a fleeting reflection crossed his mind about the possibility of them having a relationship in the future if things didn't work out between him and Valerie.

* * * * * *

Later during the week, Lance drove up to the gym at Prince George's County Sports & Learning Complex. This was the first time he had been to the gym since Reina left for Puerto Rico, and being there caused him to realize how much he missed her. When he exited his car, he spotted his friend Trey, walking towards his car wearing a black sweat suit with a towel over his right shoulder.

"Trey, what's up, man? You work out here?" Lance asked, giving Trey the black man's handshake, bumping shoulders and gripping the hands tightly and then pulling away quickly.

"Yeah, I just started a few weeks ago. It's a nice gym. It has a lot more weights and is a lot cheaper than the gym in DC."

"You are definitely right. It is one of the nicer gyms in the area."

"Yeah, I know. I've been working out more and trying to stay focused on the positive. Things have been rough lately. You know how that is, man," Trey said as he looked away from Lance, who was holding his blue gym bag in his right hand.

"What do you mean? Is everything okay, Trey?" Lance asked.

"Let me just be straight with you. I lost my security job over some petty stuff last month. On top of that, my girl and I had a little disagreement and she called the cops on me. I'm glad they didn't lock me up. I have to get away from this woman. I got locked up before over some similar shit. So…I have been spending a lot of time at the gym and looking for a gig," Trey said, shaking his head while reflecting on his predicament.

"I'm sorry to hear about that. Take care of yourself, man. I don't want to see you go to jail over a woman."

"Yeah, look at what I am going through." Trey threw his gym bag in the back of his car, leaned against his car, crossed his arms, and waited for Lance's response.

"You seem to have a tough time with the ladies. All I can say is stay focused on your goals, Trey. You will get a job eventually."

"This woman is high maintenance and very insecure. She's always nagging me and she even checks my underwear to see if I've been sleeping around. That's some crazy shit. I gotta leave her, Lance. I don't need this police drama, and I definitely don't wanna do something I will regret later," Trey said, as a look of desperation appeared on his face.

"You definitely have issues with her. Why don't you guys just chill for a while? Take a break from each other, man," Lance suggested.

"Yep, I think I'll do just that. I will probably stay with my mom for a little while until I can get things back in order financially. I hate staying with my family, though. I am too old for this shit."

"I hear you, brother, but you have to do what you gotta do," Lance replied.

"How's the business?" Trey asked, changing the subject.

"It's coming along. We're still trying to get everything together," Lance responded.

"I need work. Can you hook a brother up?"

Noticing Trey did not look very well and that he mysteriously had a black eye, Lance hesitated with an answer.

"I might," Lance finally said as he spoke in his street vernacular. "We go way back, dawg...you my boy. I'll see what I can do. I got your back, partner. I'll call you within the next few weeks once I am working in a full-time capacity. I may have something for you. Just hang in there for me."

"Thanks, Lance. I'll take whatever you got. I just need a job. Call me at my mom's house."

"Okay, Trey. Peace."

Chapter Twelve

Several days later, Lance walked into his office and noticed his office door was unlocked, which was unusual since he locked it whenever he left at the end of each day. And the only person who had access to his office was the office manager and Allen.

While Buddy was riffling through his files, Lance slowly and quietly walked up behind him. "Buddy! What the hell are you doing in my office? You shouldn't be in here!" Lance shouted.

Buddy looked around as if he was caught with his hand in the cookie jar. "Hey, Lance, you scared me," Buddy said, his face immediately turning beet red from guilt.

"What are you doing, Buddy?" Lance asked again angrily.

"I'm sorry, Lance. The office manager gave me the key to your office. This was an emergency request. Nathaniel requested a copy of your monthly sales report immediately," Buddy answered nervously, avoiding eye contact, knowing that he was actually trying to remove some of Lance's contract files in order to make him look incompetent.

"I don't believe you, Buddy. You could have obtained a copy from the secretary. I don't trust you in my office, and I will certainly take this matter up with Nathaniel. Now get out, please!" Lance demanded.

Buddy rushed out of the office. As he walked quickly down the hallway in one direction, Lance headed in the other toward Nathaniel's office.

"Nathaniel, I came in this morning and found Buddy in my office. He said you requested a monthly report," Lance said, displeased, standing in front of Nathaniel's desk.

"That's correct, but we don't need the report until tomorrow."

"That's interesting. Buddy said it was urgent and he requested the key to my office from the office manager. I don't understand. I feel Buddy's actions were inappropriate. He should have waited until I came in."

"I was not aware of how Buddy obtained your monthly reports," Nathaniel replied, appearing relaxed and not particularly concerned about Lance as he continued to type on his computer nonchalantly.

"Well, Nathaniel, I have been here for a long time, and I know an employee must seek approval through the office manager before entering another employee's office. According to McIntyre's office policy, this request for entrance must be approved by the Vice-President."

Nathaniel arrogantly pulled his eyeglasses below his eyes, turned towards Lance, and said, "I am not sure what you are insinuating, Lance, but I will talk to Buddy about this matter. I have a meeting in ten minutes, so I will talk to you later."

Lance felt immediately angry and somewhat disrespected at Nathaniel's lack of professionalism. He felt that Nathaniel, Buddy, and even Allen Frisco were not operating in his best interest. Anxious to get his business underway, he called Eddie and Kenya upon returning to his office to set up their meeting for later that evening. They decided that Houston's Restaurant would be the place to meet briefly to discuss the business of Freedom Technologies.

* * * * * *

"Eddie, you have met Kenya before, right?" Lance asked.
"Yes, it is good to see you again, Kenya," Eddie said.

"Nice seeing you, as well," Kenya replied.

Lance, Eddie and Kenya stood in the lobby area of the restaurant. After Eddie was introduced to Kenya, they all walked to the bar area of the restaurant and waited to be served after giving the waitress a guest name.

"I have heard so many good things about you. I hear you have a lot of experience in marketing and sales."

"Yes, I enjoy the process of getting customers excited about a product or service. I have worked in marketing for many years, and I'm excited about bringing my knowledge to Freedom Technologies," Kenya smiled and sipped her juice. "I hear you have a lot of experience in the area of business development over at SBO."

"Oh yeah, fifteen years' worth," Eddie replied.

"Now that we are acquainted, I want to touch on a few things regarding Freedom Technologies," Lance interrupted. "I will be the President, Eddie will be the Chief Executive Officer, and, Kenya, you will be the Vice President of Marketing and Sales. I would like to be behind the scenes for a while, especially in the IT arena. Hopefully, at our next meeting, I will be able to share the business and strategic plan I have been working on for the last two weeks. It's different from our marketing plan. Unfortunately, I still have not received the financing from State Street Bank."

"I see. So how do we effectively operate without the financing? Perhaps we need to put our focus on planning this business until we can move into an office space and hire a secretary and a technical team," Eddie said.

"Excellent point, Eddie," Lance said. "We definitely need the two hundred thousand dollars. I say we continue to plan our strategy. I have a good feeling Jim Earp will come through with the financing. I was expecting the loan approval sooner, though. If he doesn't call me this week, I will call him first thing Monday."

"It will definitely cost money for advertising and marketing. We need to print brochures, cards, and other marketing material," Kenya added.

"I agree, but I'm also curious to hear more about your new strategy, Lance," Eddie said.

"I am curious, too," Kenya voiced.

"I know you all want to hear about it, but I can't let the cat out of the bag yet. Next meeting, pal," Lance laughed. They left the bar area as the waitress seated them at a table for their evening dinner.

Even though he laughed on the outside, Lance felt somewhat embarrassed. He had assembled a great team for his business venture, yet he did not have the capital in order to move his business to the next level. It was all becoming a bit frustrating. Moreover, his relationship with Valerie was slowly falling apart.

Chapter Thirteen

It was early spring and Lance had not seen Valerie in two weeks. Sheila's Cuisine, an upscale restaurant and popular after work hangout, was crowded with mostly young black professionals. Lance and Valerie sat at a table in the restaurant.

"This whole experience has really been challenging and quite difficult for me. I've been keeping myself busy at the law firm with this case that requires me to travel to New York at least once a week," Valerie said as she crossed her legs and took a bite of her garden salad. A piece of salad failed to enter her mouth, but landed on the lower part of her lips. Primly, she wiped her mouth with the napkin and waited for Lance's response as he struggled with trying to find the words to say.

"It's good to see you, Val. I am glad we could meet and talk. I have a lot on my mind these days. I have been so busy. I haven't even called my mother in a week, and I try to talk to her at least two or three times during the week. It has been hectic," Lance said unconvincingly, failing to give Valerie direct eye contact. Instead, he kept looking towards the entrance of the restaurant as people walked in. It was a convenient resting place for his curious eyes. He then took a sip of his black tea and nervously placed a cloth napkin in his lap.

"I'd like to think that these two weeks would have given you a chance to think about us and reflect on our future," Valerie said as her probing eyes focused directly on Lance. She hesitated on her next bite of salad, anxious to see if Lance showed any signs of caring for her. For a moment, Valerie thought about her last encounter with Lance.

"Yeah, I did evaluate our relationship. Everything seems to be happening so fast. You know... the wedding. I still need time, Val. And this has nothing to do with you. You know how I feel about you. I need time to think things through and determine what is important to me.

Just like you have put yourself into your work, I have done the same thing."

"Obviously, you have not thought about this relationship seriously. What are you telling me, Lance? What do you mean by 'more time'?" Valerie asked as she placed her fork down on the table, suddenly having lost her appetite.

"That's right, Val. I have a lot going on in my life right now, especially my business. And to be honest, I am a little disappointed with this relationship. I had big plans for us. The cancellation of the wedding did not set well with me. I wanted this wedding as much as you did. However, we have been arguing way too much. I don't like seeing this side of you, Val," Lance declared.

"Your business became a priority over our relationship and I didn't like that at all. I agree, this arguing is not terribly productive. Let's face it, though. It is me who is trying to keep this relationship together. I am the one who arranged this lunch. There has to be some reciprocity here. I can't keep pursuing you like this," Valerie said with finality.

"We don't need to go there again. What you said is completely untrue. When I visited you two weeks ago, when Julia was there, it was me who came to visit you. So...I really don't want to hear that. It was you who cancelled the wedding."

"Okay...you know what, Lance? Nothing has changed since I last talked to you, and I have had enough of this blame game. I have to get back to work. When you are ready to have a real relationship, let me know. Excuse me, waiter, can I get the check," she called out while motioning for the server.

"So it's like that, huh?"

"The ball is in your court, Lance." Valerie paid the bill and they both departed in separate directions in Union Station, with Valerie returning to her law office.

She had decided not to pursue Lance at this point in her life. She thought if Lance really wanted a relationship, he would do the pursuing. Valerie felt Lance was selfish and self-centered. As she sat in her office at the law firm with her door closed, feelings of anger and being misled consumed her. She was fed up with Lance. As she stared out of her window on K Street in North West, DC, she thought to herself, "Lance isn't a man. If he was, he would know what the hell he wants. I will find a real man someday who knows how to make decisions." With that, she picked up the telephone and called Richard, an old friend who worked with her at a previous law firm.

Many thoughts went racing through Lance's mind after Valerie left the restaurant. He was greatly disturbed by the abrupt departure Valerie had made. He was also disappointed in himself for not knowing how to terminate the relationship. After a while of strolling past the stores and gift shops of Union Station, he decided to stop and sit on the bench in the mall-like setting. He thought about Valerie and tried to determine what went wrong with his relationship.

Lance felt bad about what he had done to Valerie. He tried to write it off as just bad timing. In his heart, he loved Valerie, but marriage was not for him at this particular time in his life. In a strange way, he relished his time away from Valerie because he knew she was not the right woman for him. As he sat on the bench, his thoughts suddenly shifted to Kenya. He liked everything about Kenya and was determined to get her.

At about 7:45 p.m., Lance parked his car in front of his house and walked towards his mailbox. After placing his briefcase on the sidewalk, he pulled his mailbox key from his pants pocket, opened the mailbox, and removed six pieces of mail. He scanned the first three pieces of mail while walking up his driveway. As he was opening the door of his house, he heard the phone ringing and quickly ran to answer it, throwing the mail on his kitchen counter in the process.

"Hello, Lance. I was just calling to verify the date of our next meeting. If I recall correctly, you said we would be meeting this week. I forgot to ask you at dinner," Kenya said in a professional tone.

"That was the plan, but I have to move the meeting to next week. There are a couple of business matters I have to take care of. So, it will be next Thursday."

"Okay, that works for me. Also, I wanted to tell you something about Nathaniel Watson.

"What about him?" Lance asked, full of curiosity.

"He and Buddy Poretsky are becoming real good friends. Buddy is really playing up to Nathaniel. I can't put my hands on it right now, but I just know they are up to something."

"I believe you, and I'm not surprised. I told Nathaniel about Buddy and his unauthorized entry into my office. Nathaniel's response was lukewarm, when I expected him to be more responsive. He said he would look into the matter. That took place last week, and I have not heard from Nathaniel."

"I just wanted to let you know. It probably doesn't mean anything to you at this point, though."

"I appreciate it, Kenya."

"Don't mention it. That's what partners do."

"Hey, would you like to do dinner this weekend?"

"Maybe, but I have to check my itinerary first before I commit. I'll let you know tomorrow."

"Oh...okay," Lance responded. He was hoping to get an immediate yes from Kenya. He couldn't understand why Kenya was so business like with him all of a sudden. He knew she liked him, but what would explain her change of attitude towards him?

As Kenya hung up the phone, she smiled to herself. Even though she was delighted to be asked out to dinner by Lance, she still had to maintain her strategy. Kenya felt if Lance really wanted her, he had to earn her. She wanted Lance as bad as he wanted her. However, she was unsure about his relationship with Valerie. Still, having a man pursue her, especially one she desired, made her feel good and lessened her feelings of insecurity. She smiled again as her eyes blossomed with excitement, knowing that her actions would produce results.

When Lance hung up the phone, he continued where he had left off with sorting through his mail. Within seconds, he saw an envelope from State Street Bank and immediately opened it, ripping the envelope apart like a million dollars was in it. The first sentence of the letter read: "Congratulations, you have been approved for a secured loan in the amount of two hundred thousand dollars ($200,000.00)."

Lance felt an enormous burden being lifted from his shoulders. He had waited to hear from State Street Bank for more than three weeks, and they had finally delivered. He walked into the living room, sat on his couch, leaned back, loosened his tie, and just stared at the letter as his heart filled with joy.

"Beep...beep...you may record your message."

"Eddie, this is Lance. I just called to let you know that the loan was approved. Hey, man, we definitely have to celebrate. This is a big step. Please call me when you get an opportunity."

Next, he called his parents, his mother answering on the first ring.

"Is something the matter, Lance? You don't usually call this late unless there is a problem or something," Mrs. Kojo said.

"Mom, the bank loan was approved. I am so happy about this. I can now move forward with my business plans," Lance said like a little kid who had just opened their first Christmas present.

"Congratulations, son. I knew everything would work out for you. Believe in yourself and leave the rest up to God."

"Thank you. Is Dad awake?"

"No, he's sleeping right now. But I will definitely tell him."

"Okay, thanks, Mom. I love you."

"I love you, too, son. Good night."

The next day, Lance went to Fleming Brown Barbershop to get a haircut, which was long overdue since he had not had one in about three weeks.

"You were right about Tasha. Aw, man. You wouldn't believe what happened to me. This got damn thief," Big Flem said.

"What happened?"

"She robbed me, man."

"You're kidding, right?"

"I'm serious as a heart attack."

"What did she steal?" Lance asked.

"She took my credit card and bought all kind of stuff from the internet, even used it to buy clothes. She ran up my bill to about sixteen hundred dollars." Looking visibly upset and distraught, Big Flem began to tie up his apron. "Let me cut his hair before I get to you, Lance," Big Flem said while rubbing his bald head and pointing to the one customer who was an old friend of Big Flem's.

"Sure, no problem. I knew something like this would happen. I tried to tell you about those young girls. Did you call the police?"

"Not yet. She told me that her ex-boyfriend stole my credit card when he came by to see his son. First of all, I didn't know that the "baby daddy" was coming over my house. I don't believe her, though. I know one thing. I put her ass out of my house," Big Flem said, shaking his head and looking serious, like he meant business.

"I don't think her boyfriend did it. I believe it was Tasha who pulled some bullshit scheme on you," Lance insisted as he stood next to Big Flem.

"You're probably right. I made a mistake, and to make matters worse, I found out that she was a stripper at the Playboy Club on Georgia Avenue. I had no clue she was stripping. I took your advice and went down to the Playboy Club and saw her dancing on the damn stage. That's all I needed to see. I walked out immediately. I couldn't stand to see her shaking her ass up there. I didn't feel comfortable with what she was doing, and I didn't like the idea of her outright lying to me. She made me look like a damn fool," Big Flem said.

"I am not surprised, but you should try and get your money. She can't get away with this."

"I'm going to have to figure something out real fast. I don't want the police involved. I should have been more alert. And why is she still involved with her ex-boyfriend? I heard he was a notorious drug dealer."

"She seems to be involved with the wrong crowd. You can count your loses and move on with your life. It may not be worth it. She's not going to pay you back sixteen hundred dollars. I just know it. She doesn't care."

"You may be right, Lance," Big Flem agreed, then paused momentarily as if he were in deep thought. "Well…let me finish this customer's head and I will take care of you."

Chapter Fourteen

Lance drove to Jamaica's Restaurant in Bowie to meet Eddie and Kenya, arriving thirty minutes early for the business meeting. Punctuality was an important virtue to Lance. Besides, he was keyed up over achieving a major milestone: Financing. Lance was anxious to share his ideas. He was confident, but somewhat apprehensive. Lance had put together an ambitious plan that required a lot of persuasion, but he was not sure how his plan would be received by Eddie and Kenya.

McIntyre was a major player in the IT arena. Therefore, Lance's ultimate strategy involved competing against McIntyre Corporation. His plan was to take those two contracts he had so diligently obtained as an employee of McIntyre and bring them to his company. The total value of those contracts would be worth thirty million dollars once the base year period expired. It was Lance's intent to position Freedom Technologies as the company of choice. This approach would involve a significant display of salesmanship and persuasion, which Lance felt wouldn't be hard at all since he was a masterful salesman and had an enormous track record with DOSP and DOIS.

While waiting for the others to arrive, Lance took a seat in the lobby area and stared at the background in the restaurant. The walls were painted with the layout of blue water and white sand. It appeared to be a beach in a far away place like the Caribbean islands. The scene of the beach relaxed Lance just a bit.

Maintaining his professional appearance, Lance wore a blue pinstripe suit with a gold tie and matching gold cuff links. He kept rubbing his head from front to back over his short wavy hair, a habit he had picked up in high school whenever he was nervous or excited.

As a couple entered the restaurant dressed in formal attire, Lance looked at the young lady who was standing in front of her date. His eyes widened and his mouth opened a little in shock. The woman looked like Valerie, but after a second look, he realized the woman was much shorter. He sighed for a moment and shook his head. After few minutes passed, Eddie and Kenya walked into the lobby area at the same time.

"You two must have driven together," Lance declared.

"No, we kinda arrived at about the same time. I saw Eddie getting out of his car when I was parking, so he waited and we walked in together," Kenya said.

"Oh, okay. Perfect timing, huh?"

"Yep," Eddie said.

"I am glad you all could make it here at such short notice. This means so much to me. I am really excited about this opportunity. I hope it is not an inconvenience meeting at a restaurant. I wanted this to be in an informal environment where we all could relax."

"This is perfectly fine with me," Kenya said as the waitress seated them at a table in the middle of the restaurant.

Kenya was dressed in a very revealing skirt. The short length of her skirt was generous to the roving eyes of men. She sat to the right of Lance with her legs crossed, displaying those sexy and toned legs and a tease of her left thigh. Lance hesitated for moment and reflected privately as he glanced at Kenya's legs. With the help of the restaurant's painted background, he fantasized for a moment of how it would be on an island with Kenya.

"There is nothing wrong with dreaming," Lance thought silently.

"Would you all like to order right now?" the waitress asked, jarring Lance from his daydreaming.

"Could you give us a few more minutes, please?" Lance said.

"Sure," the waitress responded.

"I have been here before with my girlfriend at a birthday party last year. The food is not bad," Kenya said.

"Oh really?" Lance replied.

"Yeah, especially the jerk chicken."

"Well, this dinner is my treat. It's a time for celebration. We have some great talent around this table, and I have thought about this plan for more than a year now.

"As a small IT company, we must be competitive by being creative and working smarter than our competitors if we are to survive. We have one big contract with the Prince George's County Public School System and it is doing very well. Now, it's time to go after the big fish. Within the last two years at McIntyre, I have obtained two big contracts with the Department of Information Security and the Department of Strategic Protection. My strategy is to persuasively and competitively take back the two contracts from McIntyre.

"McIntyre has a five-year contract with the Department of Information Security for twenty-five million dollars and a three-year contract with Strategic Protection for fifteen million. These contracts have a one-year base period with options. When there are options associated with a contract, this allows the client flexibility. The client may choose to terminate the contract after the first year or may exercise the options associated with the contract. This is where we will come into the game. Our strategy is to convince DOSP and DOIS to terminate their contracts after the first year and consider our company as the alternative. This means we could potentially obtain as much as thirty million dollars worth of business. I know this is an ambitious plan, but it can be done. This concept is very simple. It's not rocket science. I have seen this done before at McIntyre Corporation."

"Wow! Good plan and yet simple," Eddie commented. "You are right, Lance. I have seen this done several times at SBO. It is not easy because you have to convince the client that you can offer a better service at a better price. However, as a SBO employee, we tend to approach agencies from the standpoint of small business goals. It is mandated by congress that federal agencies must set aside a certain percentage of contracts for small businesses and minority firms. So, let's be realistic for a moment. Your plan will be quite challenging in terms of the implementation phase. McIntyre is a major Information Technology firm. They may have established themselves in the IT arena. The key to making this work is that we must get inside the ears of the players at DOIS and DOSP."

"I didn't say it would be easy, and you made a good point about the small business goals. You may want to approach our clients from that perspective. As a matter of fact, I read an article in the Washington Post recently which stated that many federal agencies have failed to meet their small business goals. I have established good relations with my clients over the years, and I know a lot of the people at Strategic Protection. In fact, I'm supposed to be playing golf with one of the procurement representatives at DOSP. What's his name?" Lance said while snapping his fingers. "Oh yeah, Jerry Patton. He's an excellent point of contact. I'll have to be sure to call him."

"You're right again, Lance. I have seen this happen before at McIntyre Corporation. It's all about competition. When do DOIS and DOSP's first year contracts end?" Kenya asked as she looked at Lance with admiration. Kenya had been playing difficult to get for the last month, but Lance's intellect really turned her on.

"Both contracts will end within the next three months of their base year period. So, it's time for us to get started right away," Lance said.

"When I get back to my office, I will investigate the status of both agencies. I need to determine what their small business goals are in reference to federal contracting. We have that information at SBO," Eddie added.

"I will put together a nice marketing package and market directly to Information Security and Strategic Protection," Kenya said.

"That sounds great, Kenya. Maybe you can come along with me when I do my presentations."

"Sure, Lance," Kenya replied.

"Lance, I will talk to my SBO contacts. I will stay on the case, man. Also, I know procurement people over at DOIS and they could definitely use some help in terms of small business representation," Eddie said.

"I love this. We have a plan and it's workable. Since I have both of you guys approvals, let's kick some butt!" Lance said enthusiastically as he shook hands with Kenya and Eddie.

Lance felt good about the plan. He knew this was an important first step for him, and he was willing to put everything on the line. His experience at McIntyre Corporation had been an unpleasant and entrapping one. This was now a time of liberation for Lance.

"Hey, Lance, are we all finished up here? This meeting was very productive and the food wasn't too bad either, but unfortunately, I have to make a quick stop before I go home."

"No problem, Eddie. I was just about through talking about business anyway. I will be leaving shortly myself. What about you, Kenya? Do you need us to walk you to your car or will you stick around with me?" Lance asked, hoping Kenya would chill a while with him.

"I'll stay around for a few minutes and finish my glass of wine," Kenya replied.

Lance felt good about Kenya's hesitation to leave. It would be just like a dinner date, absent Eddie. Kenya had been reluctant to go out with him lately, and he knew it probably had something to do with her not knowing what was going on between him and Valerie. However, this was his opportunity to change her mind. As far as he was concerned, his relationship with Valerie was essentially over.

"Just you and I. Almost like a date, huh? Lance said mischievously, his eyes brightening like a full moon.

"Well, I guess you could say that. I'm really impressed with your plan. I'm proud of you and love how you took charge. It is a real turn on," Kenya replied.

"Turn on? Maybe I need to talk like that more often." Lance smiled, thinking Kenya was back to her old charming self.

"I mean, not that way really. It makes me feel good. I respect intelligence."

"Now that we are alone, why have you been avoiding me lately? I asked you out at least three times and you always have an excuse."

"Well…do you really want to know?"

"Yes."

"Frankly, I did not want to interfere with your relationship. It seems like something wonderful is about to happen."

"That's over Kenya. The wedding was called off six weeks ago. We are just mere friends, although she may be expecting more. I told her in my last encounter that I wanted to focus on my business."

"Oh, really? The relationship is over? Are you sure?"

"Yes, Kenya. Let me be frank with you. I like you. I mean…I like you a lot. I think we would make a hell of a power team running this business," he confessed while reaching across the table to take hold of her hand.

"That sounds all good, Lance, and I feel the same way about you, but I want to make sure my feelings don't get hurt. I didn't want to rush into a relationship. My last relationship wasn't too pleasant, and I'm a little more careful now." Kenya thought to herself about her last encounter with Jason "But, you know, it is not easy having a personal relationship and a business relationship. It can be challenging."

"I have heard that before, but I think you and I have a unique chemistry, Kenya."

"Let's focus on this new business first and we will see how things go, okay?" Kenya said, removing her hand from his grasp ever so slowly.

"Fair enough," Lance replied.

Lance was willing to be patient and take a chance on Kenya. It was not his style to mix business with pleasure. However, Lance felt confident with Kenya.

Chapter Fifteen

"Good morning, Helen," Lance said.

"Hello, Lance. I brought in my homemade German chocolate cake. You better try some."

"Absolutely, I love German chocolate," Lance said.

"Good, the cake is in the conference room on the table."

"If you don't watch out, Helen, you are going to make everyone fat in this office," Lance said as he chuckled, standing in the hallway.

"My grandfather owned a bakery in Georgetown for many years. My mother loved to bake, and I love to bake. It runs in my blood. But you don't have to worry about your shape, Lance, because you are far from being chubby," Helen responded as she smiled.

Lance had to meet with Nathaniel Watson to discuss some new business opportunities, which he could have cared less about. At this point, Lance had little interest in McIntyre Corporation. His primary concern was to determine whether he should give Allen Frisco a two weeks' notice or thirty days. Thinking realistically, he felt he needed at least thirty days to orchestrate his business strategy. With the first twelve months of both contracts he had gained through McIntyre scheduled to end within three months, it was Lance's intent to bring his two contracts with him to his company.

Lance entered Nathaniel's office in a nonchalant manner after knocking.

"I have a new opportunity with a commercial client. This is a major opportunity," Nathaniel stated right away, without as much as a hello.

"Sounds interesting," Lance said in an unconvincing way.

"I will need two Account Executives working on this opportunity, so I have assigned Buddy Poretsky as the lead person to work with you."

"I don't understand. Why Buddy? I have more experience and my production is a lot higher than Buddy's," Lance said, knowing fully that Nathaniel was trying to undermine him. Lance thought about what Kenya had told him about the relationship between Buddy and Nathaniel. This arrangement didn't seem right at all. Still, Lance took the proposition in stride, with the comfort of knowing he would be gone in a matter of weeks.

"I understand your concern, but Buddy has some experience with this new client. Do you have a problem working with Buddy?" Nathaniel asked, shaking his head with an arrogant smile.

"No, I don't have a problem working with anyone. I'm flexible, although he can be a little difficult at times. Seeing as I'm the Senior Account Executive, I just thought I would be the team leader on this new project. But it looks like Buddy is getting all the support around here. Buddy visited my office without consulting me last week. He went through my work files. That was not appropriate, Nathaniel, and you didn't adequately deal with the issue. Did you even talk to Buddy about this?" Lance asked, becoming somewhat infuriated. He always felt he should have been the Vice President of Sales and Marketing, not Nathaniel Watson.

"Yes, as a matter of fact, I did discuss this with Buddy," Nathaniel answered as he cautiously looked at Lance. Nathaniel never appeared at ease with Lance, and he certainly was not comfortable with Lance challenging him. Clearly, there was some tension. "Lance, I think you are a little out of line to question me about Buddy. As I told you earlier, I discussed the matter with Buddy and informed him that he did not follow the proper protocol, okay?" Nathaniel said.

"Okay, but you seem like this issue is insignificant," Lance added.

"I don't need to provide you with any further explanation because remember, I am your boss and don't you ever forget that," Nathaniel warned, becoming a bit perturbed.

"Is that right? Well listen, Nathaniel, I have been trying to be as professional as possible with you. But you know something? You're a real asshole!"

"What did you say?" Nathaniel said as his neck turned red and he rose from the chair behind his desk, flabbergasted by Lance's boldness.

"You heard me," Lance said as he immediately walked out of Nathaniel's office and slammed the door.

He didn't give a damn about Nathaniel Watson. Hell, he didn't even care about his job. Lance was on his way out of McIntyre Corporation. He just needed to hang in there for at least three more weeks so he could figure out how to take the two contracts with him when he walked out the doors of McIntyre for the last time.

Allen was sitting at his desk drinking a cup of coffee when Lance entered.

"Allen, I will be submitting my written resignation to you this afternoon. I will be here for another two weeks in order to transition my projects to the new person who will be assigned to my position."

"What do you mean, Lance? Is there something wrong?" Allen asked, spilling coffee on his white shirt. "Dammit!"

"It is time for me to leave, Allen. I have not been able to achieve the upward mobility within this company. Nathaniel Watson and I are not communicating well. This arrangement will not work. I really do appreciate the opportunity."

"This is a startling surprise. I didn't know you were having problems with Nathaniel. You are a valued and very productive employee here at McIntyre, Lance. I think your decision is a bit premature. Relax, I have big plans for you. I will talk to Nathaniel, and hopefully, we can all work this out. As I have told you numerous times over the many years of your employment, if you have a problem in the office or otherwise, let me know so we can talk about it. Are you sure you want to do this, Lance?" Allen displayed a smile that was as counterfeit as a three-dollar bill.

"Yes, indeed," Lance answered confidently.

Lance felt relieved as he gave Allen his letter of resignation later that afternoon, and felt in his heart that his action was his revenge for his mistreatment. Lance knew Allen's comments were insincere and that he didn't care about his future. Lance had witnessed the deceptive nature of McIntyre's business practices. Allen had lied about Nathaniel's new position. He no longer wanted to be confined to a rigid corporate environment. Lance wanted his independence. He just needed a few weeks to execute his plan. And in an effort to execute his plan, he called Jerry Patton, the contracting officer at the Department of Strategic Protection.

"Jerry, I am in the process of transitioning to a new company."

"You're leaving McIntyre?" Jerry asked.

"Yes, I am, Jerry. As a matter of fact, I have started a new company and will bring half of the people working on your contract with me. These are some of our best technically trained people in the field of information technology. I have worked with some of them for more than twelve years," Lance informed him, knowing that Jerry's base year contract with McIntyre would end in sixty days. Lance's strategy was to sell Jerry on his company and get his business.

"Congratulations, I am happy for you. I always enjoy doing business with you. You definitely stayed on top of things around McIntyre. I am sure you will be successful in your new venture."

"Thank you. My real reason for calling was to let you know I will be in Ohio next week on business. What are you doing next Saturday?" Lanced asked.

"Hang on for a second. Let me look at my calendar." Jerry paused for a second. "It looks like I don't have anything planned for that weekend."

"Great. Let's get together and play a round of golf. How's your swing?" Lance asked, hoping to infuse some excitement in Jerry.

"Sounds like a plan. My stroke is not too bad, but it could certainly use a little improvement. I have been playing regularly at Bobby James Williams. It's a great course. Maybe I can schedule a tee time for us next Saturday. I like to play early mornings. I hope this is okay with you."

"No problem. Let's do this," Lance said enthusiastically.

Lance knew the meeting of the two would be a great business opportunity. While it appeared to be simply a golf outing, Lance's main goal was to secure a contract with Strategic Protection. Lance had proved to be an outstanding employee at McIntyre. He now wanted to prove his ability through Freedom Technologies.

* * * * * *

At lunchtime, Lance met Kenya at Lillie's Cafe.

"I have been very busy lately developing the marketing package, and I have almost completed the brochures. I'm also working on finalizing the radio ads," Kenya said as she drank her bottled water.

"I have been rather busy myself. As a matter of fact, I spoke with Jerry Patton at Strategic Protection this week. I'm planning a trip to Ohio next week and would like for you to come with me. Perhaps you can help me persuade Jerry about working with Freedom Technologies," Lance said.

"I would love to, but I have plans for next week. I will be out of town. However, I will cancel my plans if necessary," Kenya said sincerely.

"Oh no, I can handle it. I was just extending a courtesy invitation. Maybe next time," Lance added.

"Are you sure?" Kenya asked, relinquishing her "hard to get" strategy, and now willing to give Lance a chance in a relationship.

"Absolutely, I will be fine. I definitely know how to sell the company."

"I have total confidence in you," Kenya said as she smiled at Lance.

"This is the first time we have talked about the business since two weeks ago when we met at Jamaica's Restaurant."

"That's right, and I heard you are leaving in two weeks," Kenya said.

"Yeah. News travels really fast around McIntyre, but you knew I was leaving anyway," Lance responded.

"This is really funny to me because when Helen and Buddy came to my office all surprised, I pretended like I didn't know."

"Oh really?"

"Yeah."

"I think Buddy is glad to see me leave. I never really liked the jerk anyway. I had a little conflict with Nathaniel Watson yesterday. He seems to protect Buddy no matter what he does. I challenged him the other day and called him an asshole. After calling him an asshole, I went into the Allen's office and gave him my letter of resignation."

"Really? I like a man with guts. I am sure Nathaniel got the message."

"Definitely. He probably wanted to fire me, but who cares at this point."

* * * * * *

It was pouring rain like cats and dogs, even thundering and lightning. Lance could hardly see the road on New York Avenue as he drove to his parents' house in Washington. Lance needed to talk to his father, who still had contacts in the real estate business although he was retired. He wanted to find the right location for Freedom Technologies. He pulled out his umbrella and ran inside the house.

"You just have forgotten about us, son. You need to visit your family more often," Mrs. Kojo said.

"I know, Mom. I'm sorry. I have been so busy with this business," Lance said.

"That's right, son. We're getting old. You need to check in with us more often. I could use some help around the house sometimes, too. And I'm still waiting for my grandson and granddaughter. It's too bad you and Valerie didn't get married. Are you still seeing the young lady?" Mr. Kojo asked.

"Not really. It seems like we are drifting apart. Sometimes things just don't work out."

"I am sorry to hear that. Valerie is a nice girl. I just hope and pray you both can work things out," Mrs. Kojo lamented.

"Hey, I didn't come here to talk about Valerie. I came to get some information from you, Dad, about commercial leasing. Do you know where some good office space is in Maryland?" Lance asked.

"Not off the top of my head, but I wouldn't have any problem finding out, son. I can call my friend George Stein. George owns a lot of commercial real estate in Maryland. I worked with George for many years. I can get you a good leasing deal. What do you think about the Rockville area along I-270?" Mr. Kojo asked.

"It's kind of too far out from where I live. I really like the Bowie area," Lance replied.

"Okay. I will call George tomorrow and then let you know what he has available."

"Thanks, Dad."

"Are you hungry, Lance? I just cooked. I have some mashed potatoes, green beans, and corn on the cob. There's baked chicken in the oven."

"You know I love mashed potatoes, Mom."

"That's why I cooked them," Mrs. Kojo said as she chuckled.

Chapter Sixteen

The barbershop was unusually crowded for a weekday afternoon. There was a young woman seated with two of her young boys who appeared to be about four and seven years old, and at least twenty-five other individuals were waiting for a haircut with only four chairs available. Big Flem was "shaping up" an older gentleman's beard. Lance walked around the barbershop hoping to find a seat, but his search was fruitless. After about five minutes of standing near the door, Ardell, the barber, called out, "Next!" Lance rushed to occupy the seat of the young man who vacated it to get his haircut.

"How is everything going, Big Flem?" Lance asked after finally being called to the chair for his two o'clock appointment.

"I'm hanging in there," Big Flem replied, looking busy as he walked toward the cash register to return change to his customer.

"I guess business is good. You have a full house, man."

"It seems like everybody decided to get a haircut today. I'm not complaining, though. I definitely need the money. But hey, Lance, it's good to see you. Have you left your job?"

"Almost. I got two weeks before I leave. I gave my boss my resignation this week."

"Congratulations, Mr. Businessman. Are you ready for the big league?" Big Flem said as he looked at Lance in a serious manner. "You are going places, man."

"I am ready as I'll ever be. I've been preparing for this for a long time, and I'm ready to take care of business," Lance responded as he punched his right fist against his left palm to emphasize his point.

"That's the right attitude, Lance. Go head and kick some ass!"

"What's up with your girl? You know who I am talking about right?"

"You mean Tasha?"

"Yeah."

"I'm still trying to get my money back from her."

"Did you get the police involved?"

"Naw, because she said she was going to pay me back. She came by my house last week and gave me fifty dollars. Now remember, she owes me sixteen hundred dollars."

"Riiight," Lance uttered.

"Well, she came up to my door with this young guy who looked like a hood rat, his pants hanging all off his ass, but I didn't let her in. She told me she would pay me half, like eight hundred dollars. I expressed to her that I wanted my money back in full. Next thing I know, this young punk jumps into our conversation and tells me to shut the fuck up and that I should just take what I get. Then he threatened me. He even had a gun in the side of his pants. Hell, this guy doesn't even know me. Needless to say, I didn't get it yet."

"That's crazy. I told you to call the police. I wouldn't deal with that kind of drama."

"I just want my money. This young guy looks like a drug dealer. I have seen him hanging on the corner in Southeast. They don't scare me!" Big Flem looked stressed. His facial lines looked more prominent than usual and beads of sweat covered his forehead.

"I hear you, Big Flem." As Lance looked up, Trey walked into the barbershop.

"Trey, what are you doing over here, man?"

"Trying to get a haircut, just like you. How you been, Lance?"

"Not bad. Hey, man, I'm trying to get my company up and running."

"I hear you, man. I'm still waiting to hear from you about that job," Trey said.

"I haven't forgotten about you. Just hang in there. Word is bond," Lance replied.

"How you been, Big Flem?" Trey asked.

"I've been okay, man." Big Flem replied. "I see you still pumping that iron. It seems like muscles are everywhere, Mr. Bodybuilder," Big Flem said in a complimentary way

Trey had on a tight silk body shirt which exposed his upper body and enhanced the shape of his muscles. The lady with the two boys stared intently at Trey, her left hand on her chin and her legs crossed in a comfortable position. She seemed to be in awe of Trey's body. Trey had a classic body builder's shape with a small waist and well-defined, legs, chest, and arms. He wore a pair of gray baggy sweat pants and blue sneakers. In his right hand, he had bottled water.

"I have to keep the body looking good. I've been at the gym everyday. I will be competing in a bodybuilding event in three months," Trey said.

"Well, I'm going to have to see what I can do about putting all those muscles to good use," Lance said. "You know I have to lookout, 'cause you're my boy. Call me in about two to three weeks."

"Alright, man, I'll call you."

Big Flem brushed the hair off Lance's shoulder and face and shouted the proverbial statement, "Next customer!"

As Lance was walking to his car, his cell phone rang.

"Ola! How are you, Lance?"

"Who's calling?" Lance asked cautiously.

"It's Reina. How you doing, Lance?"

"Reina...hey, baby, I'm fine. I didn't recognize your voice. Wow! This is great. I am so glad to hear your voice. How have you been?"

"I'm okay. Things are a little somber, but we are trying to move on. I have been real busy with trying to resolve my grandmother's estate and sell her house. I thought it would only take me about two or three months to finalize her business, but it's going to take at least another six months. On a brighter note, I think about you a lot, Lance. I miss you."

"Oh yeah? That's sweet. The feelings are mutual."

"I also miss being at the gym, although I still work out. What about yourself?"

"I still go to the gym, but it's not the same without your beautiful face. I don't like the new spinning instructor. She never shows up on time."

"You still know how to make a woman feel good, huh?"

"I'm just telling you how I really feel."

"I know. Well, I have to go now, but let's keep in touch."

"Okay, Reina. Take care and I'll be talking to you soon."

* * * * * *

It was a warm and sunny day, the temperature about eighty-four degrees, a perfect day to play golf at Enterprise Golf Course in Mitchellville, Maryland. Lance was an avid golfer and played regularly with Eddie. He was particularly concerned about playing this week because he had plans of playing with Jerry Patton next week in Ohio. He wanted to be sharp with his golf game.

"So how is your golf stroke, man?" Eddie asked in an attempt to size up his competitor.

"Good enough to beat you, Eddie," Lance said as he laughed.

Eddie and Lance were both passionate about their golf game and competitive on the golf course. They respected each other, but were just like little boys when it came to golf competition. They both were dressed like serious golfers. Eddie wore a yellow short sleeve golf shirt with matching yellow pants and a white cap. Lance wore a blue shirt with a Ralph Lauren symbol embroidered on the left pocket. His cap was navy blue.

"I don't want to hear any excuses from you when I beat you, okay? You know what you usually say when you lose. 'My stroke was off today. I have not played in a while. I don't like this golf course'...yadda, yadda, yadda," Eddie replied.

"I have no excuses today. Let's just play. How about eighteen holes?"

"Alright."

"I spoke with my father last night and I think we may be getting some office space soon," Lance said as they walked over to retrieve a golf cart.

"Good. I am working on some things myself. I met with the IT Director over at the Department of Information Security. We talked about using Freedom Technologies as a possible 8A vendor after the first year of McIntyre's contract. However, he is not sure if he wants to terminate McIntyre after the first year. He said he had not encountered any major performance problems with McIntyre. So, I may need your help in convincing him to do business with us."

"I think all three of us should meet with him when I get back from Ohio," Lance suggested.

"Good idea. There is some good news, though. They are trying to maintain their small business goals, and they are not doing too well in that category. They need more 8A and minority IT firms. They are required by law to have a certain percentage of 8A contracts. Not just DOIS, but all federal agencies. We need to stress this as a selling point with DOIS," Eddie said.

"We need to do all we can do within the next thirty days. McIntyre's contract ends in about one month. We have to stay on top of this situation."

"Definitely," Eddie agreed.

"You know, I'm happy to have Kenya on our team. It doesn't hurt that she is very attractive, either," Lance said as he became excited.

"You like her a lot, don't you? I mean, in a different kind of way Let's be honest," Eddie insisted.

"Yes, I like her a lot. She is my kind of girl. We have a lot in common. I have not met a person like her in a long time," Lance responded.

"How is Valerie doing? Have you totally forgotten about her? Just about a year ago, you guys started planning a wedding."

"I know, Eddie. I really loved Valerie, but we just drifted apart. I spoke with her about three months ago and told her I needed some time and space. I think about her a lot and feel really bad about the situation. It's been difficult for me, especially after the wedding cancellation. We didn't see eye to eye about my plans to start my own business, but I later realized she wouldn't fit into my lifestyle at this point. She wants stability in her life, and I couldn't guarantee her that. I have to pursue my dream. Valerie is a wonderful woman, though. I respect her, especially a woman like her who has her act together," Lance said passionately.

"Maybe you do need time, and besides, it seems like Kenya has your interest at the moment," Eddie replied.

"Frankly, I think Kenya and I are a lot more compatible, but I haven't gotten over Valerie. I still love her."

As he privately reflected on Eddie's comments, he knew he could be very indecisive at times and was cognizant of the fact that he had caused pain in Valerie's life. Lance accepted his weakness. He knew he had difficulties ending relationships.

"I saw how you were staring at Kenya when we were having dinner at Jamaica's Restaurant. It's quite apparent. I knew you were up to something, man. But do you believe you can be a lover and boss to Kenya? Don't get caught up with the drama. Keep your eyes on the prize."

"Yes, it can be done, Eddie, if both parties are mature and have a clear sense of what their priorities are. I will never let a relationship preclude me from pursuing my business dreams. I am focused."

"Good, then I support you in whatever you do."

Eddie stood straight and concentrated on the white golf ball positioned on the white tee. He held the golf club tightly in a proper position and swung with great precision and intensity. The ball went straight down the middle, about 250 yards down the fairway.

"Good shot, Eddie!" Lance yelled with surprise. "For right now, my business is first priority. I need to get these two contracts from McIntyre. This will authenticate Freedom Technologies as a major player in the IT arena."

"I am with you, man. We will make this happen together."

After they reached the eighteenth hole, Lance hit the golf ball and it went into the trees.

"Dammit! I can't hit the damn ball straight. This has not been a good day of golf for me."

Eddie gave a victorious smile to Lance. "I know. Good game. Keep practicing, man."

"Sure, right," Lance responded.

"Loser buys winner a cold beer," Eddie said.

"Yeah, yeah, let's check out this new bar in Southwest," Lance said, not knowing what predicament awaited his friend.

"Cool," Eddie replied.

Chapter Seventeen

Eddie walked in the bar and immediately, his attention was drawn to a young woman sitting at the bar alone. The young lady appeared to be in her late twenties. She had short curly hair, a light brown complexion, and was dressed in a very revealing way. She had on a pair of white jeans and a purple blouse. Her hip hugging jeans revealed a tattoo on her lower back, which looked like a butterfly. Her blouse was extremely short and stopped mid-range on her stomach. The string of her purple thong could be seen from the back as she straddled the barstool. While approaching her, Eddie took in the deep curves of her butt.

"Lance, Lance," Eddie whispered, trying to get Lance's attention.

"What's up, man?"

"Check this honey out at the bar. She looks interesting. She looks like a freak, man. You can see the crack of her ass. Isn't that some shit?"

"Man! She is fine! Go for it, Eddie. I'll order us a beer," Lance said.

Eddie knew this young woman was his type. He liked adventurous women. He believed they had more fun. Conservative women didn't excite him. Eddie decided to approach the woman, easing up on her in a real smooth way.

"How you doing?" Eddie asked.

"I am good, and yourself?" the young woman said.

"Are you with anyone?" Eddie wanted to make sure the coast was clear and that she was not with a friend. He didn't want to get beat up by a jealous boyfriend like before when he was at a bar. He learned his lesson.

"No. I decided to come out for a drink alone. I just moved from L.A. about two weeks ago, and I am still trying to find my way around DC," the woman said.

"I'm sorry. My name is Eddie, and yours?" Eddie said as he extended his hand out like a seductive player and smiled.

"Tia. Tia Simmons. "

"Can I buy you a drink, Tia?"

"Sure, an Apple Martini, please."

From the way she kept smiling at Eddie, Tia appeared to already be a little tipsy. She was extremely friendly and inviting.

"Thanks, man," Eddie said as Lance handed him his beer. "Tia, this is my friend Lance. Lance, this is Tia."

"How you doing, Tia?" Lance sat back and chilled at the bar, content with just listening to Eddie charm the young lady.

"We just came from playing golf as you can see," Eddie said, pointing to his shirt and shoes.

"Yeah, golf, huh? I would love to learn how to play golf one day. It looks like a very interesting sport," Tia said as she sipped her Apple Martini. Eddie sat next to her in close range and quickly took a glance at her butt when she sipped from her drink.

"I like the game and have been playing for a while."

"I'm sorry, Eddie. Please excuse me while I go to the ladies room. I will be right back, hun." As Tia stood up, Eddie got a full view of her apple-bottom curves from the back. This woman had Eddie's full attention.

"Bartender, can I get another beer?" Eddie asked, now on his fourth beer.

"You should go light on the drinks, Eddie. I don't want you to get drunk in here. You remember what happened the last time?" Lance warned.

"I can definitely hold my liquor, man," Eddie insisted.

"I don't know about that, Eddie. Just don't get wasted. I remember the last time we were at the Upper Nile you got tore up, man."

"So what do you do, Tia?" Eddie asked as she returned to her seat.

"I am a makeup artist for a local cable TV station in DC. When I lived in L.A., I use to do the make up for a lot of prominent celebrities."

"That sounds hot. I bet you know a lot of people."

"I know a few people. I have a small circle of friends. I could actually count them on my fingers. I love to party and have a good time, though. What about you?"

"Well...I love to party. I love to live life to the fullest. Career wise, I am a businessman in the IT business with my friend here."

"That's nice. I like men with ambition and who are not afraid to live a little."

Eddie could feel his "buzz" coming on and became more talkative and inquisitive towards Tia. "Do you have a boyfriend?"

"Well...aren't you curious? I broke up with my boyfriend after a two-year relationship. This move to DC was good for me 'cause I needed to get away from L.A. for a while. What about you?"

"I'm not dating anyone at the moment. I am free as a bird," Eddie said as he started to laugh in a goofy way. "Hey, bartender, can I get another beer?"

Eddie was now on his seventh beer, and he was putting them down like he was drinking sodas.

Lance became greatly concerned about Eddie's behavior. He looked drunk and he was saying all kinds of complimentary things to Tia, who was enjoying it. On top of that, Lance was concerned greatly about Eddie's safety since they had come in separate cars.

"Excuse us, Tia," Lance said as he pulled on Eddie's arm and walked him to the bathroom. "No more beers, man."

"I'm okay, Lance. I'm having a good time talking to Tia. Isn't she sexy? I will get those digits tonight, my man," Eddie slurred, then started singing in an awkward way.

"Yeah, yeah, she's nice. Just don't get carried away. I don't want to see you fall on the floor," Lance replied.

"I'll be okay, Lance. Trust me, okay? This is my last beer." After convincing Lance he would be okay to drive home, he returned to the bar.

After saying goodbye to Tia, it took Eddie several minutes to locate his keys, which he had dropped on the outside driver's side of his car. Eddie was so intoxicated he didn't even hear when they dropped. He stumbled into the front seat of his car and sat quietly for about five minutes while rubbing his head. The alcohol he had consumed was creating a spinning effect in his vision. Doing a U-turn and spinning off from the bar, Eddie turned on his radio full blast and headed in the direction of his home, which was no more than twenty minutes away.

As he entered Seventh Street, he started to swerve, crossing the median strip numerous times. Suddenly, bright lights started flashing behind him. Eddie went into panic mode. "Oh shit, it's the cops," Eddie said to himself while looking in the rear view mirror. "I have to be cool."

After pulling to the side of the road, an African-American female cop got out of the police car and approached. "Can I see your license and registration, sir? I followed you for about a half mile, and you kept driving in and out of lanes. Is everything okay, sir?" the heavyset DC cop asked.

"Officer, I am sorry. I'm fine. I was driving and using my cell phone at the same time. I guess I got a little clumsy," Eddie said, hoping she would buy his explanation since he had his cell phone lying in the front seat on the passenger side of his car. The last thing he wanted was for the officer to know that he had been drinking.

"You have to be careful about using the cell phone while driving. You can easily get in an accident," the officer responded as she looked at his driver's information and then shined the flashlight in the back seat of his car.

"You are right, officer. I should have used my earpiece," Eddie said nervously.

"What's that smell?" she asked while handing him back his license and registration.

"What smell?"

"Have you been drinking? I smell alcohol."

"Just a beer!" Eddie answered quickly.

"Now that I am closer to you, your eyes look red, and I think you have been drinking more than one beer." She shined her flashlight into Eddie's face. "You know it's illegal to drink and drive, sir, right?"

"Yes, I do, officer, but I am fine. I am only about ten minutes from my house. I don't want any problems, officer. I just want to go home," Eddie pleaded.

"Sir, you know I could arrest you for driving under the influence, right?" she threatened.

"I know. Please don't. I am a decent and hardworking man," Eddie said as his heart started beating faster. He even broke out into a sweat.

"Where do you live, sir?"

"I live right down the street in Northwest."

"Get out of the car," the officer instructed.

"Is there something wrong, officer?"

"Sir...get out of the car," she said in a more demanding tone.

"Please don't arrest me, officer. Just let me go home."

"I need to determine your alcohol content, but first, I need for you to walk straight on that white line."

"I am not drunk, officer. I just had a beer at the bar," Eddie whined as he exited his vehicle.

"I want you to walk on the white line for thirty seconds," the officer said, ignoring Eddie's comment.

As the officer reached the count of five, Eddie staggered miserably until almost falling.

"That's enough, sir. It appears that you are over the alcohol limit. I can determine this and I haven't even given you a breathalyzer test yet. You should not be drinking and driving. You could be in an accident, or worse, endanger the lives of other innocent people." She paused, looking Eddie in the eyes, and thought this was just the scare he needed in order not to risk driving under the influence in the future. Besides, she really didn't want to be stuck at her desk doing the paperwork for his arrest an hour after she was supposed to already be off duty.

"Mr. Patterson, you are lucky I am in a good mood tonight. I will not take you in, but I will give you a warning and a ticket for not wearing your earpiece. I don't want to see you drinking and driving on these streets again. Do you understand that, Mr. Patterson?"

"Yes, thank you, thank you, thank you," Eddie said repeatedly, relieved that the officer had been lenient.

"Since you live only ten minutes away, I will follow you home to make sure you get there without an accident."

As Eddie climbed back in his car, he was shaking and appeared confused. He had never been to jail, nor did he have a desire to go. As he continued his drive home, with the officer following closely behind, he kept thinking about Lance's advice about his drinking. Eddie considered this a lucky and eye-opening night. But he knew his ways would have to change, because the next time, he may not get off with just a slap on the wrist.

Chapter Eighteen

Lance's plane arrived in Ohio at 9:03 a.m. He was excited about meeting with Jerry Patton, an opportunity that may prove successful in securing a major contract with the Federal Government. He walked into the fifteen-story building at the Department of Strategic Protection dressed in a dark brown suit with four gold buttons in the front and well groomed with a two-day-old haircut. His light silk brown tie blended nicely with his suit, and his shoes were shiny black with a buckle on the side. His briefcase and leather notepad was checked in by security of the building.

Glancing around the lobby, he located the appropriate elevator which would take him to the desired floor. As he waited for the elevator, he saw a lot of military people dressed in their uniforms and those not wearing uniforms. The others he noticed looked dignified or displayed a sense of importance. As he entered the elevator, a gentleman came up behind him and stood next to him on the elevator with a nametag on the right side of his uniform that read, "Lieutenant Colonel William Davis."

Once he departed the elevator, Lance approached the secretary and told her about his appointment with Mr. Patton, at which time she directed him to the conference room down the hall. Two minutes later, Jerry Patton walked in, informing Lance the conference room had been scheduled for an event and that they would have to move to his office.

"How are you doing, Mr. Kojo? Finally made it, huh? Please, have a seat."

"Oh yeah. It's good to meet you in person. I can now put a face to the voice," Lance said. "Um, do you mind if I put this file on the table?" Lance asked cautiously in regards to the contract file that was in the seat Jerry had offered.

"Sure. I'm sorry, Lance. I have to apologize for my unorganized office. I try to keep things in place, but it gets a little crazy around here sometimes."

With Friday being dress down day at Strategic Protection, Jerry had on a pair of jeans with a collarless blue casual shirt. Jerry was a short and stocky guy, standing at about five feet six inches tall with a slightly protruding stomach. He displayed a broad smile that exposed most of his front teeth.

"Yeah, I know what it's like when things get busy," Lance said while looking around at the pictures, certificates, awards, and the college degree from Tuskegee University that covered Jerry's office wall. "I see you are well recognized at this organization," Lance commented with admiration.

"The awards? Oh yeah, I try to take care of business around here. I have been working in government contracting for the last sixteen years. I like what I do. It's better than working on my granddaddy's farm back in Alabama," Jerry said in his heavy southern accent, expelling a high-pitched laugh.

"Yeah, I think this job may be a lot less physical. But you see, I don't know much about farming," Lance said as he laughed with Jerry. Lance felt at ease with Jerry and his down-to-earth nature.

"Trust me. This job is a lot better. So, Lance…what can I do for you today?" Jerry asked, getting right to the point.

"First of all, I am no longer with McIntyre Corporation," Lance replied.

"Okay, I see you have made the big step," Jerry said.

"That's right, Jerry."

We have a lot of opportunities for small businesses. I receive requirements and work statements from our program office almost everyday, especially in the area of IT."

"That's good to know. Most of the technical crew who worked with me at McIntyre will be coming with me over to Freedom Technologies. My team has acquired a certain amount of expertise on this current contract. We understand what DOSP wants, and I feel we should not break this continuity of experience."

"I absolutely agree. Let me ask you, is Jeffrey Smith coming with you to Freedom Technologies?"

"Yes, indeed," Lance responded.

"Jeff does outstanding work as a Project Manager. We have a good working relationship with him. He helped us resolve some of our software problems with this new system we have. His skills are invaluable. You are lucky to have him at your new company."

"Oh yeah, he does good work. He will be a great asset to Freedom Technologies. It's my understanding that the first year of the contract you have with McIntyre will be ending in about thirty days. At that time, I would like for my company to complete the last two years of the contract. I am certain we have the capabilities and expertise to perform on this contract."

"I agree. However, this is an issue where I need to discuss the logistics of this project with my program office. I can't make any promises to you. I have to allow the contracting process to take place, and I can't favor any particular contractor because that would be illegal. However, I will take your experience under consideration. Our office is trying to promote more opportunities with small businesses and this can certainly put your company in a favorable position. I also would have to verify with senior management whether or not we should maintain our contractual relationship with McIntyre."

"Okay, I understand. I'll wait for your official response."

"Now, are you ready to play some golf?" Jerry asked as he stood up from his desk and pretended to swing a golf club.

"Sure, I got a little practice in last week while playing with my buddy."

"Good. I'm sure you will like this golf course. "

The next morning around eight o'clock, Lance met Jerry at the golf course in Dayton, Ohio, and they played eighteen holes of golf. In the end, Jerry had a more impressive score than Lance Lance attributed this to his focus on developing a business relationship with Jerry than winning the game. His competitive juices had taken the back burner.

"Good game, Lance," Jerry said as he wiped sweat from his forehead and gave Lance the closed fist shake. "I need to let you know that I have to keep a low profile when talking to contractors outside of work."

"What do you mean?" Lance replied.

Jerry shifted his weight to lean over his golf bag and directed a sincere look at Lance. "We have procurement regulations to adhere to. We can't socialize outside of work when it is not official government business. It has to do with the appearance issue. We can't be perceived as doing any special favors for contractors. In this case, we just played golf which may not have been my better judgment, but it's all good."

"I understand, Jerry, and I respect your rules."

"I knew you would. Just call me. You can call me on my cell phone. I would like to see you succeed. Not enough African-American businesses make it in this fierce, competitive IT arena. I am here to help small businesses do business with the government."

"Thank you. I'm glad your heart is in the right place. I know it's tough in this business, but if given an equal opportunity to play on the field, I will do my best. That's all I ask."

"Alright, Lance. You sound like a winner already."

* * * * * *

"Lance! I have been trying to reach you all day, man," Eddie said in an urgent tone, sounding upset and nervous.

"Is everything okay, Eddie?" Lance asked while moving from the edge of his bed in the hotel room to the desk chair.

"Yeah and no. I almost got arrested the other night after I left the bar in DC. I got stopped by the damn police," Eddie said as he walked outside of his apartment toward his car with the cell phone.

"Hey, Eddie, I'm really sorry about that," Lance said, turning the television volume down a little so he could hear clearly.

"You know what you told me about drinking? This experience has definitely opened my eyes. I could have gotten arrested. I was scared as hell when the cop pulled me over. This black cop, who happened to be a woman, gave me a break. She made me take a test of walking a straight line, which I failed, but she let me go, thank goodness," Eddie said, opening the door of his car.

"You're lucky. It could've been a lot worse. You really shouldn't drink and drive and I don't mean this to be a campaign slogan. You have to be careful these days."

"You're right, Lance. I can't afford to put myself in that type of situation again. I definitely don't want to be locked up in some jail with a cellmate named Bubba," Eddie chuckled.

"I hear you, man," Lance said as he hesitated for a moment. "How's the young lady you met at the bar the other night doing?" Lance asked as he smiled, hoping to get some juicy information.

"Oh, Tia? I called her today. Man, I tell you...she is something else. She's a fun girl. She wants to hangout with me this weekend."

"Oh yeah? Moving right on it, huh?"

"Yep. I'll see what she is really about this weekend because big daddy is getting ready to put down my skills. You hear me, bro?" Eddie said.

"Do your thing, man. You sound like a brother on a mission." Lance chuckled slightly. "On a serious note, I had a good meeting with Jerry Patton."

"Is he interested in doing business with us?"

"He's willing to explore the possibility of doing business with us. However, he has to speak with his program office. I'll touch base with him within the next week."

"Sounds good to me. Well, I have set up a meeting with DOIS. They have some serious problems with their minorities contracting goal. They award less than one percent of government contracts to African-American firms. I believe the agency's goal is twelve percent based on the information I received from SBO. It's important that we make this a part of our sales presentation," Eddie said.

"Good idea. We can all meet with them next week. I'll let Kenya know. By the way, Eddie, Jerry has a good golf game. He had a better score than I did. I need to practice and get my stroke down."

"It looks that way, Lance," Eddie replied smugly as he drove off in his very clean looking Mercedes.

"Okay, Mr. Tiger Woods, I'll be ready for you the next time we hit the green," Lance countered.

Chapter Nineteen

The next day, Lance flew back to DC and decided to drop by the Upper Nile that night. While sitting at the bar listening to a poet, he recognized Kenya sitting at a table with her girlfriend. From where he sat, her back was to him, and she could not see him. He sat there at the table for a moment admiring Kenya who was fashionably dressed. He observed the woman she was talking to at the table. Lance watched Kenya converse with excitement. After a few minutes, Lance walked up to Kenya's table and tapped her on the shoulders.

"Hello, Kenya," Lance said.

"Hi, Lance. What are you doing here?" Kenya asked. She was surprised, but glad to see him.

Lance bent down, giving her a hug and kiss. "I felt like hearing some Jazz and poetry after I got back from Ohio. I took an early morning flight and just felt like hanging out. I thought about calling you. But look, here we are together. Strange things do happen."

"So I see, but you could have at least called me. We could have come together. Lance... this is my girlfriend Diane. Please, join us."

"Hi, Diane. How are you?" Lance replied while lowering himself into the empty seat at their table.

Diane was a petite woman and stood about five feet tall. She was attractive with a beautiful ebony complexion. She seemed to be the quiet type who didn't say much, but instead listened.

"I am fine, just enjoying the music. It's nice to meet you," Diane said as she extended her hand to Lance.

"Diane is a TV producer at Channel Nine," Kenya said.

"Okay…this is the friend you told me about. I remember you talking about her many months ago, but I forgot her name. So how do you like being in the news business?" Lance inquired.

"Well, actually, I really enjoy what I do. I have been in this business for the last seven years, and it has been an interesting ride."

Kenya looked at Lance and smiled, displaying the joy in her heart. She was very proud of her best friend Diane.

"It's really nice that you enjoy your career. It makes life intriguing. How long have you and Kenya known each other?"

"I have known her for a couple of years. I believe since college, right, Kenya?"

"Yeah, that's about right...five years," Kenya answered as she put her right hand on Lance's shoulder and looked him in the eye. Then, without warning, she kissed him in the mouth in front of Diane.

Even though he was taken by surprise, Lance enjoyed the sudden kiss. However, he thought it was a little uncharacteristic of Kenya since she had been somewhat reserved.

Kenya's main reason for kissing Lance was to prove to her friend that she had an intimate relationship with Lance. She had told Diane so much about Lance, but there was no evidence of her dating him. Diane honestly did not think the relationship existed. Therefore, Kenya wanted to prove to Diane that she had a man.

"Oh really? Five years, huh?" Lance finally responded after recovering from her spontaneous kiss.

"How was your business trip?" Kenya asked in an attempt to help him recover from her unexpected kiss.

"It was productive. Hopefully, we will get a contract. I will tell you more about it later. Eddie scheduled a meeting next week with DOIS," Lance said as he rubbed lipstick from the corner of his mouth.

"Okay, now, I see that we are taking real action," Kenya said.

"We have no choice. By the way, you look really nice tonight," Lance complimented.

"Thank you," Kenya replied shyly, feeling like a school girl.

"Excuse me, guys. I will be right back. I have to go to the ladies room," Diane said, perceptively, wanting to give Lance and Kenya a moment of privacy.

"Okay, Diane," Kenya replied. After Diane left, Kenya leaned over and whispered in Lance's ear, "Are you still with your girlfriend?"

"No. I told you it was over between us."

"It just seems that things turned around so quickly. What happened?" Kenya asked, as she felt momentarily insecure.

Kenya wanted to make sure she had what it took to satisfy Lance. She knew she had an uncompromising way of loving a man. She put her heart, emotions, everything into her relationships, and in some, her past lovers were not reciprocal. Thus, she was devastated emotionally, and in many ways, this created her insecurity with men.

"She didn't understand me and we had different priorities. But in the case of you and me, I feel we have so much in common. I truly believe you are my soul mate. I feel it in my soul."

"I feel the same way, Lance. Honestly, it's kind of scary because it seems too good to be true. I have been somewhat reluctant to be in a relationship because of some bad experiences, but I feel secure with you," Kenya replied as she rubbed his hand, showing her affection.

"You are amazing, Kenya. You never cease to amaze me."

After several minutes of Lance and Kenya engaging in small talk, Diane arrived back to her seat.

"It's getting really crowded in here, but the band sounds good," Diane said.

"The band does sound good. I like that John Coltrane piece. And is that my favorite poet, Balil, coming to the stage?" Lance asked.

"Yeah," Kenya replied as they all sat back, relaxed, and took in the soulful poetry.

* * * * * *

Casually dressed in a blue blazer and a light blue shirt, Eddie was excited about meeting with Tia. He picked her up at her apartment in North West, DC and had reservations for two at Legal Seafoods in Georgetown. For some strange reason, Tia requested that Eddie call her when he arrived in front of her apartment, not wanting him to come inside. Following instructions, Eddie sat in his car and waited for Tia to come out. Within five minutes, she emerged from the building.

It was mid summer and the weather was accommodating for summer clothing, which Tia was dressed in. Her attire consisted of a short skirt with no stockings, a white blouse that exposed her cleavage, and a pair of black high heel shoes with matching purse. The perkiness and fullness of her breasts would have one think they were surgically altered, which they very well could have been. Her legs were light brown, shiny, and guiding her as she walked to his car with a commanding strut. Tia opened the car door, the scent of her perfume saturating the air within, and sat in the front seat, her beautiful legs exposed even more as her skirt came up about three to four inches. Eddie enjoyed a woman who dressed provocatively.

"Where are we going, Eddie?" Tia asked.

"We are headed to Legal Seafoods in Georgetown. You will like Georgetown. It's a trendy section of DC with plenty of restaurants and bars," Eddie said with confidence.

"Sounds good to me," Tia said as she looked at Eddie and smiled seductively. Tia appeared carefree, the type of woman that "went with the flow."

After arriving at the restaurant, it took them at least thirty minutes to locate a parking space. Once inside, Eddie and Tia had to wait another twenty minutes before the waitress showed them to their table, even though they had reservations.

"Menu, please," Eddie said to the waitress while making a poor attempt to hide his irritation from having to wait so long to be seated.

"Coming right up, sir," the waitress replied.

After placing their drink and dinner order, they fell into a get-to-know-you-better conversation.

"So, Eddie…what type of women do you like?"

Eddie stared at Tia in amazement and then thought for a moment.

"I like women who have a sense of humor, are adventurous, and sexy. Women like you."

"Oh really? I'll take that as a compliment," Tia said, looking around the restaurant and then opening her purse as if she were searching for something.

"Please do. I didn't give it to you to be taken any other way."

Tia was a very inquisitive woman and wanted to know what Eddie was really about. So, she became bold and uninhibited in her statements.

"What about the physical characteristics? Let me be more specific. Are you a tit or ass man?"

"Whoa! You caught me off guard with that question." Eddie was shocked she had asked such a question, although he was clearly interested in her sexually. "Let me think. I like both. A nice round butt is nice no matter what size. And what do you like?" He started to think her aggressive questioning was an indication that she was not as sophisticated as he had imagined.

"I like money. Looks and physical characteristics are secondary," Tia said as she drank her rum and coke.

Stunned by her response, Eddie looked at her with an incomplete smile. "So it's all about the money, huh?"

"You could say that. Money makes the world go round. I just moved from Cali and my living expenses are high. I have expensive taste in clothing and jewelry. I guess you could say I'm high maintenance. I enjoy the nicer things in life."

"You like living large, eh?" Eddie was quickly becoming disappointed in his date.

"I have to be straight up with you, Eddie. I am not the fake type. I am honest about my desires and wants."

Eddie immediately started to view Tia as a gold digger. However, she was fine and good-looking. Eddie was not sure of her motives, but he knew she had an agenda.

"This blackened salmon is delicious," Tia said, wiping her mouth with a napkin and looking at Eddie intently trying to ascertain what turned him on.

"The food is not bad here, especially the fish. I come here all the time," Eddie responded as he drank his white wine.

"Oh yeah? Tell me, Lance, what do you like doing when you are not working?"

"Well, as you know, I play golf and I love to travel."

"I like traveling, also. I was in the Bahamas last month with a friend of mine," Tia said as she opened her purse again and pulled out some mints, placing them on the table.

"I have been there a few times. What about yourself? What do you like to do?"

"Do you really want to know?"

"Sure, come with it."

"You remember I told you that I like money."

"Yes."

"Well, I work for an escort service part time. I entertain men."

"You're kidding, right?" Eddie put his fork down, his facial expressions going south. He was disappointed with her announcement, but tried to play if off like it was nothing to him.

"Nope, I started doing this back in California. I met a lot of clients through my job as a makeup artist. You wouldn't believe how my male clients 'hit on me' all the time."

"When you say entertain, do you mean you have sex with your clients?"

"Not all of my clients want sex, but affection. My clients are usually wealthy, middle-aged white men who are just in need of some attention. Many of them just like my company. These men want me to dress skimpy and dance for them. I do have sex with some of them for the right price, though."

"Okay, I see how it works," Eddie said, trying to sound understanding. "This sounds a little freaky, but you are just doing your thing. Do you like this gig?"

"It pays the bills. I am sort of an exhibitionist, so I find it a real turn on for me. I am comfortable with my body, I like to perform, and I like satisfying my clients. Some of these men travel a lot and are really lonely. They don't have a lot of time for their wives and girlfriends. You wouldn't believe what these old white men want me to do for them. It's pretty wild."

"I can imagine. Freaky stuff, huh?"

"Yeah, I have a little freak in me."

"Interesting. But hey…different strokes for different folks. Whatever rocks your boat is cool with me. You just don't strike me as a person who would be in that type of business."

"It's my innocent look. They say I look like the girl from around the way."

"My thoughts exactly."

"Well…do you like me, Eddie?" Tia asked with feigned interest. Although she liked his company, Tia looked at Eddie as a potential client. She was not interested in developing a serious relationship with any man. She only wanted the money.

"Yes. The first time I saw you I thought you were really hot."

"Are you looking for a good time tonight, Eddie?"

"Well, I really just wanted to talk and get to know you," Eddie replied, sensing what the conversation was leading to. It wasn't his thing to pay for sex, and as far as he was concerned, he didn't want to be associated with a girl from an escort service. His whole perception of Tia being a freak changed to her being a sophisticated prostitute. He was not looking to be a victim of any sexually transmitted disease because of her promiscuous behavior. He was looking for a girlfriend to have fun with.

"I guess that's a no, Eddie. I understand, but I am not into relationships at this point in my life." She paused. "My price is reasonable," she added, hoping to convince him to sample her services.

"I don't think so, Tia. I'm gonna chill for now. Check, please!" Eddie called out to the waitress.

After leaving the waitress a generous tip, Eddie drove Tia back to her apartment, walked her to her door like a gentleman, kissed her goodnight, turned to walk away, and never looked back.

Chapter Twenty

It was around 11:20 p.m., and the neighborhood was fairly quiet. No one could be seen hanging on the corner of Joyce Street in Southeast. A black Mercedes car slowly drove onto Joyce and parked about two blocks from Big Flem's house. Two young black men in their twenties and dressed in dark colored clothing got out of the car. Stealthily, they cut through an alley of a nearby apartment complex and entered the backyard of Big Flem's house. As they sneaked up onto the deck of Big Flem's house, they pulled the black masks over their faces.

"Are you sure this is the fuckin' house?" the one guy whispered to the other.

"Damn right. This is the address Tasha gave me. Plus, I was here a few weeks ago with her," Tasha's boyfriend whispered back.

Tasha's boyfriend unlocked the back door of the deck using a set of keys that Tasha had given him. They then eased into Big Flem's house walking slowly and looking around carefully in the dark. They looked upstairs and saw a dim light on and proceeded to walk upstairs.

"She told me this motherfucker got money. Let's get his shit and get the fuck out of here," Tasha's boyfriend said.

"Shh, shh, be quiet."

Thinking he had heard someone in his house, Big Flem woke up and sat straight up in his bed. He thought for a moment that it was just his imagination until he heard someone walking up his stairs.

"Who's there?" Big Flem yelled out into the darkness.

As the footsteps continued to approach, Big Flem turned on the nightstand lamp and reached inside for his gun.

"Now, now, you don't want to do that," the guy said as he pointed the .38 pistol at Big Flem.

"What do want? Please, don't kill me!" Big Flem pleaded with his arms held up high while his weary eyes raced from left to right trying to determine the next move of the burglars as his face crumbled with fear.

"Shut the fuck up and tell me where your money is stashed, old man!" the armed perpetrator ordered.

"I have a couple of hundred dollars on the table behind you in a brown envelope. Just get it and leave!"

As the guys momentarily turned their backs to get the money, Big Flem reached for his gun. However, Tasha's boyfriend was quicker with draw and pulled the trigger, shooting Big Flem in the chest as his big body fell to the floor with his head hitting the floor first. The nightstand lamp fell on top of his body due to the enormous impact of the fall. Big Flem's body trembled for one breath of air and his life quickly ended.

"Get the money and let's get the hell out of here!" Tasha's boyfriend said. He took a glance at Big Flem's body and quickly exited the house along with his crime partner.

* * * * * *

Lance drove down the street where Fleming Brown's Barbershop was located. As Lance got closer, he noticed a crowd of people standing outside. Curious about the scene, he parked his car on the street and walked over to the crowd to see what was going on. Lance thought that a special celebration was going on. He knew Big Flem occasionally had parties, but this was early afternoon during business hours. Lance then saw a woman crying and weeping as she leaned against her car, and immediately, he became suspicious. After spotting the two police cars parked in front of the barbershop, the idea of a celebration quickly disappeared from his mind.

"Is everything okay, young lady? Why is everybody standing out here?" Lance asked.

"Big Flem is dead. I can't believe this. They better find out who did this and make them pay for this murder!" the lady said as she threw her arms up in air.

"What do you mean Big Flem is dead? Oh my God! This can't be true," Lance said, stunned at the tragedy. He rubbed his hand over his head and shook it in sadness. He soon spotted Ardell in the crowd and waved him over.

"Ardell, what's going on, man?" Lance demanded sharply, and then said disbelievingly. "This lady is telling me that Big Flem is dead." But the look on Ardell's face as he approached warned Lance that she spoke the truth.

Ardell grasped Lance's shoulder and quietly confirmed. "I am sorry, Lance. Big Flem was found dead in his home last night on Joyce Street. Word is someone broke in his house, robbed, and killed him." Lance's blood ran cold as Ardell relayed the news. Ardell continued, his face contorted in horror. "This is horrible, man. I can't believe someone would do that to Big Flem. We will find the killer. You better believe that! I am tired of brothers killing brothers," Ardell vented angrily, his hands shaking and fists clenched.

"This is messed up, man. Who do you think did it?" Lance whispered as his face announced a sense of disbelief. He still couldn't believe that big Flem was gone, just like that.

"I don't know, but it's probably about Tasha. That bitch!" Ardell spat venomously. "I was told by a friend that the guy Tasha was hanging out with is probably responsible. He had an ongoing beef with Big Flem. I knew some shit went down between Big Flem and that guy," Ardell responded heatedly.

"Yeah, that's right. Last time I spoke with Big Flem, he told me that Tasha had come over to his house with that guy and he threatened Big Flem. That asshole gave him a hard time. I tried to tell him. I knew something wasn't right with that girl. Big Flem was a good man. He didn't bother anybody. He was the pillar of this community. Everybody liked Big Flem." Lance's voice broke on this last comment. His face crumbled and his brown eyes filled with tears.

"I am feeling you, Lance. As you can see, everybody out here is in shock. They don't believe what has happened. Why Big Flem?" Ardell said in utter disbelief.

"Have you heard from Tasha? The police should question her. She probably knows who did it. Gold digging bitch!" Lance spat.

"Definitely, I told the police about Tasha's association with Big Flem. They will be on her case."

Out of nowhere, a twenty-something young guy came up to Lance and Ardell. "I think J Quick had something to do with this killing. He has a reputation in the streets. You know, he is a big-time drug dealer."

"Who is J Quick?" Ardell asked, trying to determine who this short, dark skin guy with braids was volunteering information.

"He was fuckin' around with the girl Big Flem use to hang out with?" the informant said.

"You mean Tasha?" Ardell asked.

"Yeah, I think that's her name," the guy said as he started looking around, hoping no one could see him snitching.

"The guy's name is J Quick, huh?" Ardell asked again.

"Yeah, that's his street name. He will smoke a brother in a minute. That's the kind of rep he has."

"Thanks, man. I will pass this information on to the police. What's your name?"

"I'm out, man. Peace," he said, refusing to give his name, and disappeared into the thin air as he made his way through the crowd.

"So...the name is J Quick," Lance said.

Lance was grief-stricken, as well as angry. Not only had Lance been a long-time customer of Big Flem's Barbershop, Big Flem had been like an uncle to Lance, giving Lance a lot of advice over the years. Although Lance had moved out of Southeast, DC when he was a young teen, he kept close ties with Big Flem and the people of that community.

******

Tasha sat at a table behind a glass wall in the police station. She was being questioned by a police officer in a small room. She looked confused and nervous. Her face was moist from a mixture of perspiration and tears. The police officer was trying to get information out of her regarding J Quick and determine her involvement with the murder of Big Flem.

"Ms. Tasha Hall, do you know a young man by the name of J Quick?" the big burly officer asked, walking slowly towards Tasha.

"Yes, sir," Tasha replied in a trembling voice as she avoided eye contact with the officer. She stared at the wall looking confused.

"What is your association with him?"

"He is a friend of mine," Tasha answered.

"Was he your boyfriend?" the officer asked putting his hand on the table trying to get direct eye contact with her.

"No, he is just a friend."

"Ms. Hall, various sources have informed me that you and J Quick had a relationship. Prior to dealing with J Quick, you were involved with Fleming Brown. As a matter of fact, I was told that you lived with Fleming for six months. Is this correct?"

"Yes, you could say that. I lived with him for about five and a half months."

"Is it true that J Quick had an argument with Fleming Brown when you visited him last week?"

"I don't remember any argument."

"What did you discuss with Fleming Brown when you talked with him last week? Did J Quick accompany you on that visit?" the officer asked, continuing his line of questioning as he stood in front of Tasha with his arms folded.

"I came to get my clothes from Fleming's house. He would not let me get them. I just wanted to get my clothes. J Quick was with me when I saw Big Flem."

"Are you sure you came to get your clothes? A well-placed source told me the visit was about money or some credit card problem."

"I didn't owe him any damn money!" Tasha said as she briefly gave the officer eye contact in an effort to make her point.

"Are you sure, Ms. Hall?"

"Yeah!"

"We have researched Fleming Brown's credit history for the last six months and noticed an outstanding debt of approximately sixteen hundred dollars. Most of these creditors are women clothing stores and jewelry shops. Now, I'm going to ask this question again, Ms. Hall. Did you owe Fleming Brown any money?"

Lowering her head and looking at the wall to avoid eye contact, Tasha hesitated for a few moments before answering. "He told me I could use his credit card, okay! I didn't take any money from him," Tasha said unconvincingly.

"I don't believe you, Ms. Hall. Where is J Quick?" the officer asked looking a bit frustrated. He banged on the wall in an attempt to intimidate Tasha and then he looked through the glass window at the other officer standing outside listening.

"I don't know," Tasha replied flatly.

"Where does J Quick live?"

"I don't know."

"What do you mean, you don't know? This man is your boyfriend. It does not add up, Ms. Hall. Are you hiding something from us? You have a boyfriend and you don't know where he lives? You gotta come clean, young lady."

"I don't keep up with J Quick, and he is not my boyfriend. He is just a friend."

"Did J Quick kill Fleming Brown?"

"I don't know."

"If we find out you were an accomplice to the murder of Fleming Brown, or you had anything to do with the death of Fleming Brown, you definitely can expect to spend the rest of your life in prison. So again I ask you, where's J Quick?" The officer banged his fist on the table where Tasha was sitting.

"The only thing I know is that he lives in Baltimore, but I don't know where in Baltimore."

"Where were you on the night of Fleming Brown's murder?"

"I was home with my son."

"Can you prove it?"

"Yes. My girlfriend was over my house playing cards that night."

"What's your girlfriend's name?"

"Carolyn."

"Okay, Ms. Hall, we will investigate this matter, and if I find out you were lying to me, you can expect the worse. Do you understand that?" the officer said in a loud voice as he pointed his finger in her face.

"Yes, sir…I mean, officer," Tasha replied in a frightened manner.

Chapter Twenty-One

Lance was determined to keep focused on reaching his goal of starting a successful business despite all the recent distraction. He was tired of corporate America's false promise to black people. He knew equality would never be achieved in a corporate structure or any organization where blacks were a minority. McIntyre Corporation had imposed limitations on his career because of his race, and this was Lance's opportunity to get revenge for his discrimination.

The relationship with Valerie was over. Valerie gave Lance an ultimatum and he refused to respond to her call for a true commitment. Instead, he wanted to pursue a relationship with Kenya.

Lance was brokenhearted by the death of Big Flem, who was a confidant and anchor in his life. Wanting to show his appreciation for him, Lance considered establishing a scholarship fund that would serve as a memory and honor to Fleming Brown. He made a mental note to talk with Kenya about getting with her father, who was active in assisting students with scholarship money at Morgan State University, in order to see how to put his idea into motion.

******

A week later, Lance, Eddie, and Kenya met with the Director of the Information Technology Division at the Department of Information Security in Arlington, Virginia.

"I need to see each one of your identifications, and I also need the three of you to sign in at the desk," the lobby security officer said as they entered. Security was strict and cautious, especially after the 9-11 tragedies.

After signing in, Lance, Eddie, and Kenya entered the elevator and rode to the ninth floor where the waiting receptionist showed them to a conference room overlooking the Potomac River. The room provided an excellent view of the blue sky and billowy clouds of DC from Virginia. Soon, a man who appeared to be in his early fifties, wearing thick black glasses, entered.

"Hello, Mr. Kojo. My name is Joseph Glover. I am the Director of the IT Division."

"How are you? This is Kenya Harden and Eddie Patterson, my management team."

"It is my understanding you are currently working with McIntyre Corporation," Joseph said.

"Actually, I resigned. I am now working in a full-time capacity at Freedom Technologies," Lance replied.

"Great. So how do you like being in business?" Joseph asked while straightening his tie.

"It's fantastic and somewhat challenging, but never a boring day. This is where I want to be," Lance said confidently as he clenched both of his hands together.

"I can imagine. I gather you are seeking business opportunities with DOIS." Joseph was very business like, not the friendliest guy, and displayed a kind of no-nonsense attitude.

"Yes, very much so."

"Mr. Kojo, we are pleased with the performance of McIntyre Corporation at this time. McIntyre has a five-year contract with us, and the first year of the contract will be ending soon."

"That is why I am here, Mr. Glover. I believe we can offer you a better service," Lance said.

"Call me Joseph."

"Okay, Joseph. We would like to provide an alternative to McIntyre. Many of our technical people from McIntyre will be joining me at Freedom Technologies. We have the best technical expertise that any company can offer. I have had a long-standing relationship with DOIS, and would like to maintain the continuity of service to your organization. I know the people very well at DOIS and our technical team has consistently delivered over the years. I have worked with them even on previous contracts," Lance said as he looked at Eddie and Kenya.

"I am familiar with your work, Lance. You managed this contract quite well. I am sure that the management at McIntyre will continue to provide quality service to DOIS, but do you foresee a change in their service now that you have resigned?" Joseph asked.

"I cannot say for sure what changes will come about with McIntyre in regards to their service performance. However, I am aware of the cost McIntyre Corporation is charging your organization for these IT services, such as help desk support and hardware/software purchases. We can provide you and the taxpayers with the same services at a better price," Lance said in his best salesman's pitch.

"I agree, Lance. Price is an important factor. However, quality service is just as, if not more, important," Joseph countered.

"As I said before, most of the people who are working at my company has worked with McIntyre on some of your previous contracts. These individuals know how to deliver a quality service and product."

"I see, Mr. Kojo."

Eddie finally broke from his silence. "Also, I researched your agency's policy with respect to contract awards. Your agency stresses small business participation in many of these contract awards."

"That's correct, Eddie. We have a goal of about twelve percent for small business and minority participation."

"Have you achieved those goals?" Eddie asked.

"I am afraid not. However, we are making small strides," Joseph replied.

"We would like to be in the position to be a provider of IT services to your agency. Why don't you take some of our brochures about our company? We have done business with the Public School System in Maryland. Although we are a new company, we have a lot to offer," Kenya insisted.

"I must admit, you guys are quite impressive. I will review your material, consider your recommendation, and pass this information on to my staff," Joseph said as he stood up and gave Lance, Eddie, and Kenya a firm handshake and a fake smile.

As Lance, Eddie, and Kenya walked to the car, Lance commented about Joseph's attitude. "I don't know, guys, but this guy comes across as a stuffed shirt. He didn't seem too excited about meeting with us."

"I agree. He looked a little hesitant. He didn't even look that comfortable. That guy probably goes home at night, puts on his hood, and meets with the KKK," Eddie said as he started laughing.

"He sure didn't make any promises," Kenya added.

"You guys may be right, but let's don't judge him yet. Let's try and get this contract first," Lance said.

After Lance dropped Kenya off at her apartment in Northwest, DC, Eddie moved to the front seat of the truck. As Lance drove down 16th Street, he inquired about Eddie's weekend.

"How was the date with Tia?"

"Do you really want to know?" Eddie said, rubbing his right hand over his face like he really didn't want to talk about it.

"Hey, man, what happened?"

"I was a little disappointed with Tia. She was not the type of woman I thought she would be."

"What are you talking about, Eddie?"

"Here's the deal, Lance. This woman is a gold digger. She is into material things and she made that very clear to me. She likes money. If a woman is preoccupied with money, it immediately turns me off."

"Oh…that type, huh? Did she ask you for money?"

"Yes. She propositioned me for a date."

"What do you mean she propositioned you? There's nothing wrong with that. Maybe she was offering you some booty."

Eddie's tone was one of disgust. "Yeah, offering some booty for rent. The woman works for an escort service. She told me she entertains men."

"Oh really. Um...? It's about the money. You will be surprised how many women work in the escort business."

"Oh really? But isn't it just another form of prostitution?" Eddie asked naively.

"Yeah, but it's not always about sex. Many businessmen travel a lot, and they make arrangements in different cities to see women simply for their company. This is big business, especially in Las Vegas. Escorts make a whole lot of money," Lance eagerly explained.

"I understand. Tia did say she loves the money. But for me, Lance, I am not in the market to buy sex. I think it cheapens the experience. I am not that hard up. At least, not yet, and I'm hoping I'll never be."

Chapter Twenty-Two

*N*ot long after Lance dropped Eddie off in DC, his cell phone rang.

"Yo, Lance. This is Trey, just checking in. Did you hear about Big Flem?"

"Yeah, man, I was down at the shop yesterday. I'm really upset about it, too. Big Flem was like family to me," Lance replied. "The police are trying to find out who killed him. I heard they took Tasha down to the police station, and the word is that either she or that guy named J Quick did it."

"Yeah, I heard that, too. J Quick probably did it, or he had one of his boys do his dirty work. You know Big Flem didn't like J Quick, right? J Quick was trying to pimp Tasha," Trey divulged.

"What do you mean?"

"This beef between J Quick and Big Flem goes way back. Big Flem was in love with that young girl, man, even before she moved in with him. He tolerated her lifestyle as a stripper, but who knows what else Tasha was doing. She was probably cheating on Big Flem all along."

"This is news to me," Lance said as he shook his head.

"Dig it. She was playing Big Flem," Trey said.

"Yep, it certainly looks that way. By the way, I do have a job for you, Trey. I hadn't forgotten about you. I want you to do some security work for me in my building. It's a small building, two levels, but I will need security. I also need for you to help market my business by distributing flyers and brochures. I guess you can call it some public relations work for Freedom Technologies. Kenya can give you some instructions."

"Kenya?"

"Yeah, Kenya is my Vice President of Marketing and Sales. I just move into a nice office located in Bowie. Why don't you come by my office next week so I can give you a start date?"

"Okay, man. You don't know it, but you just made my day."

Lance ended the call with Trey a few minutes later when Jerry Patton from DOSP in Ohio beeped in on his other line.

"I have some information for you, Mr. Kojo. I talked to the people in my program office, and it seems we may be able to accommodate your request. However, we will have to seek full and open competition. Unfortunately, we can't do a sole source contract."

"Okay. Does it have to be competed?"

"No, but a decision was made by management to put a contract in place in this case."

"So when do I get the solicitation?"

"We will probably issue a bid package within the next two weeks."

"I look forward to receiving that package."

"I will be talking to you soon, Lance. Good luck."

"Take care, Jerry."

Upon hanging up with Jerry, Lance immediately called Eddie.

"Hey, Eddie. I just spoke with Jerry Patton over at DOSP. He is willing to give us an opportunity, but we will have to compete for this business. He could not issue us a sole source contract."

"Well, I wish it were a sole source contract, but what the hell. We will compete."

"The good thing is we understand the requirements. I have previous experience with McIntyre. I know what DOSP is looking for," Lance said.

"Yeah, there is nothing easy in the business world. On top of that, this is a fiercely competitive environment," Eddie commented.

"I hope we can get the same opportunity at DOIS. That is a tough one to call."

"If not, I will talk to some people at SBO. DOIS has a lousy track record with minority contractors," Eddie said.

"Alright, man."

* * * * * *

Nathaniel Watson was terribly disturbed by a recent phone call from Jerry Patton, informing him about the status of McIntyre's contract. Jerry told Nathaniel that DOSP was considering approaching their IT needs in a different direction based on funding and budget projections, but that nothing was definitive.

Being a little concerned and cautious, Nathaniel decided to visit Allen Frisco in his office and speak to him about the situation.

"I received a call from Jerry Patton of DOSP today. He said they were exploring options in terms of IT services and he mentioned our contract with them."

"Which contract are you talking about?" Allen asked.

"It was Lance Kojo's contract. Well…the one he helped obtain through DOSP."

"Oh? There shouldn't be any problems with that contract. Lance discussed this contract with me before he left," Allen said.

"Yeah, and we don't have any performance issues. However, Jerry did mention budget and funding concerns, but said nothing was definitive. Do you think they may be having funding problems with this contract?" Nathaniel asked, his face showing concern.

"I don't think so. Lance never told me about any funding problems, and I don't have any evidence of such issues," Allen replied as he rose from his desk, putting his right hand on his face and engaging in deep thought for a second.

"I still think we should pay close attention to this contract."

"I wouldn't worry too much about it at this point. Keep me posted on any new developments concerning this contract, though," Allen said, concluding their conversation.

* * * * * *

Earlier that day, Kenya had spoken to Lance in regards to her delivering a package to him during the evening. This would be her first visit to Lance's house. It was almost seven o'clock in the evening when she pulled up to his house in the nice upscale community of Lake Arbor.

Lance answered the door dressed in sweat pants and a tight body shirt, his small muscular body pronounced after an afternoon workout.

"Hello, Kenya. I'm glad you could come by," Lance said in an excited voice, unable to resist the charm of Kenya.

"Nice place you have here. You are an art lover, too, huh?" Kenya said as her eyes investigated the beautiful art hanging on the walls of Lance's house.

"Oh yeah, I love art," Lance replied.

Kenya looked fabulous dressed in a form-fitting business suit. Her eyes were radiant as she looked at Lance. Kenya seemed a bit more relaxed than their previous encounter. She had never seen him without his business attire and it made her feel even more comfortable.

"Have a seat and let me take a look at the new brochures."

"Sure." Kenya handed over the package, their hands touching during the transfer, then they both proceeded to sat on the sofa in Lance's living room.

"Nice. These are a lot more colorful. It gives our company a wonderful image," Lance said, examining the brochures carefully.

"Yeah, I thought so, too."

"How are the radio ads coming along?" Lance asked.

"Great. We have an ad that will be running on the local station, WOK," Kenya responded enthusiastically.

"We have to get the word out. I hope we will be able to get these two government contracts. However, I also want to explore the commercial market."

"Absolutely. I am optimistic about the future of Freedom. I gave my resignation today, so I will be joining you full time," Kenya announced.

"Welcome aboard!" Lance gave Kenya a congratulatory hug. "I will definitely make it worth your while," Lance said as his heart danced with joy. He thought to himself how lucky he was to have a woman like Kenya. At that moment, he felt total happiness. "We have to celebrate. Can I get you something to drink? I have a bar on the lower level. Why don't you come downstairs with me?"

"Okay," Kenya replied.

"What will it be?"

"I'll have a glass of red wine."

"Red wine it is."

"What have you been up to lately other than being a workaholic?" Kenya asked while sipping from her wine.

"Well, I had a close friend who was killed recently. I had known this guy for over twenty years, so I have been a little out of it lately."

"I am so sorry to hear that, Lance. Hang in there. Was the killer apprehended?" Kenya asked, showing concern for Lance by grabbing his left hand and rubbing it.

"No, the police are still investigating the case. My friend, Fleming, was a productive member of the society and he contributed to his community. This killing in the black community has to stop. It seems to me that something has gone wrong and there is no respect for human life."

"I agree, Lance. Something has been lost in our community. There is a spiritual void and breakdown in our value system. Many of our communities are plagued with social problems that need immediate attention."

"Yeah, and instead of just talking about it, I plan on taking action. I have been thinking about starting a scholarship fund in Fleming Brown's name for our inner city youth who graduate from high school. The scholarships will be awarded to low income African-American students who live in urban areas, who have at least a 3.5 grade point average, and who score at least nine hundred on the SAT. What do you think?"

"It's a good idea, Lance. I think it would be a good way of giving back to the community."

Lance smiled at Kenya's response. He was so impressed with her support for his endeavors. Once again, he was convinced Kenya was the woman for him.

"Maybe you can give me some ideas about structuring the fund. We need to establish a non-profit organization for this scholarship fund and also start doing some fundraising. I will donate the first one thousand dollars to start," Lance said.

"My father works with the United Negro College Fund and helps locate students who might qualify for these UNCF scholarships, so he will be more helpful than me. But I will help out in any way I can. I will talk to my father about how to establish a scholarship fund since he has a lot of experience."

"Didn't you tell me his name was Professor Kwame Harden?"

"Yep, that's him."

"This is so strange. We have something else in common," Lance said as he reflected for a moment.

"What's that?" Kenya asked as she finished her glass of wine.

"We both have African names. My last name is an African name."

"I know. Is your father from Africa?" Kenya asked as she crossed her legs at the bar.

"No, he is African American. However, my father was very active during the civil rights movement and really into this black consciousness movement, so he decided to change his last name from Williams to Kojo. Isn't that something?"

"Yeah. I think your father would like my father because he teaches African American history at Morgan. They would have a lot to talk about."

"I am sure. My father is a retired real estate broker."

"So he was into business, too. Like father like son."

"Yeah, I guess so." Lance paused. "Can I say something special to you?"

"Go right ahead."

"I have had a lot of girlfriends in my short life, but you are indeed special," Lance said as he looked Kenya in her eyes.

"I feel the same way because I believe we are truly soul mates, Lance," Kenya responded, smiling as she rubbed Lance's hand again.

"I agree, baby," Lance said affectionately.

To Lance's dismay, Kenya rose from her seat and prepared to leave. "It's getting late, so I really should be on my way."

"Thank you so much for coming by to see me. This meant so much and I really enjoyed the conversation," Lance said as he walked her to the front entrance of his house.

Before reaching the door, Lance grabbed her by the hand and then gently wrapped his arms around her waist. For a brief second, they stared into each other's eyes and then, without any hesitation, they kissed goodnight.

Chapter Twenty-Three

The police were looking for J Quick, the murder suspect in the Fleming Brown case, but were unable to find him for several days. While driving to New York on the New Jersey Turnpike, J Quick and a female friend were stopped for speeding. The state trooper notified police that James Holmes, a.k.a. J Quick, had several outstanding warrants, and he was transported back to Washington DC and brought to the police station on New York Avenue for questioning.

"Mr. Holmes, where do you live?"

"I live at 29 North Avenue in Baltimore, Maryland."

"Are you sure that's the correct address?"

"Yeah, and you don't have to ask me twice. Now, I need to call my lawyer."

J Quick had an angry attitude. He had on a big white T and baggy Jeans. He had a tattoo on the right side of his neck. His head was shaven bald with two earrings in both ears. He looked like a New York City rapper without the microphone.

"Let me just ask you a few more questions, Mr. Holmes," the young muscular built officer asked while sitting at his desk.

"I do not want to talk to you, officer, unless my attorney is present," J Quick said sharply. This was familiar territory for J Quick. He had been in and out of jail most of his life and knew how to manipulate the police.

"Where were you the night of Fleming Brown's murder?" the officer asked, ignoring J Quick's request.

"I was in New York that Saturday."

"Have you ever confronted Fleming Brown about his relationship with Tasha Hall?"

"No, and I don't have anything else to say," J Quick said while looking at the officer in a cocky way and shaking his head.

"Did you ever threaten Fleming Brown?" the officer continued, pushing some papers to the side of his desk.

"Hell no!" J Quick responded as he turned his head away from the officer.

"It is my understanding that you threatened to kill Mr. Brown on several occasions. A well-placed source said you came over to his house last week with Tasha Hall, and apparently, there was an argument between you and Fleming Brown. I was told it was about money. Is this true?"

"No, and I don't have to answer these questions. I am done. I need my attorney. I am not saying shit else to you," J Quick said abruptly.

"What is your relationship with Ms. Tasha Hall?"

J Quick sat in silence in a stoic manner, putting his head down.

"So you want to play tough guy, huh? We are going to lock your ass up. Now…deal with that, tough guy," the redheaded officer threatened.

"I want my goddamn lawyer!" J Quick hollered out as the police officers standing behind J Quick handcuffed him and rushed him out of the station.

J Quick was kept in custody.

******

A large congregation of people formed outside of the large New Hope Baptist Church in Southeast, DC to attend the funeral of Fleming Brown. Big Flem was well known throughout DC, Maryland, and Virginia, and at least five hundred people come out to pay their respect. The mayor of DC even attended the funeral of Fleming Brown. The death of Fleming Brown had gained wide spread media attention in DC. To make matters even worse, DC had been rated as the murder capital of the nation based on recent crime statistics and reports.

As Lance walked towards the church, he recognized many people who frequented Fleming Brown's barbershop.

"Hey, Lance," Ardell said as he attempted to park his car.

"Oh, how you doing, man?" Lance replied as he looked closer to ascertain who the caller was exiting the car.

"I'm trying to hang in there, man. It hasn't been easy lately. The barbershop has been closed for the last week, and I don't know what Big Flem's daughter is going to do. She is taking care of all his business. She told me she will probably close it or sale it," Ardell said.

"That's tough. So what are you going to do?"

"I'm not sure, Lance. I don't have the money to buy it. I will probably find another job. Maybe I need to move on with my life. Hey, did you hear about J Quick?" Ardell asked.

"Yeah, he's locked up, right?" Lance said.

"No, J Quick is out of jail and back on the streets. They couldn't find enough evidence to keep him in jail."

"This is unfortunate for Fleming's family. Do they have another suspect?"

"Not really. They probably won't ever catch the killer."

"And you're probably right! They never do, especially when it's black on black crime."

"You hit the nail right on the head. Listen, Lance, I'm going into the church so I can get a seat. This place is going to be packed. I will see you inside, buddy."

"Alright, be safe."

Several great speeches were made at the funeral, including that of the mayor which stressed the importance of ending the violence in the community. Also, Lance made a brief speech announcing the Fleming Brown Scholarship Fund, and he received a loud applause from the congregation. Afterwards, Lance was personally congratulated by the mayor and Fleming Brown's family.

* * * * * *

To the disappointment of many, Fleming Brown's daughter sold the shop to a Korean family and it later became a liquor store.

Chapter Twenty-Four

"Can I speak with Lance Kojo, please?"

"Speaking."

It was Lance's first day working in a full time capacity at Freedom Technologies, located in a quiet business park right off of US 301 in Bowie, Maryland. When he arrived at 9:12 a.m., he dropped his briefcase on the chair as he hurried to answer the ringing phone. "Well, hello, Lance. This is Joseph Glover from DOIS. I am calling to follow up on a meeting we had last week. I have reviewed your request for a sole source contract. At this time, we have decided to continue our business relationship with McIntyre Corporation."

"Okay…um…if that's your decision, we have to honor it. I was hoping to hear something more encouraging, but perhaps we can do business in the future."

"Okay," Joseph responded after hesitating for a moment. "I will put you on our bidder's mailing list for future consideration. I wish you well in your future business endeavors."

"Thank you. I appreciate your consideration," Lance said. "Take care and have a good day."

Lance hung up the phone and stared at it for about five seconds. "Damn! I will get that contract," Lance whispered to himself. He knew it would be difficult to convince DOIS to change contractors. However, he was determined to get the business from McIntyre.

Lance sat down in his chair and meditated, looking around at the few pictures, used leather chair, desk, two chairs, and three boxes of unopened office material that made up his office. At the far end of the office was a small window with a view of the highway. No doubt, this office was less than impressive as compared to his office at McIntyre.

After the passing of several minutes, Lance picked up the phone to call Eddie at SBO.

"Eddie, I received a call from Joseph Glover and he rejected our proposal. He wants to stay with McIntyre Corporation."

"Glover is full of it. I have looked at their profile on minority businesses, and quite frankly, it sucks. They have awarded less than two percent of government contracts to minorities firms and less than one percent to African-American businesses. I have documentation to support these statistics. They award most of their contracts to large defense contractors. At any rate, we have to come up with another approach. We can't give up on DOIS," Eddie declared.

Lance felt relieved after hearing Eddie's encouragement. "Okay. Shoot. What do you have in mind?" Lance asked, placing his elbow on his desk and resting his chin in the palm of his free hand.

"There are two issues we should examine. I will send an e-mail to the Director of SBO and see if he can contact the agency head at DOIS. My objective is to convince DOIS to seek out small business participation for this opportunity. The other thing we should do is contact our local congressman."

"Good idea! Hopefully, this will make them reevaluate their decision," Lance replied.

"It's certainly worth a try. So let me get busy. I will keep you posted."

"Okay. Let's rock and roll, baby!" Lance responded.

******

"I enjoyed talking to you last night. Have a wonderful day," the card read.

Kenya smiled and smelled the two dozen roses that had been delivered around noon from Sonja & Stephanie's Florist Shop to her office space on the second floor of Freedom Technologies. This gesture from Lance filled her with joy. She leaned back in her chair and stared at the wall for a few moments, reflecting on her encounter with Lance over the weekend.

Trey reported to work dressed in his security uniform. "How you doing, man?"

"I'm alright, Trey. And yourself?"

"I'm here to take care of business," Trey said confidently.

"Your desk will be located in the lobby area of the building. Please make sure you answer the phone if I am not here because we don't have a secretary at this time and I may need some help. Also, I might need you to make a few deliveries from time to time or even pick up some computer equipment," Lance said.

"Whatever you want me to do, I'll do. I like the building. Two levels, huh?" Trey said.

"Oh yeah, I need all the space I can get. Kenya's on the second level. Let's go upstairs so I can introduce you to her."

******

"Nice flowers. Now who might they be from?"

"I believe they are from a secret admirer," Kenya said as she smiled and chuckled a little.

"Do you like them?"

"Yes, I love flowers. How sweet. Thank you."

Trey stood right next to Lance and witnessed the interaction between the two of them. Immediately he knew that Lance liked Kenya. Trey smiled to himself, reminiscing back to when they were younger and pursuing girls.

"Kenya, this is Trey Wilson. We grew up together. I have known him for most of my life."

Kenya extended her hand. "How are you Trey?"

"I am fine. It's a pleasure to meet you," Trey replied, shaking her hand gently.

"Trey will be protecting us. He is our security guy. He will also be assigned to other duties as well," Lance said.

"Great. I look forward to working with you," Kenya said, displaying a warm smile.

* * * * * *

Allen Frisco sat in his office staring at a letter he had received from Jerry Patton of the Department of Strategic Protection. The letter was addressed to Allen Frisco, President of McIntyre Corporation, and informed him that DOSP had decided not to renew the second year of the contract. Allen was totally perplexed by this news and could not understand why DOSP would suddenly terminate his services.

Allen understood the potential financial impact of this decision, and he was furious. He would lose approximately ten million dollars worth of business over two years. For a moment, he thought about Lance in a favorable way. He knew Lance had great skills in terms of the project management and thought that maybe Nathaniel Watson was in part responsible for McIntyre losing the contract. Utterly confused and befuddled, Allen called Nathaniel to his office.

"Nathaniel, have you read this letter?" Allen asked.

"No."

"DOSP will not be renewing our contract for the second year."

"You and I discussed this contract last week. I warned you about this possible outcome."

"That's correct, Nathaniel. Do you have an explanation for this letter?"

"Not really. There were no performance problems with the contract, and we were not notified of any problems from DOSP."

Nathaniel sensed a discomfort in Allen's voice and felt that maybe Allen was placing the blame on him, but he knew he was not responsible.

"There has to be some reason. A client typically does not terminate a good contractor without a reason. This letter said they wanted to go into another direction in terms of their IT needs. Do you buy that, Nathaniel?" Allen asked, his eyes expressing defeat and disappointment.

"No. I have a suspicion that Lance Kojo may have something to do with this, but I can't prove it at this point. It's just a little strange this came about as soon as Lance resigned."

"Ah-huh, are you sure?" Allen asked.

"I just have a sneaky suspicion. Buddy Poretsky told me some things about Lance, and they were not positive. Lance is capable of doing anything. Not to mention, my last encounter with him was not very good. I remember him calling me an asshole. Can you believe that?"

"I don't recall you telling me about that incident," Allen said, leaning back in his chair.

"Yeah, I know. It happened the same day he submitted his resignation, so I let it fly."

"What could Lance do? Isn't he working at another firm?" Allen asked.

"I am not sure. When he resigned, he didn't tell me about his plans," Nathaniel responded.

"Well, I need some answers fast, and I expect you to get them for me. I am furious as hell and I hope this decision by DOSP is not a reflection of McIntyre's inability to satisfy a client," Allen expressed in a not-so-pleasant tone.

Chapter Twenty-Five

Lance enjoyed the ocean. For Lance, being near a body of water had a calming effect on him. It was a place he could sort out his thoughts and attempt to provide solutions to his problems he was experiencing. In short, it was a place for reflection.

After receiving the "green light" from Kenya expressing her interest in a relationship, Lance thought that being near the water would be a good place to chat with Kenya and get to know her better. Therefore, Lance decided to take Kenya to a early evening dinner at a restaurant near the water on North Beach, his favorite place to visit even during the fall and winter season. North Beach was located forty minutes south of Washington, DC in the state of Maryland.

"This is incredible. The water is so amazing. What a treasure. It looks like a little quaint beach town," Kenya said, getting out of Lance's car.

"Yeah, I love this place. I come here a lot. I'm glad you like it," Lance replied.

"I really do. It reminds me of Cape Cod. When I was a kid, my parents use to take me and my brother to Martha's Vineyard in the summer. My father loved the Cape."

"Oh really? That must have been nice. But you know…it's not quite the Cape. Cape Cod has a lot more to offer."

"Yeah, I guess so. I'm really in a good mood, Lance. Do you think we could walk along the beach when we finish our dinner?"

"Sure, that was part of the plan…for me to give you a walking tour after dinner."

"Great," Kenya said as she grabbed Lance's hand and walked into the restaurant.

"Hello, and welcome to Mildred's Restaurant. Would you like to sit in a smoking or non-smoking section?" the bubbly little waitress asked.

"Non-smoking, and if possible, can you get us a table near the window. We would really like an oceanfront view."

"No problem. I have the perfect place for you."

After they were seated, Lance and Kenya engaged in some small talk while taking in the great view of the ocean. In no way did Lance want to discuss business on this evening when he was surrounded by the breathtaking view of the beautiful woman before him and the calming ocean in the background. Periodically, Lance would look out the window and Kenya did the same.

Soon, the waitress returned with their drink order she had taken upon seating them. "Are you guys ready to place your order for dinner?"

"Yes," Lance replied.

"I'll have the lobster with baked potato. Hold the sour cream, please," Kenya said.

"And I have a taste for shrimps, so it will be the jumbo shrimp platter for me," Lance requested.

During dinner, Kenya couldn't help but to stare at Lance's hairy chest. His white shirt was loosely buttoned, enabling her to easily see his well-defined chest. She tried not to make her staring so obvious by allowing her eyes to rove, but ultimately, they always managed to focus back on his chest, which was starting to turn her on a little.

About an hour later, Lance and Kenya left the restaurant and walked along the beach, taking in the dazzling sunset. It was picture perfect. For a few minutes, Kenya and Lance walked in silence along the beach and held hands as they looked at each other and continuously smiled.

"I am going to take off my heels and walk in the water," Kenya announced.

"Okay. Go for it!"

"Don't you want to join me?" Kenya asked. Kenya held onto Lance's shoulder for support as she removed her shoes.

"Well...that means I have to take my socks off and get that gritty sand between my toes," Lance reluctantly said.

"Come on. It won't hurt you," Kenya said as she grabbed Lance's hand, pulling him closer to the shoreline.

"Okay, okay. Let me remove my shoes, socks, and roll up my pants first!" Lance insisted.

Lance and Kenya walked along the shore hand in hand for several minutes before she splashed a little water on him to break his stiffness. He splashed back at Kenya and then he ran over to the small water fountain to rinse his feet off.

"Hey, Kenya, let's sit on the bench for a few minutes and just look at the water," Lance requested as he waved at Kenya while she continued to walk in the water.

"Do you see those huge waves?" Kenya asked, sitting next to Lance.

"Yes, I love the sound of the waves. Listen," Lance replied as they sat for a few moments in silence with nothing but the crashing of the waves against the rocks to be heard.

By now, it had gotten completely dark. However, the lights along the boardwalk shined brightly towards the ocean. Lance placed his arm around Kenya's shoulder and held her in silence while they sat on the bench together. Within seconds, they looked into each other eyes and kissed passionately.

An elderly black couple walking past stared and then quickly looked away.

"We better calm down, baby," Kenya said, regaining her composure.

"You're right. If we don't, we may soon have an audience." Lance chuckled.

"Besides, it's getting late and we probably should go," Kenya said.

After driving Kenya safely home, he walked her to the door and then planted another kiss on Kenya's receptive lips, his way of saying goodnight without the actual words.

Chapter Twenty-Six

The next week, upon walking into his office, Lance noticed a large brown envelope from Jerry Patton on his desk. Inside the envelope was a "solicitation" and bid package. Since this was Lance's first opportunity to bid on a federal government contract, he had to develop a technical and cost proposal and send it to Jerry Patton for evaluation.

After leaving his house, Eddie stopped by the office.

"I received a bid package from Jerry Patton today. We have ten days to prepare a technical and cost proposal. Hey, Eddie, this opportunity is the big one for us."

"Okay, so we need to present a good price and a strong proposal to Jerry. By the way, I have sent both my Director and Congressman Barron Tyler a letter. I am going to stay on top of this," Eddie said, determined to win the contract with DOIS. "And as a matter of fact, I have some people at SBO who are helping me. This may take a while, but we must be patient."

"Alright, Eddie. We know what we have to do to make this work."

"For sure. The plan is in effect."

"So, have you heard from Tia?" Lance asked, changing the subject from business.

"No. That's history. I'm already working on something new. I met an interesting young lady last week. We are just talking right now. I take it one day at a time. Women come women go," Eddie replied as he gave a little smirk, indicating confidence.

"I hear you, man."

"I have to keep a little honey in my tea, ya know," Eddie said as he leaned back in the chair in front of Lance's desk and laughed.

"Okay, player," Lance replied.

******

At 6:30 p.m., the doorbell rang.

Lance had invited Kenya over to his house for a second time to cook his favorite dish of akee and codfish with vegetables for her. Cooking was one of his hobbies. Since he was an only child, his mother of Jamaican descent taught him how to cook when he was young.

"I had to take you up on your offer," Kenya said as she walked into the entrance of Lance's house.

"Well, I'm glad you did. Can I get you something to drink?" Lance asked.

"Sure. For now, some bottled water would be fine."

"No wine?"

"It's a little too early, and as you know, I am really not that much of a drinker."

"Alright, I will get you some water. Let's go in the kitchen area. Have a seat."

"Something smells really good," Kenya said.

"I am cooking some akee and codfish. It's the sauce you smell."

"What is akee?

"Actually, akee is a vegetable. It's a pretty common dish in Jamaica. My mother use to cook this dish all the time."

"Well, if it tastes as good as it smells, I can't wait to eat it," Kenya said as she stared at Lance with a look of admiration.

"Why don't you taste the fish? Take a bite." Lance grabbed a fork with a small plate and fed Kenya a piece of fish and akee. Kenya opened her mouth slowly and chewed the food, shaking her head with approval.

"Mmm, not bad."

"You like it, huh? Do you mind if I light some candles and put on some Maxwell?" Lance asked as he smiled.

"Sure, baby. I love Maxwell's music."

Lance's intent was to set a romantic mood. He knew Kenya was the romantic type and wanted to make her feel comfortable. Not to mention, he had a strong desire to make love to her. It was something about the way she looked in her beautiful fuchsia skirt which stopped right above the knees, white silk blouse that exposed her cleavage, and her "naked" legs, their smooth appearance making Lance want to stroke them.

"Kenya, I have a special gift for you," Lance said as he stood in front of her with his purple silk shirt and pair of nicely-fitting blue jeans on.

"Gift? Did I do something?" Kenya asked as her eyes sparkled with surprise.

"Yeah, this gift is for being sweet. Open it."

Kenya experienced mixed emotions as she held the gift wrapped in an unusually small box. "Is Lance asking me to marry him already? Is this an engagement ring?" she thought to herself. As Kenya opened the gift, a beautiful gold necklace appeared. She held it delicately in her hand while her eyes and heart immediately embraced it.

"Lance, this is so nice. Thank you. I love it, but you really didn't have to do this."

"I did it because I like you a lot. This is what I call a friendship necklace. I want you to think about me when you wear it. Let me put it around your neck for you." After Lance slipped the necklace around Kenya's neck, she got up from her seat at the kitchen table, kissed Lance, and then gave him a hug of appreciation.

After finishing their dinner, they went into Lance's living room to relax and allow the food to digest. They just stared and adored each other while the music played. The light from the muted big screen television illuminated the room.

Becoming more relaxed, Kenya decided she was ready for a drink. "Can I have some wine now?" Kenya asked.

"Sure, baby. I think I will have some, also," Lance replied eagerly, rushing off to return with two glasses of red wine.

"Let's toast to our relationship."

"To our relationship," Kenya echoed as the two glasses softly collided with each other.

Once they had sipped from the red potion, Lance set both glasses on the coffee table in front of the couch. Then, he put his arm around Kenya, rubbed her shoulder, and gave her a superficial kiss on the lips.

Kenya leaned her head on Lance's chest as they sat next to each other on the leather couch. "You know, Lance…I feel really comfortable with you. I have not always felt secure in relationships, but you have a special way of making me feel like no other man has been able to do." Kenya's eyes sparkled with a look of sincerity as she gazed directly into Lance's.

"I feel the same way, Kenya. I see a great future for us. What I want is for us to take our time and develop a good relationship, because I don't want to make the same mistakes I did in my previous relationship."

"Amen to that, Lance. Once I am in a relationship, I give it my all, and I just don't want to get hurt. Do you understand?"

"Yes, baby. Everything will be fine. Trust me." Lance's words gave Kenya a dose of reassurance.

Looking at Kenya's sensual lips excited Lance, and he no longer could hold back his desire to have her. While holding her soft face with both hands, his thick tongue explored the depth of her small mouth, his tongue and her tongue flickering back and forth. Kenya then began to gently kiss Lance's lower lip, delivering soft nibbles in the process. Soon, she returned to the deep kissing they had started with.

Lance suddenly stopped for a moment, grabbing Kenya by the hand and guiding her as he walked. "Let's go to my bedroom where it is a lot more comfortable."

"Okay," Kenya replied with total surrender.

They entered the room and sat on the edge of Lance's queen size bed, resuming their heated kissing while Lance slipped his hand inside

Kenya's blouse and started to caress her breast. Feeling the avalanche of foreplay, Kenya's nipples immediately became hard.

"Oh, Lance...oh, Lance. You're making me so wet, baby. Damn! It feels good when you touch me like that," she whispered in sounds of sexual pleasure.

Wanting to explore other parts of her sexy body, he slid his strong hand between her legs and pushed aside her bikini underwear, finding his way to her erotic zone of wetness. He gently massaged her with his middle finger, generating a roar of passion.

Once again, Lance and Kenya ceased their exploration of pleasure for a moment as they removed their clothing. Lance completely unbuttoned his shirt and threw it on the floor. After struggling to take off his jeans, he realized he still had his shoes on. Kenya took her sexy panties off and put them on a chair along with her skirt and blouse, folding them in a neat and meticulous way.

Lance had waited for this moment for a while and was anxious to make love to her. As he kissed her breast, Kenya resumed her erotic sounds of lovemaking. His tongue was relentless and it brought pleasure to her sensitive and beautiful breast.

"I want you inside of me now," Kenya moaned in a demanding way as she massaged her swollen bud. Kenya leaned back on the bed, moaning and groaning continuously, as Lance continued to massage her breast before entering her. Lance's muscular body stroked her lovingly, his body moving in and out of her with the perfect rhythm.

With her legs spread wide open, Kenya responded with equal passion as she rotated her lower body. Lance increased his movement, and sweat dripped from his face as he continued to administer pleasure to Kenya. Resuming his multi-tasking, he kissed her on the lips and periodically caressed her breast while maintaining his hard penis inside of her. Kenya held both of her hands on Lance's shoulder with a tight grip and screamed in delight as her body trembled with prescribed satisfaction.

At last, they had become one.

Chapter Twenty-Seven

Lance had submitted the proposal to DOSP and was waiting on a response. He knew this contract would catapult his business into financial stability and, more importantly, fulfill his mission of financial independence at the expense of McIntyre Corporation. In addition, he was waiting on Eddie's efforts with the Department of Information Security to pay off.

"How are you adjusting to your new work environment?" Lance asked as he walked toward the front office with a notepad in his hand. He wanted to get a better profile of Trey within the workplace.

"Everything is cool," Trey replied.

"If you have any problems, let me know. I'm here to help."

"Good looking out," Trey responded.

"No problem. I want to make sure the security is tight. We are kind of isolated out here, and I don't want any unauthorized people entering this building."

"Okay, man. Don't worry about the security side of things. I got you covered," Trey said confidently.

After walking back into his office, Lance listened to the voice mail from the call he had missed. "Hello, Lance. This is Jerry Patton. Please give me a call at your earliest convenience." Lance immediately returned the call, hoping to receive good news.

"Hello, Jerry. This is Lance Kojo. I am returning your call."

"Oh yeah, let me get your file. I was calling you about your contract. Freedom Technologies was the successful winner on this "re-compete" effort. Congratulations," Jerry said as he shuffled through the clutter on his unorganized desk in order to get the complete file.

"Thank you so much. This is great news," Lance said, touched by the announcement and feeling proud. He quickly wiped his watery eyes.

"Yes, indeed. You had a strong proposal. The reference from the Prince George's County Schools was favorable. You were highly recommended. In addition, you offered a very good technical solution to our IT needs."

"I remember you calling me last year when I worked for McIntyre Corporation and announcing the same good news. But it is even more amazing now because I have my own business. Thank you so much for your assistance in this matter. Is there anything I need to do at this point, Jerry?" Lance asked enthusiastically.

"I need for you to come in and sign the contract. Next week, we need to schedule a meeting with you to go over our requirements in detail. This initial meeting is quite typical with most of our contractors. I will keep you posted."

"Okay, Jerry. Again, thanks for the opportunity."

Lance sat at his desk and reflected on the good news, thinking of how far he had come from when McIntyre Corporation had denied him opportunities on the basis of his race. He rubbed his face, closed his eyes for a moment, and then took in a deep breath. Lance thought out loud, "You can't keep a good man down. I am winning, Allen Frisco!"

Wanting to share the news, Lance went upstairs and approached Kenya's office with a huge smile on his face. As Lance walked into her office, she looked up from her computer and adjusted her fashionable reading glasses slightly below her eyes so she could see Lance from a distance.

"We have just won our first big contract with DOSP," Lance informed her.

"Fantastic!" Kenya responded as she jumped up and ran from behind her desk to hug him.

"Thank you," Lance said while holding her close.

After looking around her office to make sure no one was present, she gave him a quick peck on the lips before backing off and returning to her seat. This good news further reassured her that she had made the right decision to be with Lance. Once he left from her office, the smell of his cologne lingering behind, Kenya began daydreaming about her and Lance living in a big house in the suburbs with three children. In her eyes, they certainly had much to look forward to.

* * * * * *

To celebrate, Lance and Eddie walked to a local bar on Seventh Street. This bar was unique because it was a restaurant, but after 10:00 p.m., it became a nightclub. Lance walked into the bar with his necktie loose in a carefree manner. His walk was a smooth strut of confidence, much like that of a movie star. There were a small number of people at the bar drinking and talking loudly. One young lady in particular smiled and looked Lance up and down as he entered, her eyes shimmering in delight. She whispered something to her girlfriend and started laughing, although Lance was unaware of her apparent admiration of him.

"Our plan is working. I knew we could do it. We took his business away from him. You know, success is the best revenge. The best way to retaliate against a man like Allen Frisco is to hit him in his pocket where it hurts," Lance said in a braggadocios manner. He playfully gave Eddie a light boxer's punch on his right shoulder, emphasizing his point.

"Hey, Joe Frazier, don't knock me out. I hear you, man. Another victory for Freedom Technologies," Eddie said jokingly.

"Riiight, and if we get that DOIS contract, we will have completed our initial plan," Lance said.

"Phenomenal! We are beating out the competition. You know, I wouldn't be surprised if McIntyre started to spy on us."

"I wouldn't put anything pass them. We can't worry about them, though. We have to stay focused on our mission. What are you drinking, Eddie?"

Eddie nodded his head in agreement of what Lance had said. "I'll have a cranberry juice. I have to take it easy for a while. I am working on my overindulgence so to speak."

"I'll have a beer, and my partner here will take a cranberry juice on the rocks," Lance said to the bartender.

"Draft or bottle," the bartender replied.

"Bottle will be fine. And good for you, Eddie," Lance said.

"I'm trying. It's not easy, but I don't need to be stopped by anymore police."

"That's right, because we are on our way. Can't have you trying to run things from behind bars like Suge Knight," Lance chuckled as he held his beer in the air and gave cheers to Eddie.

Chapter Twenty-Eight

At the moment, Lance didn't know what to think. It was ten-thirty on Thursday morning, and they had a ten o'clock meeting scheduled for that morning. Yet, Lance had not heard from Kenya. He dismissed her lateness as her just being caught in the traffic on 301, which could get a little congested during early morning rush hour. Time passed quickly, and it was now an hour later. Still, no word from Kenya. Lance became exceedingly concerned about her whereabouts and started calling her cell phone repeatedly. Still, no answer. A half hour later, his telephone rang.

"Hello, sir. My name is Topper Johnson. I am a police officer with the Prince George's County Police Department, and I'm calling to report an accident. I found a business card that belonged to Kenya Harden."

Lance's heartbeat increased.

"Ms. Harden also had a notepad with letterhead that read Freedom Technologies."

Lance's palms became sweaty.

"Can you tell me if Ms. Kenya Harden is employed with this company?" the police officer asked.

"Yes, sir, she works here. Is Kenya okay, officer?" Lance asked in an anxious tone.

"And whom am I speaking with?"

"My name is Lance Kojo. I am the owner of Freedom Technologies."

"I am afraid to report to you that Ms. Harden was in a very bad accident. The ambulance is here and they are about to take her to PG Hospital. The other driver who hit her died at the scene."

"This can't be. Where was the accident?" Lance asked in disbelief.

"The accident occurred on Central Avenue and 193 in Upper Marlboro, Maryland. Apparently, a car ran a traffic light and hit Ms. Harden. This is all I know at this time."

Lance abruptly hung up the phone without saying another word to the police officer and drove down to PG Hospital's emergency room. Before leaving the office, he told Eddie and Trey what had happened to Kenya. Eddie, who happened to be working at McIntyre that day, although he was on his way out of SBO, offered to go with him to the hospital, but Lance instructed him to stay behind and handle business.

Lance was visibly shaken, upset, and nervous. He could not conceive of Kenya being dead. Once he arrived at the emergency room, he hurried to the nurses' station.

"My friend was involved in an accident on Central Avenue. Her name is Kenya Harden. Can I see her? Is she okay?" Lance's words came out rushed as he stood in front of the nurse looking troubled and disconcerted, his tie loosened and his shirt hanging from out of his pants. He kept frantically looking down the hallway of the emergency room hoping to see Kenya.

"Calm down, sir," the Korean nurse said politely.

"Her name is Kenya Harden," Lance repeated, afraid the nurse had not heard him the first time.

The nurse scrolled down a list of names on a clipboard and then did a search on the computer. "I have not received a patient in by that name, so I am not sure if she is here," the nurse said.

Just then, a middle-aged black nurse walked up to the front desk and handed a chart to the front desk nurse.

"Oh, wait, sir. Here's her chart. Apparently, she has just arrived."

Lance then turned to the other nurse. "Is she okay? Is Kenya alive?"

"I don't know, sir. If you'll please have a seat in the waiting room with the rest of her family, the doctor will inform you of her condition soon."

"Can you tell me anything? Tell me something," Lance demanded.

"Like I said, I don't know, sir. The doctor will let you know. Just hang in there for a few minutes. I don't want to give you any false information until we know for sure, okay?"

"Alright, but please let me know as soon as possible," Lance replied in irritation, frightened at the nurse's avoidance in answering his question and making him think the worse for Kenya.

"We will, sir."

As Lance entered the waiting area, he saw three individuals seated: a middle-aged man, woman, and a young man in his twenties. The woman was quietly weeping.

"God, please, don't take my daughter away from me," the woman whispered repeatedly while rocking back and forth and wiping the tears from her eyes.

"Excuse me, are you related to Kenya Harden?" Lance asked softly.

"Yes, we are her family. This is her father and my son, Clay. And you are?" Ms. Harden asked.

"I am the close friend and employer of Kenya. My name is Lance Kojo."

"How are you doing, Lance? My name is Professor Kwame Harden." He extended his hand for a firm handshake.

"And I am Alice Harden. Kenya has told me so much about you. As a matter of fact, she mentioned something about bringing you over next week to meet us. This is so terrible," Ms. Harden cried out as Mr. Harden reached over to comfort his ex-wife by rubbing her back.

Clay, Kenya's brother, simply sat in silence.

"It is a pleasure to meet you all under an unfortunate situation. I do hope Kenya is okay. She is very special to me."

After an hour of waiting, Dr. Lee, a short Asian-American who wore black rimmed glasses, walked in the waiting room to provide an update on Kenya's condition.

"My name is Dr. Lee. Are you all the family of Kenya Harden?" he asked while walking toward Professor Harden.

"Yes, we are, and this is her friend Lance," Professor Harden replied.

"Well, the first thing I would like to report is that she is alive."

"Thank goodness." Lance sighed as he bent over and put both of his hands over his face.

"However, she received trauma to the head and is in a coma. We are going to do a CAT scan to determine the degree of injury," Dr. Lee informed Kenya's loved ones.

"How long will she be in a coma?" Ms. Harden asked.

"I can't say with certainty. It's really a bad injury, and there is some internal bleeding, as well. Many times with an injury of this nature, the patient may never come out of the coma. She may recover, but it is largely dependant on the seriousness of the injury. At this point, I can't allow you to see her, so why don't you all get some rest," Dr. Lee said as he folded his arms, waiting to hear a response.

"Okay, Dr. Lee, I guess the only thing we can do is wait and pray," Professor Harden replied.

Lance was devastated by the doctor's statement. He couldn't imagine not being with Kenya. He knew there was a distinct possibility that she may never recover from the coma. Lance was deeply hurt yet again, experiencing a second blow to his spirit...first, Fleming Brown and now, Kenya. It was at that moment he realized just how much he was in love with her.

* * * * * *

Meanwhile at McIntyre Corporation, Allen, Nathaniel, and Buddy were sitting in a conference room seeking answers to questions and pondering strategy. The Department of Strategic Protection's sudden decision to terminate their contract bothered Allen immensely.

He had been sold on the idea that Lance Kojo was behind this scheme. However, he couldn't validate it until Nathaniel and Buddy gathered up some information. Needless to say, Buddy was excited about the opportunity to dig up some dirt on Lance.

"I don't like how this contract was handled with DOSP. They did not give us adequate notice of the termination. Do we have any legal recourse?" Allen asked.

"Perhaps, but unfortunately, DOSP has a right to terminate after the first year of a contract. Federal agencies terminate contracts for many reasons. I think they call it termination for convenience. I have done a lot of work with the government, and learned they do it all the time," Nathaniel said.

"It's fierce competition. People will do anything to gain an advantage, business-wise. I've noticed four of our technical people have resigned since Lance left, which I find to be a little strange. They all say they will be working for another firm, but they never disclose the name of the firm. We need to investigate these four employees who resigned recently," Allen said while rubbing his lower face with his right hand.

For a minute, there was silence in the room. Nathaniel looked at Buddy with a confused expression on his face. Again, Nathaniel felt that Allen wanted to place the blame on him.

"Yeah, I know it seems strange," Nathaniel voiced, breaking the uncomfortable silence. "In the IT business, however, there is a high turnover of people. They come and go. They are always seeking better opportunities. Numerous times I have seen people leave firms and take people with them."

"You seem to have an explanation for everything, Nathaniel, but I smell a rat and want answers. Let me know what you find," Allen said sarcastically before abruptly exiting the room.

Chapter Twenty-Nine

The next day, Lance visited Kenya at the hospital. His trip was filled with mixed emotions as he chronicled the experiences and good times he had shared with her. He thought about what their future would be like and envisioned a life of happiness and peace. He had never met a woman who shared his interest like Kenya. Lance was an eternal optimist and was convinced she was his soul mate.

Why did this happen to her? Why did God create this wretchedness in my life? Is this all for a reason? Lance thought to himself.

He walked to the front desk of the hospital and inquired about the location and room number of Kenya.

"Can you tell me the room number of a patient?" Lance inquired at the hospital's information desk.

"Name of the patient, sir?" the receptionist replied.

"Kenya Harden."

"She's in room 1924. Take the elevators to the right of you to the nineteenth floor."

As Lance exited the elevator, he proceeded to walk reluctantly to Kenya's room. He did not want to see her in an incapacitated state. It was not the Kenya he wanted to see and he expected the worse.

After entering her room, he stared at Kenya who was lying in bed with a large white bandage around her head and IVs stuck in her arms. It appeared that she was hooked to a life support system. She attempted to open her eyes, but was unsuccessful. A cold chill raced through his body as he walked slowly towards her in a skeptical manner Not knowing what to do, he stared at her for a while and then sat in the chair next to her bed. He silently prayed and wished that Kenya, in a miraculously way, would acknowledge his presence. The only sounds were that of the life support monitors which kept track of her vital signs. Soon, a nurse came in the room to fix her pillow, examine the monitors, and write down some information on Kenya's chart.

"How is she doing?" Lanced asked cautiously.

"Her vital signs are good, but she is still in a coma," the young nurse replied with a friendly smile.

"Do you see any signs of recovery?"

"Not yet. It's still early. She is heavily medicated right now, so we will have to wait and see how this medication works. The doctor wants to run some more test on her. Just hang in there. I hope she will come through all of this," the nurse replied in a kind and comforting West Indian accent.

As Lance sat there, he continued to stare at Kenya and then stood to kiss her on the cheek, breaking into a sob he could not stop. He was wounded in his soul. After sitting in her room for about an hour, he left, emotionally drained, and went home.

The next day, Eddie accompanied Lance to the hospital for emotional support. When they entered Kenya's room, she appeared to be in the same condition. Her head still had bandages and half her face was covered with an oxygen mask. Quietly, Lance walked over to her bedside table and placed the flowers he had brought amongst the many other flowers, baskets of fruit, and get-well cards loved ones had left behind. He then turned and looked at Kenya once again, lying so helpless.

Eddie joined him by Kenya's side. "She is going to be fine. Just have patience and faith," Eddie whispered.

"I will. God will take care of her."

After leaving her room, Lance and Eddie stopped by the nurses' station to obtain the status of Kenya's condition.

"Hello, I was here to see the patient in room 1924. How is she coming along?" Lance asked.

"Oh yeah, Kenya Harden. I remember talking with you yesterday. Ms. Harden is opening her eyes frequently and showing some progress. The preliminary results of the CAT scan indicate that her head injury was not as severe as we expected. We were able to stop the internal bleeding rather quickly," the nurse said.

"Does that mean that she will recover from her condition?"

"I can't say for sure. Perhaps, you should talk to the Dr. Lee about the specifics of her recovery," the nurse replied.

"Thank you. You've made my day," Lance said, a bit more optimistic now than he had been when he first entered the hospital. In his mind, he believed Kenya would make a full recovery and become a vital part of his life.

******

Having called a meeting with Nathaniel Watson and Buddy Poretsky to discuss the problem at hand, Allen Frisco was determined to find out why he lost the contract with the Department of Strategic Protection.

"I have some good information for you. I took a look at DOSP's procurement bulletin on the internet. This website announces contract awards for that agency. A company by the name of Freedom Technologies received a contract award last week for the same services we were contracted to do. I researched this company and found out that Lance Kojo is the president and owner of Freedom Technologies. Can you believe that, Allen?" Buddy informed him.

"You are kidding, right?"

"No way. As I said, Freedom Technologies is doing the same work we were contracted to do. How he was able to do that I don't know."

"This is unbelievable. This nigger took business from me, huh? Well, I am not going to just sit here and take this from Lance. We fight for every piece of business we get through McIntyre Corporation. I am not going to take this lying down," Allen said.

"I knew this little friggin' scum bag was up to something. I just knew it. That's how these people operate," Nathaniel spat.

"I could have told you that a long time ago. I worked with that pompous and arrogant nigger. He thought he was so damn smart," Buddy added, gladly contributing his racist comments.

"Well, he must know something, because how in the hell did Lance take this business from us? Can anybody answer that question?" Allen asked, turning his head left and right, looking perplexed at Nathaniel and Buddy.

"I don't know. I guess he convinced DOSP that his company could do a better job." In all honesty, Nathaniel was clueless as to what marketing strategy Lance had implemented, but felt that Allen's question warranted an answer.

"Maybe he slandered McIntyre's name. Lance is capable of doing anything. Who knows? What I do know is that we are talking about ten million dollars worth of business lost," Allen said in an angry and unprofessional manner, his true racial feelings emerging. Allen knew then that his misdeeds had come back to haunt him.

Chapter Thirty

The drama-filled week had come to an end. Upon waking Saturday morning, Lance felt he was strong enough mentally to go and visit Kenya. After his last visit, the nurse had given him tremendous hope and lifted his spirits. It appeared a full recovery for Kenya was eminent.

Lance knocked on the slightly closed door of room 1924 of PG Hospital.

"Come in," a soft, friendly voice responded.

When Lance opened the door, Ms. Harden was sitting on the edge of Kenya's bed. Kenya was sitting up in the bed and not lying down as usual. She only had one tube attached to her right arm, unlike the previous encounter when she had tubes in both arms. The oxygen mask had been removed. When Lance looked at Kenya, her eyes were wide open. Lance walked over to her bed and gently kissed her on the cheek.

She acknowledged Lance's presence with the familiar dimpled smile, but didn't speak a word.

"Hello, Ms. Harden. How are you today?"

"I'm fine, Lance. Kenya is responding very well. She recognized me, and certainly, she knew who you were when you walked in the room. This is real progress. Thank God."

"This has really been a tough week, but I knew Kenya would come through. Prayers do work."

"Yes sir, young man. God does answer prayers. I prayed for my daughter every night. I ask God to not take her away from me and he answered my prayer. I spoke with Dr. Lee before I came to see Kenya, and he said that he expects a full recovery. It's still going to take a little while before she leaves this hospital, though. She has to regain her strength."

Suddenly, Kenya struggled to speak. "Thanks for coming," she said, forcing the words, then started to cough violently.

"Take it easy, honey. Don't strain yourself. You don't have to speak now. We would like for you to get well soon. Let me give you some water." Ms. Harden placed a straw in a cup and gave it to Kenya. She then rubbed her back. "Take it easy."

Lanced nodded in agreement of what Ms. Harden was saying.

"I really thank you for giving Kenya so much support. You are a nice young man. I hope everything works out for you and my daughter. She seems to really care about you."

"I really care about her, too, Ms. Harden. Kenya has always been supportive of me, especially with my business. She is a wonderful woman and I will do anything to make her happy," Lance said as he looked at Kenya. Kenya's eyes brightened as she heard the sweet words that escaped Lance's lips. Aside from her accident, that moment was the closest she had ever come to feeling like she was in heaven.

******

Saturday evening, Lance and Eddie sat dining and discussing business at Copeland's Restaurant. Eddie was a little concerned about whether he could convince Joseph Glover to do business with Freedom Technologies. He had informed his senior management at the Small Business Organization about the opportunity at DOIS and had contacted Congressman Tyler's office. Eddie was glad to receive a contract from DOSP, however, it appeared that his efforts with DOIS were not happening fast enough. He wanted the second big contract, which would be worth twenty million dollars.

"I received a letter from Congressman Barron Tyler's office. Perhaps there is a possibility we may get some business from DOIS," Eddie informed Lance.

"Yeah, maybe something will happen," Lance replied.

"I don't know. It probably is going to take a while."

"Don't worry, Eddie. You are doing your best. Let's wait and see what happens."

Excusing himself, Lance went to the men's room of the restaurant. As he was returning to his table, Valerie and a tall man entered the restaurant holding hands. It had been over nine months since they broke up, however, Lance felt a little strange. Just less than a year ago, they were planning a wedding.

"Hello, Lance. How are you?" Valerie said cordially.

"Hello, Valerie," Lance replied in a hasty manner, and then continued on to his table.

Lance was not jealous of Valerie being with another man, but he was just a little startled, not expecting to see Valerie at this particular restaurant. For a moment, he wondered whether he should have married Valerie. "Eddie...did you see Valerie with her new boyfriend? Check that out." Lance nodded his head in the direction of Valerie and her date seated two tables away from them.

"Are you okay, man? It seems that Valerie has moved on with her life. Don't sweat it."

"Yeah, it seems that way. Hey, man, she is old news. We once had a relationship, but that's the past."

Lance glanced over at Valerie's table. She was laughing about something and appeared to be happy. The two were quite engaged with each other.

"Are ready you to leave, Eddie?" Lance asked, now uncomfortable with the surroundings.

"I'm ready when you are, man."

"Check, please!" he called out to the Indian looking waitress.

Before departing from the restaurant, Lance glanced once more over to Valerie's table. Without so much as a goodbye, Valerie looked at Lance and smiled as he walked out of the restaurant.

Chapter Thirty-One

Three months had passed since Kenya's accident. She had fully recovered and things were back to normal with her life. This unfortunate incident, which could have ended her life, had brought Lance and Kenya closer together. Things were getting serious with them, and she soon moved from her apartment to live with Lance. They had a great relationship and were able to operate in a dual capacity as lovers and business associates.

While Lance's business had begun to experience promising opportunities, Allen Frisco had just received a called from Joseph Glover who informed him that DOIS would not be renewing their contract with McIntyre. Immediately, Allen knew Lance was responsible, and he didn't take kindly to losing business. He had lost business before, but he could not take losing thirty million dollars from two contracts, especially as a result of Lance's doing. Allen felt it was now time to exercise his corrupt side. He knew how to orchestrate harm to a person if necessary. Picking up the phone, he called security up to his office.

"Tommy Slate, how you doing?" Allen said, directing Tommy to the chair in front of his desk.

"How you doing, boss?" Tommy replied as he immediately sat down looking eagerly at Allen wondering why he was called to his office.

"Not too good. I have a former employee who has literally stolen thirty million dollars worth of business from me."

"What do you mean stolen?"

"Well…not really stolen, but he created some type of scheme and now he has my damn contracts. Isn't that a son of a bitch?"

"Shit! That's a lot of money," Tommy replied.

"That's why I need your help."

Tommy had worked for Allen for the last five years as a security guard. Tommy served eight years in prison on an armed robbery charge, and Allen, knowing of Tommy's reputation, enlisted him to do his dirty work. It was even said that Tommy had killed a man on a previous job.

"What do you want me to do, boss?"

"I had an employee that resigned from here a few months ago. His name is Lance Kojo. He owns a company in Bowie, right off of 301 near the Mercedes Benz dealership. Do you know where that location is?"

"Oh yeah, I know where it is," Tommy said, rubbing his fingers through his blond hair.

"Well, I want you to shake him up a little. I want you to make a statement. I don't want you to kill him, but scare the shit out of him. And if that doesn't work, I will let you know the next order, okay?"

"I understand. I know how to handle this type. When I finish with him, he will wish he was dead."

Tommy stood about 6'3" tall and had a rather large body frame with a snake tattoo on his left wrist. He wore dark sunglasses a lot, even during the winter months. It was part of his low profile image. He had dealt in criminal activity for many years, so he knew the rules and what was required to get the job done. Tommy was a man of few words.

"How much?" Allen asked, eager to end the conversation and put things into motion.

"My price is fifteen thousand dollars. It takes me a full two months to execute my plan. I don't want the police on my trail."

Allen reached into his briefcase and pulled out a checkbook and wrote a check to Tommy.

"Here's a check for fifteen thousand. I want to see results in sixty days. I want to teach this nigger a lesson."

"Consider it done."

* * * * * *

While Allen was plotting Lance's fate, Lance was celebrating at his office with Eddie, Kenya, and about fifteen of his employees. There was plenty wine, champagne, and food. The cause of celebration was due to the phone call they had just received from Joseph Glover offering Freedom Technologies a sole source contract. The contract was worth twenty million over four years. Apparently, Eddie's efforts had paid off along with the fact a favor was owed to Eddie from Congressman Tyler who assisted in gaining the DOIS contract.

The evening grew old, and by eight o'clock it was pitch dark. By this time, all of the employees had left the office except for Trey, Lance, and Eddie. Even Kenya had decided to leave early. Lance was sitting in his office talking to Eddie while they summarized the daily events.

Suddenly, a loud noise was heard. BOOM! BANG! BOOM! The noise was so loud until they could hear it from Lance's office.

"What the hell was that?" Lance asked to no one in particular as he rushed out to Trey's desk where he was sitting.

"Did you hear that noise, Trey?"

"Yeah," Trey replied, then quickly ran out of the building to the front parking lot where Lance's BMW truck was parked with a busted windshield. Apparently, someone had thrown a huge brick into Lance's car. The alarm was beeping. Trey's eyes scanned the front of the office building, but he did not see anybody. However, he did hear the sound of a car speeding off quickly, but could not determine the make, model, or color of the vehicle because it was too dark. Lance and Eddie stood silently behind Trey as he pulled out his gun and looked in the back of the office building. No one was in sight. He quickly ran back to Lance's truck and approached with caution, the glass crunching beneath the weight of his body. Trey examined the truck and he saw a big brick in the driver's seat with a note attached which simply read: NIGGER MONKEY.

"I'll call the police," Eddie said, going back into the building as Lance deactivated the alarm and then approached Trey to read the note.

Lance read the repulsive statement. "What in the hell is this? It must be some KKK extremist who did this. Man, this is some crazy stuff."

"Yeah, it could be a white supremacist, some redneck, skinhead, or terrorist. Who knows? It definitely looks like someone is trying to make a statement or start trouble," Trey replied while shaking his head in disgust.

"Why would someone do this?" Lance asked rhetorically.

"Hate, jealous, or just flat out bored," Trey replied.

Lance put his hand on his waist and shook his head, wondering who could have done such an act.

"I spoke with the police. They should be here in a few minutes," Eddie announced as he emerged from the building.

After about twenty minutes of waiting, a police car pulled up with its siren blaring and lights flashing in a circular motion. Two white male cops got out of the car.

"We received a call about a truck being vandalized."

"Yes, sir, we called you," Lance responded.

"Who is the owner of this vehicle?"

"I am, officer," Lance replied.

"And what is your name, sir?" the officer who was filling out the report asked.

"Lance Kojo."

"What time did this occur?"

"Approximately twenty minutes ago. We heard a loud noise and came out to find my windshield broken. Someone threw a fifty-pound brick into my windshield with this note attached to it," Lance informed them while handing over the torn piece of paper.

The one officer read the note while the other wrote down information.

"Is this a hate crime, officer?" Eddie asked.

"It's too early to tell. I can't say," the officer replied.

"What else could it be?" Lance said with a tone laced with anger.

"In order for me to complete this report, I need to get more information from you, Mr. Kojo. Did you see who threw the brick in your vehicle?"

"No, the car had driven away. I didn't see the person," Lance replied.

"What are you doing here at this building?"

"I work at this location," Lance said as he pointed to the big sign that read: Freedom Technologies, Inc.

"Okay, and who are these gentlemen with you?"

"These are my colleagues. They also work here," Lance replied.

"What do you do here, Mr. Kojo?"

"I am the proprietor of Freedom Technologies."

"Uh…owner? Are you sure?" The Officer seemed to be shocked at this revelation.

"What do you mean?"

"Well, let me just say it differently. Can you provide any documentation to show you are the owner of this company?"

"Now officer, why do I have to do that?" Lance asked while looking at Eddie and Trey as if to say, "*This racist motherfucker doesn't think black folks can own anything*."

"Mr. Kojo, I am just doing my job. I am required to verify these things," the officer said.

"Well, here's my business card as proof," Lance responded with major attitude.

"This will help, but I need more substantial documentation."

Trey stepped forward. "I am the security person for this building, and am employed by Mr. Lance Kojo, who is in fact the owner. Mr. Kojo has given you his business card, and that should be sufficient." Trey shook his head and sighed.

"Okay, gentlemen, I won't push this issue any further. We will investigate this matter and I will be in touch with you in the next couple of days. Have a good night."

Lance became infuriated after his encounter with the police. While reporting a crime of vandalism and conversely, he was questioned by a police officer with suspicion and doubt. He believed their questioning was another case of racial profiling.

"Who do you think did this, Eddie?" Lance asked, hoping he could shed some light on why this had happened to him.

"It has to be somebody that doesn't like you. Who are your enemies?"

"I don't have any that I know of," Lance responded.

"Well, I have an idea of who might have done it," Eddie said, looking at the vehicle and inside of the car for any further damage.

"Tell me."

"I believe it was some of McIntyre's people."

Lance snapped his fingers. "Why didn't I think of that?"

Eddie continued with his theory. "Think about it. We have taken a substantial amount of business from them. This happens all the time in the business world, but maybe McIntyre is a little upset. Well, that may be an understatement. They are pissed. Remember now, we are talking about thirty million dollars worth of government contracts. That's enough to cause even the most law-abiding citizen to seek revenge."

"You're probably right. What I did might be perceived as a little unscrupulous, but certainly not illegal. Well, I will not be intimidated. We just have to watch our backs and tighten the security. Competition is American as apple pie or baseball. When this kind of thing happens between two white corporations, the unsuccessful company, many times, will offer their services to subcontract or partner with the successful company. In this case, Allen can't accept defeat by a black man."

"Preach, brother! I hear you loud and clear," Eddie said, nodding his head and smiling.

"You guys are right. Your former employer is mad as hell, and I don't think they will stop with their attacks. We definitely need more security," Trey said as he stood with his hands in his pockets.

"I am not afraid of Allen Frisco and his people, but I do agree we need more security."

"I know some people who would be good. I use to work with them," Trey replied.

"Okay, give me their information and I'll call them."

"You bet," Trey responded.

Lance had secured two government contracts through his clever negotiations and persistence, along with some luck. However, this accomplishment would be at a price. Allen Frisco was determined to make his life difficult. He was not going to back off Lance. Tommy Slate had implemented his first plan of action, and this was only the beginning of the havoc he would create for Lance and Freedom Technologies.

Chapter Thirty-Two

Two weeks had passed since the car incident. Tommy's approach was to allow everything to cool down for a few weeks and then continue his plan of intimidation and vandalism.

It was midnight. Traffic on 301 was slow. There were no cars parked near the building of Freedom Technologies. After circling the building twice in his black Chevrolet SUV with tinted windows to make sure no one was around, Tommy parked in the back and sat for about five minutes. In the rear seat was a gallon of gasoline. It was time to execute the second phase of his thought-out plan.

Tommy emerged from the truck with some knife-like instrument in hand, picked the lock of the building, walked in the lobby area, poured gasoline everywhere, and then put fire to the gasoline at the entrance of the door. The flame ignited and the fire alarm sounded as Tommy ran to his truck and drove away. Within fifteen minutes, the Bowie police and fire department were on the scene.

Ironically, about thirty minutes later, Lance drove up with Kenya.

"Officer, what happened to my building?" Lance asked with trepidation as he watched the firefighters scurry about.

"What is your name, sir?"

"I am Lance Kojo. My business is located in this building."

"Well, Mr. Kojo, it seems like this is the work of an arsonist."

"What?!"

"Someone tried to burn your building down, but fortunately, we were able to get here within a fairly quick time. Another ten minutes, and the damage could have been worse. It seems the fire was confined to the lobby area of the building."

"Did anyone see who did this?"

"Well, my partner questioned the gas station attendant across the street who said he saw a black Chevrolet SUV with tinted windows drive out of your parking lot about forty-five minutes ago. That's all the information we have so far."

"Two weeks ago, my car was vandalized in this parking lot...and now this. I need some type of police protection for the safety of my employees and myself. As you can see, this building is located in an isolated location," Lance pleaded.

"Mr. Kojo, I can put in a request for police presence. However, we cannot be on duty at this location twenty-four hours a day. We don't have the resources or manpower. We can have a police present in the late afternoon and evening hours when people are leaving, but that's all we can do at this point. Do you have security in this building?"

"Yes, I do, but it's probably not enough."

"Well, you need to hire more."

"Is this type of crime common in this area?" Kenya asked.

"No, ma'am. Bowie is considered a low crime area. This type of situation is a bit unusual. These acts of violence indicate that someone may be trying to cause harm to you. We will conduct an investigation, though."

The next morning, Lance received a call from George Stein, the owner of the building, who assured Lance he would have the lobby area renovated within a week.

* * * * * *

"My car has been vandalized. We have been hit by an arsonist. What's going to happen next? Will they put a hit out on me?" Lance asked. All dressed in casual attire, Lance, Trey, and Eddie hung out in the evening on the patio of a restaurant in Bethesda trying to create a strategy to Allen's harsh actions.

"If they wanted to kill you, it would have already happened. In the street game, when someone wants you, they will come right after you and even your family. Believe me, I know how gangsters and thugs operate. What these cowards are trying to do is intimidate you and run you out of business. They want to break your spirit and frustrate you because you were smart enough to compete and win their business," Trey said while looking back and forth between both men through his dark sunglasses. Trey was now operating in Freedom Technologies' inner circle of management and advising on security strategy.

"I have an idea, Lance. Let me provide you with personal security for a while. I could be your driver and provide security at your home up until midnight everyday. And you could let two other security guards take care of securing the office building," Trey suggested.

"Hmmm, not a bad idea. I promised Kenya I would increase security. You would be like a bodyguard, right?" Lance replied while dipping his buffalo wing in the ranch dressing.

"Exactly. I could do this until things cool off."

"Perfect, I'll take you up on your offer, and of course, I will pay you more."

"Yo, Lance, I got your back, dawg. Besides, I could use the extra cash."

"Good idea. We have put a lot of time and energy into this enterprise, and we're not going to let them punk us right out of business," Eddie said.

"Hey, guys, those two ladies have been staring at me all evening. What's up with that?" Trey said.

"They're digging you, Trey. They're looking at your big muscles busting through that tight ass shirt and are probably having freaky thoughts. You better go over there and get those digits. You want me to come over there with you? You know me. I'm not one to let a fine young cutie slip through my claws," Eddie said as all three men burst into laughter.

* * * * * *

Trey had protected Lance since his childhood and when he was involved in street fights with guys back in Southeast, DC as a teenager. The two men had a long-standing relationship. Equally concerned about

Lance's safety as he had been back when they were growing up, Trey decided to call Allen Frisco the next day and issue him a warning to back off, without mentioning Lance's name, of course.

Practicing caution, Trey placed his call from a phone booth to ensure it wouldn't be traced back to him.

"Hello. McIntyre Corporation. How can I help you?"

"Can I speak with Mr. Allen Frisco? It's an emergency."

"May I ask whose calling?"

"Yes. Mr. Johnson. I am one of his clients, and it's very urgent," Trey replied, providing a false name.

"He is on the other line. Can you hold for a few moments?"

"Sure."

After a few moments of waiting, Allen picked up the line.

"Allen Frisco speaking."

"Mr. Frisco, I am calling to warn you that if you continue with your threatening acts of violence, you will be dealt with. And not in a very nice manner, either. You will become non-existent. Do you fucking understand?"

"Who is this? What are you talking about?" Allen asked nervously, caught off guard.

"You know what I am talking about! Keep doing the shit you're doing and you'll be issued a death sentence."

Click!

The caller was right. Allen knew exactly what the anonymous caller was referring to, and he was now visibly shaken. Immediately, Allen called Tommy to inform him of the phone call.

"Tommy, I received a threatening phone call a few minutes ago. I didn't recognize the voice, but it did not sound like Lance. Do you think he's on to us?"

"Of course, Allen. I think by now he has narrowed down his suspects."

"Well, he's threatening my life, and nobody, I mean no-bod-y, threatens my life," Allen said, letting go of his fear and finding his balls once again.

"So what do you want me to do?" Tommy asked.

"I'm not quite sure just yet."

"Well, I have one more phase of my plan to execute. The decision is yours if you want me to carry it out or not. I know the police are on my trail, so maybe I should lay low for a while and then strike."

"My goal was only to intimidate him and destroy his business. However, if this doesn't stop him, we may have to go one step further and eliminate him."

"Like I said, I will wait for a few weeks and then strike again, unless you instruct otherwise."

* * * * * *

After picking up Lance from his home, Trey informed him of his call to Allen.

"I gave our friend a little call yesterday," Trey said.

"Who?"

"Allen Frisco."

"Oh really? What did you say to him?"

"First of all, I did not identify myself or mention your name, but I did give his ass a pretty good scare by way of threats."

"That's good, as long as he doesn't know who is doing it. So Allen Frisco is officially on notice, huh?"

"That's right. I made it very clear to Mr. Frisco about my intentions."

Lance sighed heavily. "I just hope he gets the message."

Chapter Thirty-Three

Despite the recent incidents that had happened, Kenya and Lance grew closer. Lance felt it was time for them take a break from work and spend some quality time together, so they decided on a midnight cruise in Baltimore at the Inner Harbor. The summer night was peaceful and the ocean breeze embraced the night and created a sense of comfort and relaxation. The moon was full and bright and the light reflected off the water, giving the atmosphere a serene and romantic feeling. As the ship sailed smoothly along the ocean waters, they listened to the sounds of Coltrane and Monk being played by a live Jazz band emanating from the ship's sound system.

Both were dressed to impress. Lance in his white shirt and white pants, and Kenya in a light blue, body-hugging, mid-length dress. Her cleavage prominent for Lance's viewing pleasure. Her black heels finished her look, exposing her well-manicured feet.

"Waiter!" Lance called out, trying to get the attention of the waiter who was serving dinner on the ship.

"Yes, sir. Are you ready to be served?"

"Not yet, but I see you have flowers for sale."

"Yes, sir, we do. Would you like me to order some flowers for the lovely lady?"

"Yes, could you have a dozen of red roses on our table before dinner is served?"

"Certainly. I will get those for you right away, sir," the waiter replied.

"Oh, Lance, that's so sweet. You are really full of surprises." Kenya blushed a shade of crimson.

"You are my princess and deserve the best."

"Well...if I'm your princess, then you are my prince. Lance, I haven't felt this way in a long time, and I am so glad to have you in my life. We have gone through so much. I want us to be together no matter what happens in our life."

"I feel the same way, Kenya. I realized how much you meant to me when you were lying in the bed at the hospital fighting for your life. I feared I would lose you. I am a lucky man, and to show you my appreciation, I have something special for you."

Despite his crisp, clean white attire, Lance rose from his seat and got down on bended knee.

"Kenya, will you be my wife and partner for life?" Lance asked while looking directly into Kenya's anxious eyes.

For a moment, Kenya seemed to be in a state of shock. Then her eyes became watery, indicating she had been a witness to the proposal. "Yes, baby, yes. I will marry you."

Lance reached into his pants pocket and pulled out a black velvet box. "I hope you like it."

Kenya gasped as she opened the box and examined the ring. "This is so beautiful, Lance. I love it. I love you. I am so happy." Lance stood from his kneeling position and Kenya quickly rose to hug him and plant a kiss on his welcoming lips.

"I thought maybe we could get married next year in the spring."

"And spring can't come fast enough for me, dear."

While they sat quietly and stared at each other, Kenya periodically broke their gaze to look at her dazzling ring as the ship sailed further down the ocean.

Chapter Thirty-Four

The office had been officially renovated after the fire, and having resigned from the Small Business Organization, Eddie was now employed full time at Freedom Technologies. As Chief Executive Officer, he was running things at the office.

One morning, Jeffrey, the project team leader, entered Eddie's office and submitted his resignation. His reason, as stated in the letter, was he felt uncomfortable working at Freedom Technologies after the most recent attacks. This was a big loss to Freedom because Jeffrey was very talented, dependable, performed his job well, and had worked with Lance for over ten years.

"We have lost two employees today," Eddie said as he sat in his new office talking to Lance.

"I'm sorry to hear about this. Did they give a reason why?" Lance asked.

"They didn't feel safe working at Freedom because of the recent incidents."

"This is exactly what Allen Frisco wants. He wants to destroy my business. But you know, Eddie, we have to roll with the punches. We have two big government contracts and our focus is to continue providing good service to our clients."

"I agree."

"Well, on a brighter note, Kenya and I are engaged and plan to get married next spring."

"Hey, that is good news. Congratulations, man. I have a good feeling about her. I think she's the right one for you," Eddie said as he stood from his desk and gave Lance a handshake.

"Thank you. It's amazing how things can change in one year, huh?"

******

Later that day, Lance decided to visit the gym since he hadn't been in two weeks since attending Reina's welcome back party from Puerto Rico. At first, he was reluctant to go because of Reina, but then he decided he wanted to do things the right way and clear up any misunderstandings. He had been very indecisive with women and more specifically with Reina, giving her the impression there may have been a chance at the two of them having a relationship. He didn't want to lead her on any further. He wanted to redeem himself and become the one woman man. There was no doubt that Kenya was the only woman for him.

After entering the gym, Lance proceeded upstairs to the second level. He walked in the spinning room where the class would be starting in fifteen minutes, but didn't see anyone. Within minutes, a black woman came in the room with her bag and a CD player. She appeared to be the spinning instructor.

"Isn't Reina teaching this spinning class?"

"No. Reina moved to New York. She was offered a position to run a fitness club in Manhattan. It was an offer she couldn't refuse," the instructor informed him.

"When did this happen?"

"She left two weeks ago."

A wave of disappointment washed over Lance at not having had the chance to say goodbye. In a strange way, Lance felt guilty. Deep down inside, he felt the reason she took the job was because she was hurt over his new relationship.

Lance took a gulp from his bottled water and then climbed on the spinning bike.

"I'm ready when you are. Let's do this."

Chapter Thirty-Five

"**H**ello, Mr. Kojo. This is Chief John Banister of the Prince Georges County Police Department. I am calling to let you know we may have a possible suspect responsible for the vandalism of your car and your place of business. We were able to trace the license plate number of the suspect's vehicle given to us by the gas station attendant near where the acts took place."

Lance exhaled a huge sigh. "I'm glad to hear something is being done."

"Yes, sir, we are trying our best to solve this crime."

"Who is the suspect, Chief?"

"Well...the truck is registered to a Mr. Thomas Slate."

"Did you arrest him?" Lance asked with anxiousness.

"No, sir. This is only preliminary information. Our investigation is not complete, but we do know the suspect has a criminal record and has spent eight years in prison on an armed robbery charge. We are trying to locate Mr. Slate for questioning, but have been unsuccessful thus far. As soon as we apprehend him, though, I will let you know."

"Do you know if this Thomas Slate works for a company by the name of McIntyre Corporation?"

"Do you know him, sir?"

"No, but my previous employer was McIntyre Corporation, and I use to see a vehicle parked in the garage of this company almost everyday that matched the description of the one in question."

"The preliminary reports revealed that he was unemployed, but we will check other sources. I will keep you posted on the outcome of this investigation."

Lance did not have to wait for the outcome. He already knew that Thomas, a.k.a. Tommy, Slate was connected to Allen Frisco's dirty game…a game which was time to come to an end.

******

As Lance and Kenya redirected their focus from the vandalism to planning the Fleming Brown Scholarship fundraiser, Tommy was plotting another destructive act. Tommy had not attacked in three weeks. Aware that the police was looking for him, he had gotten rid of his black Chevrolet SUV and was keeping a very low profile. He took up residence in the basement of his girlfriend's house, only coming out at night. While sitting in the basement, he oiled his .38 special, prepared to kill if necessary.

Meanwhile, Trey had adjusted to his new security shift. He drove Lance and Kenya to and from work and remained on duty about one block from Lance's house from eight o'clock p.m. to twelve midnight each day. Trey was licensed to carry a firearm and was prepared to respond to any suspicious behavior.

Back at the office, the business at Freedom Technologies was escalating. The two government contracts required a lot of manpower, and Eddie, being effective, had hired five additional employees to support the work for DOIS and DOSP.

"Hey, guys. I just want to let you know that our profit has doubled since last quarter. These two contracts have really made a different," Lance announced to Kenya and Eddie who were seated in his office.

"Yeah, that's good. The work load has increased dramatically," Eddie responded.

"Oh yeah, it has. I just want to make sure we have everything under control. Things seem to be running smoothly despite our recent arson attack, even though we lost some of our employees and the morale of the remaining employees was tested." Lance stood up and talked as he walked around his office with his hands in his pockets giving accolades to his management team.

"Business goes on. I try to keep the employees motivated," Kenya said.

"And I would like to thank you both for all your help. The success of Freedom Technologies is the result of the hard work each of our employees, including you, put in. On another note, I spoke with the police yesterday and they have a suspect. However, they have not completed the investigation."

"Who do they think is responsible?" Eddie asked.

"Some guy by the name of Thomas Slate. I don't know the guy, but the description of his truck sounds familiar. I would bet all my life savings that Allen Frisco has hired this character to do his conniving deeds."

"I wouldn't be surprised," Kenya said. "And I have a feeling it's far from over."

Chapter Thirty-Six

The time was eight o'clock on Saturday night, and the Upper Nile was crowded with people from all walks of life. Many of them were previous patrons of the Fleming Brown Barbershop. In fact, more people than Kenya and Lance expected had came out for the event. This was clearly a demonstration of support for the Fleming Brown Scholarship Fund.

The Upper Nile had been decorated to a more formal setting, the tables with white cloth, flowers small candles, and most of the attendees were dressed in formal attire. A Jazz band played on the stage next to a sign on an easel which read Fleming Brown Scholarship Fund: Choose Education over Violence. Lance was stopped repeatedly in his tracks by those congratulating him for establishing such an opportunity for inner city high school students.

As Lance stood watching the people enter the establishment, Ardell tapped him on the back.

"I see you put me on the program. Who said that I was a speaker, Mr. Kojo?" Ardell asked as he let out a friendly laugh.

"I had to draft somebody," Lance replied, imitating the laughter.

"I'm just kidding with you. I'm honored to be on the program. Thank you for including me."

"Yeah, I thought you would like to say something about Fleming Brown since you worked with him for so many years," Lance said as he adjusted the necktie of his black suit.

"I'm looking forward to it."

"Good. As you see, I have others on the program. I will speak for a few minutes. I have Dr. Kwame Harden, a professor over at

Morgan State University, who will talk about the importance of recruitment from high school to college. Felicia Thompson, Fleming's sister, will say a few words, and Kenya Harden will be the Master of Ceremony. She will introduce the speakers and the ten scholarship recipients. In addition, we have plenty of food and good music."

"Sounds like you planned well. Good job, Lance," Ardell replied.

Spotting Kenya talking to her father, Lance excused himself and made his way to where they were standing. Kenya was looking beautiful, dressed in her formal attire of a conservative black dress with a short sleeve matching jacket. Her hair was neatly arranged.

"Professor Harden, how are you? Thank you for agreeing to participate in this program." Lance extended his hand.

"I am honored to be here for such a wonderful event," Professor Harden replied while taking Lance's hand into a firm shake.

"We definitely need to hear your perspective. I have been working on this scholarship fund for the last four months. Again, thank you for your input."

"Not a problem."

"I must say that your daughter is responsible for putting together this fabulous event. She is such a great organizer."

"But it was all your idea, dear," Kenya replied modestly.

"Well, congratulations to you both for organizing such a worthy event. Also, I would like to congratulate you once again on your recent engagement. I wish you the best."

Together, Lance and Kenya expressed their thanks.

Having Professor Harden's blessings was just the beginning of the beautiful evening ahead.

Chapter Thirty-Seven

The next week, Chief John Banister called Lance to update him on the investigation.

"When we spoke last, Mr. Kojo, you inquired about Thomas Slate's employment, and I told you that we could not determine his place of work. Since then, we have checked with McIntyre Corporation and a representative from the Human Resources office verified that Thomas Slate was employed as a security guard."

"Bingo! I knew McIntyre Corporation was behind this!" Lance shouted.

"What do you mean?"

"When I resigned from McIntyre Corporation, I started my own business about a year ago, taking a lot of McIntyre's business and clients with me"

"Okay, so what's wrong with that? Did you break a law?"

"No, sir, but Allen Frisco, who is the owner of McIntyre, apparently viewed me as a threat to the future of his business."

"So you think he is trying to cause harm to you, huh?"

"Yep."

"Well, I don't know what his motivations are, Mr. Kojo, but I will look further into this matter. I just wanted to let you know that Thomas Slate does work for McIntyre Corporation. Now we have another lead: McIntyre Corporation."

"Any luck on finding him?"

"Not yet. The personnel file says he took a leave of absence from McIntyre Corporation, but does not provide any explanation as to why he left. We believe that Mr. Slate is hiding from the law."

* * * * * *

That same night, around 11:20 p.m., Tommy Slate decided to pay Lance a visit at his home. As Tommy approached the back deck to Lance's house, Trey, who was on guard duty and sitting in his parked car on the corner, spotted him and right away became suspicious of the character dressed in all black, including his cap. Immediately, Trey picked up his phone to call Lance, but no one answered. Emerging from the back of the house, Tommy looked around to make sure the coast was clear. By now, Trey had gotten out of his car and was now crouched down behind a large flower bush, watching as Tommy pulled out a long knife-like object. Trey waited for a few minutes to ascertain his actions, and once he saw Tommy attempting to pick the lock of Lance's back door, Trey pulled his gun from his waist and jumped out from his place of hiding.

"Hey! What the hell are you doing?" Trey shouted.

Startled, Tommy swiftly turned around, pulled his gun from underneath his black sweatshirt, and shot Trey in the leg. Trey fell and rolled behind a tree, firing return shots in the direction of Tommy. One bullet hit the window of Lance' house and the other shot hit Tommy in the abdomen.

Hearing the gunshots, Lance quickly ran downstairs. Upon opening the door, he saw Tommy lying dead at the back entrance of his house, his blood splattered all over the screen door.

"Oh my God! Oh my God! I don't believe this. Kenya! Kenya!" Lance shouted.

Kenya rushed down the stairs while putting on her robe. As soon as she saw the body, Kenya let out an ear-piercing scream, backing away as she covered her face with both hands.

"Lance...Lance…what happened? Who is this? Who shot him?" Kenya asked, hoping to get an immediate response. Kenya grabbed Lance's hand and started crying uncontrollably.

"My leg, my leg," Trey whispered from beside the tree he was lying next to.

"Oh my God! Look, Kenya." Lance ran over to help Trey. "Trey, are you alright?"

"I was hit in my right leg, and damn, it hurts like shit. Lance…that man was trying to break into your house, but I shot him before he could get in." Trey grimaced from the pain of his wound. "Is he dead?"

"He looks dead, but I'm not going to touch him to find out. Let me call the police and get an ambulance." Lance hesitated before going into the house. "Trey, thank you for saving our lives. This guy could have killed us."

On the lawn, Kenya stood behind Trey in her bathrobe, visibly shaken and nervous, while Lance ran inside to call 911.

The next door neighbor emerged from her house. "What's going on? I heard gun shots."

"Someone tried to break into our house," Kenya responded, pointing to the dead body.

"Oh my!" She clutched at her chest. "Is there anything I can do?" the neighbor asked, looking at the dead body.

"No, I just called the police and ambulance," Lance replied as he returned.

Within minutes of the phone call, three police cars drove up to the front of Lance's house with their lights flashing. By this time, more neighbors had come out of their houses to find out what was going on. Two police officers entered the backyard by way of the wooden fence and approached Lance with their flashlights blinding him temporarily. Suddenly, the loud shrill of a siren sounded and two paramedics rushed out of the ambulance and were escorted immediately to the back of Lance's house by another officer on the scene.

"Who is the owner of this property?" the burly, Caucasian police officer asked with authority.

"I am."

"And what is your name, sir?"

"My name is Lance Kojo."

"What's going on here? It looks like a shootout went down here." The officer shined his flashlight in the direction of the deceased, and then pulled a notepad from his pocket.

"Someone tried to break into my house and the gentleman lying over there near the tree shot him before he could enter my house," Lance said. Lance used hand gestures as he pointed from the dead trespasser to the hero.

"Who is that man over there?" the cop asked, pointing toward Trey.

"The wounded gentleman is part of my personal security team. He was on duty when he saw this man breaking into my house," Lance said as he stood with his arms crossed over his bathrobe.

"What time did this shooting occur?"

"I'll say within the last thirty minutes."

The paramedic rose from his kneeling position beside Tommy's body. Shaking his head, he announced, "He's dead. Let's get this body into the ambulance."

"We have to ask you some questions, Mr. Kojack," the officer said, mispronouncing Lance's last name.

"It's Ko-jo."

"I am sorry, Mr. Kojo. We have a dead man and a wounded person on your property, and we need explanations," the officer apologized as the other cops examined Lance's house and the area of the dead body.

Just then, an unmarked police car pulled up and a gentleman dressed in a cheap suit got out and walked hurriedly to the back of Lance's house.

"I am looking for Mr. Lance Kojo," the man said as he approached the two police officers questioning Lance.

"I'm Lance Kojo."

"Are you okay, Mr. Kojo? My name is Chief Banister. I spoke with you on the phone earlier today. Is anybody else hurt?"

"My security assistant is wounded in the leg." Lance pointed to Trey who had been placed on a stretcher.

As the paramedics were placing the body into the ambulance, Chief Banister stopped them and pulled back the white sheet covering the face of the deceased. "Is this Thomas Slate?"

"Yes sir, Chief. We have his identification," one police officer said.

"Lance, it looks as though this guy will not be causing you anymore problems," Chief Banister commented.

"Thank God," Lance sighed with relief.

Dismissing the officers, Chief Banister took over with the questioning. Lance felt a lot more comfortable talking to him as opposed to the other aggressive police officers. Stepping over the white outline of where the body had fallen, the two men retreated to inside of Lance's abode away from the nosey neighbors, flashing lights, and cameras of the local news crews on the scene.

* * * * * *

Within hours, Chief John Banister had Allen Frisco down at the precinct asking him questions about his association with Tommy Slate. Allen was dressed in a gray business suit with a red tie. A man with influence, he had hired the best attorney who was present in the room with him where suspects were questioned by law enforcement officials.

"Mr. Frisco, do you know Thomas Slate?"

"Yes."

"Thomas Slate was killed last night while breaking in the house of Lance Kojo," the Chief announced.

"I am sorry to hear about that," Allen responding less than genuinely, already aware of Tommy's death.

"It is my understanding that Thomas was employed in the security division at McIntyre Corporation. Is that correct, Mr. Frisco?" Chief Banister asked, looking at Allen's attorney who was dressed in a double-breasted blue suit. He was an older gentleman in his sixties with silver gray hair.

"Yes, he was employed as one of our security people," Allen replied.

"Do you know Lance Kojo?" Chief Banister's six feet one inch frame towered over Allen who was seated. He was a medium built man and quite imposing.

"Yes, he was a former employee of my company," Allen responded nonchalantly, rubbing his chin and looking at his attorney.

"What was his official job title?"

"Senior Account Executive."

"Please explain his job responsibilities."

"He managed our commercial and federal accounts. He was involved with the marketing, negotiating, and acquisition of contracts."

"Were you upset about Lance leaving your company?"

"No."

"Is it correct that Mr. Kojo, after leaving your company, was able to acquire a significant amount of your contracts with his new company?"

"Excuse me, sir. My client doesn't have to answer that question. What are you implying officer?" the lawyer interrupted, starring at Chief Banister.

"I am trying to get to the bottom of this matter and solve a case. Just answer my question, Mr. Frisco," Chief Banister said, pointing his finger at Allen Frisco, expecting to get a quick response.

Allen paused for a second, looking at Chief Banister and his attorney as he turned his head left to right.

"No comment."

"Is it true you hired Thomas Slate to commit violent acts against Mr. Kojo?"

"Of course not. Why would I do such a mean spirited thing?"

"Why was Thomas Slate on leave of absence from work when these violent acts took place?"

"He told me he had to take care of some family business up in New York and needed some time off."

"What kind of family business?"

"I don't know."

"I know what kind of business it was Mr. Frisco. You could not accept the business success of Lance Kojo, so you made his life difficult at the expense of Tommy Slate."

For several weeks after the questioning, Prince George's County Police Department pursued Allen, investigating his phone logs, bank accounts, and travels. They even interviewed Nathaniel Watson about his association with Tommy, but were unsuccessful in finding evidence. Believing that Allen Frisco hired Tommy Slate to kill Lance Kojo, Chief John Banister was fighting for a trial. But with good legal representation and lack of evidence, Allen was able to escape going to court. Still, he would be kept under close surveillance by the Prince George's County Police Department for a long time.

Soon after the killing of Tommy Slate, Chief Banister met with Trey to discuss in detail the shooting incident. Knowing of the previous acts against Lance, and after verifying Trey's gun permit, he was able to conclude that Trey acted in self defense and therefore would not be charged with any offense.

******

Later that week, Lance arrived home from work to find Kenya waiting for him at the front door. She had decided to take a few days off after the incident.

"Hey, honey, how are you?" Lance asked, placing a kiss upon her sweet lips.

"Lance, we need to talk." There was a look of concern in Kenya's eyes.

"What's the matter, baby? Is everything okay?" Lance took her hands in his.

"Lance, I have had nightmares almost every night since the attempted break-in and I just don't feel safe here anymore. I was thinking we should leave Maryland."

"Why, Kenya? The perpetrator is dead. Everything will be fine."

"I told you I'm still paranoid with Allen still on the loose. I believe that man is capable of doing anything. If he tried to get rid of you once, what makes you think he won't try again?"

"Kenya, it's not easy to just pick up and move a business like that. I refuse to run. I will not allow Allen to destroy what I worked so hard to build. I have to face him head on."

"But it's not just you affected by all of this. This is stressful for me, and it does nothing to lessen my onset of panic attacks. Besides, you won't have to move the business. Just open up another location wherever we decide to move to. I need to get away for awhile. Let's take a little vacation so we can put this behind us. Sometimes a vacation gives you a fresh perspective on things."

"A vacation sounds like a good idea. Maybe it will give us some time to think about all of this. I love you, Kenya, and want you to be happy." Lance pulled her into him. "If it means that much to you, I will consider your suggestion to move, but I can't make any promises. Just out of curiosity, where were you thinking we could relocate?"

"Atlanta."

"Hmm, not a bad idea, but why Atlanta?"

"It's a great place to do business, especially for African Americans, the housing is cheaper, and the weather is great."

"Sounds to me like you've done your research, but I still can't make any decisions at this point. I need a little more time."

* * * * * *

The next day Lance talked with Eddie about Kenya's concerns.

"Kenya is unhappy with living in Maryland. These series of events have really shaken her up. She is so paranoid right now," Lance said as he paced around Eddie's office with a document in his hand.

"I can understand that."

"We have been talking about going on a vacation for two weeks."

"You guys could really use the time away. You have been through so much. Go for it. Business is doing well, and I can handle it," Eddie insisted, dressed in a tan suit and showing a smile of confidence while comfortably settling into his new role as CEO.

"You really think I should?"

"No doubt."

"Kenya's also talking about relocating to Atlanta. She thinks we should open up a new office in the Southeast. Maybe this will increase our bottom line and allow us a greater percentage of the market. A successful business must expand in order to grow," Lance said while walking towards the water cooler in Eddie's office and pouring himself a Styrofoam cup of water.

"Intriguing, but do you think the timing is premature?" Eddie asked, putting his right elbow on his desk and his hand on his chin.

"No, not really."

"Well, if you don't think it is, why don't we explore this expansion concept with our marketing and budget team?" Eddie suggested.

"I was thinking the same thing. It has always been the policy at Freedom to consult with the team. It makes good business sense."

"We could do some financial projections. If it proves feasible, then I would feel a lot more confident," Eddie added.

"I'll give this more thought while on vacation."

"Where are you guys going?"

"Mexico."

Chapter Thirty-Eight

The weather was pleasant in Cancun, Mexico. Kenya was sitting on the deck of her hotel suite facing the clear blue waters of the ocean. With an exotic island beverage in hand, she lay relaxed in a white tee shirt and a pair of white shorts. To compliment her island look, she wore sunglasses, a pair of brown sandals, and a big white sombrero. Kenya was enjoying her vacation. There was a slight breeze that wrestled its way through the air and created a relaxing effect. Inside the room, Lance was sprawled across the bed shirtless with a pair of light blue trousers on, flipping the cable channels of the TV in search of a program for his viewing enjoyment.

"Hey, baby, come check out this show," Lance demanded.

Kenya placed her drink on the patio table and entered the room, taking a seat on the bed's edge.

"Look at the way they dance in Mexico."

"Wow, it looks like they are having fun." Kenya reached out to stroke the hairs on his back.

"Definitely, they have this type of event every day on the beach. It's kinda like the Mardi Gra back in New Orleans."

"Yeah, that's what it reminds me of. Maybe we should go there tonight after we come from our tour."

"Cool. I'm up for it."

"Thank you for bringing me here, Lance. I was just a little stressed out back home."

"I understand. But you know we have to make some major decisions about our life and business future."

"Yeah, Lance, we do."

"We've come a long way, baby. I remember when you first started working at McIntyre Corporation. You were assigned to work with me as a Junior Account Executive. Now look at us. You're still with me, and we're engaged to be married. I am so proud to have you in my life. It's amazing," Lance said, wrapping his arm around her lower half.

"I always liked you from day one, but I didn't want to be too aggressive because of our work relationship. I admired your courage. I will never forget when you stormed out of the office that day. I felt your pain. And now look at what you have accomplished. We are doing well at Freedom Technologies and I expect great things to continue. The Atlanta market is booming for IT business. So are you ready to make this move?" Kenya asked.

"I thought about this long and hard, Kenya, and maybe you are right. A change of pace may be good for the both of us and the business. I can always travel to Maryland from Atlanta on a weekly or bi-weekly basis. Eddie is doing a wonderful job in running the Maryland office."

"So does that mean yes?"

"Why not? If things don't work out in Atlanta, we can always come back to Maryland. We have that choice."

"I believe growth and expansion is always a good thing if it is calculated. Those two contracts with the government have already made you a millionaire. You had a brilliant plan, which you implemented and executed with great success. Success is a great revenge. Now let's move on with our life. No matter what happens, Lance, I will always be there for you. And you know, baby, you are my hero," Kenya said, leaning her head against Lance. She genuinely cared for Lance and was a true supporter of his endeavors.

"I'm sure the move to Atlanta will be healthy for you. I want you to have piece of mind, not feel unsafe."

"You know what will make me happy right now?" Kenya asked as she pulled Lance to a standing position and pressed her body up against his.

"What?" Lance replied with a devilish grin, thinking an afternoon romp was on the agenda.

"Dancing the Salsa!"

Lance grabbed Kenya by the hand and started to do a poor imitation of the Salsa as they danced around clumsily in the hotel room trying to get into rhythm of the popular dance. They laughed and danced with joy. They were a powerful couple who loved each other immensely and their future was as bright as the afternoon sun.

* * * * * *

Two weeks later, a meeting was held in the conference room of Freedom Technologies to announce Lance's plan to open up another location in the Atlanta area. Many employees congratulated Lance and Kenya and shared in their joy. Afterwards, Lance, Kenya, Eddie, and Trey went to the Upper Nile to enjoy a private evening of celebration.

One month later, Kenya and Lance were packed and heading down 301 to Maryland 202 via 95 South to Atlanta, Georgia. It was a beautiful day for traveling. Holding hands as they rode down the highway, they listened to singer, Tracy Chapman's song, blasting through the truck's Infinity speakers.

"DON'T YOU KNOW, THEY'RE TALKIN' BOUT A REVOLUTION, IT SOUNDS LIKE A WHISPER, DON'T YOU KNOW, THEY'RE TALKIN ABOUT A REVOLUTION, IT SOUNDS LIKE A WHISPER."